rustic log chapel on the outskirts of Red Lodge. No stained glass was needed, with the natural beauty streaming through, signifying God's approval of the scene below.

Wearing the Victorian wedding dress she had found in Red Lodge, Sue Ann was strengthened with the knowledge that Miss Lily, another strong, independent woman, had worn this dress a hundred years ago. Sue Ann could almost feel the presence of the pioneer woman.

But she would never forget Shade. As she looked down at her empty ring finger, she remembered Shade asking her why she did not wear rings. Her reply had been, "Empty finger...empty heart." There would always be an empty spot in her heart for Shade, but her ring finger was about to be filled with the ring given her by another man she loved, one who was about to become her husband. Shade's blue diamond now held its place of honor on her right hand.

It was time to take her vows, vows she should have taken a lifetime ago, and she was proud to have her children there to walk her down the aisle.

Sue Ann had made her decision, and in a few minutes, she would have the man she could not live without beside her for the rest of her life. It was a difficult decision choosing between the two men she loved, but she knew it was the right decision.

Mountain Mists

by

Dr. Sue Clifton

Daughters of Parrish Oaks, Book 4

Mountain Mists

Cover Art by *Kim Mendoza*

The Wild Rose Press, Inc.
PO Box 708
Adams Basin, NY 14410-0708
Visit us at www.thewildrosepress.com

Publishing History
First Mainstream Women's Fiction Rose Edition, 2016
Print ISBN 978-1-5092-0566-0
Digital ISBN 978-1-5092-0567-7

Daughters of Parrish Oaks, Book 4
Published in the United States of America

Dedication

Sue Ann's story is dedicated to my friends
Barbara Payne and Diane Coleman
and to all women fighting to be survivors
of breast cancer.

~*~

Dr. Sue supports Casting for Recovery, a national organization providing fly fishing retreats for survivors of breast cancer. Ten percent of the profits from her Daughters of Parrish Oaks series goes to Casting for Recovery.

Acknowledgements

To my son Jeff Gentry and daughter Niki Clifton Burchfield.

Thank you, Jeff, for your wonderful writing and graphic telling in the letters from Vietnam. Once again you have helped me tell Sue Ann's story as only a son could help, especially one who was with me from the beginning in our story *THE GULLY PATH.*

Thank you, Niki, for being my true life Betsy. You are embedded in these books with me in so many ways. Thank you for always being my number one reader and fan.

I love you both.
Mom

Go Forward with Courage

When you are in doubt, be still, and wait.
When doubt no longer exists for you, then go forward
with courage.
So long as mists envelop you, be still;
Be still until the sunlight pours through and
dispels the mists—
as it surely will.
Then act with courage.

~Chief White Eagle

Prologue

Montana

Custer pushed back the buffalo skin that covered the aspen and pine limbs of the sweat lodge. He felt purified, ready for any vision the Great Spirit would present. This was the most important vision quest of his life, and he would follow the traditional ways of his Crow ancestors, omitting no part, regardless of its severity.

Leaving his modern-day clothing and his food and water in the sweat lodge, Custer wore only moose-hide britches and moccasins and carried only those items needed for such a spiritual journey: his ancestral pipe and sacred tobacco; a large piece of moose hide to be used as cover while he slept at night and to make a medicine bag, or bundle, for amulets, sacred reminders of the quest, provided by the Great Mystery; a small moose-hide pouch he always carried containing a personal object of great importance; and his knife sharpened to perfection before he left, to make it easier to cut off the tip of a finger, a sacrifice no longer used by his people but which Custer hoped would be deemed acceptable by the Great One as a symbol of his suffering and seeking of answers for Sue Ann, the reason for his quest.

Custer put his hand over his eyes and gazed

upward, tilting his head back in order to see the high peak, his destination, as close to the Maker of All Things above as he could get. As he began his trudge upward, a mist surrounded him, a sign that the Great Spirit was with him. As he walked, the mist moved ahead, guiding him to the spot where he would fast and pray, fast and pray. As he reached the top, Custer gathered wood for campfires, sweet grass and cedar to add to it, and sage to form a circle around his prayer and meditation site. Custer would allow himself only two campfires each day, one at sunrise and one at sunset, using his ancestral method of knife and stone to produce the sparks needed.

****

Custer lost track of time as he sat naked, his body smudged with burned sweet grass and cedar. He had smoked his pipe before beginning his daily prayers and now sat with his eyes closed, waiting for darkness. When his second campfire had almost burned out, he still did not succumb to the cold. Soon he would cover with the moose hide and allow his dreams to guide him. Perhaps tomorrow the mist would rise and he would receive the vision he was seeking.

Sunrise was barely visible through the mist that still lingered. No dreams had come, but Custer was patient. It was only day two, and it often took many days to receive answers on a vision quest; sometimes no vision came, which meant future quests must be made. The sunlight added little warmth through the thick swirling mass that still blocked its rays, but Custer was not deterred as he went about his rituals.

Again his second campfire, now just coals, did little to warm him as the day grew to an end.

****

Perhaps today will be the day.

Custer remained hopeful as he began his third day, but this day, too, yielded no answers. Still Custer fasted and prayed. He knew that, if given the right sign, he would sacrifice a bit of his own flesh to assure the Great Spirit of his sincerity and selflessness, since the answers he sought were not only for himself. Another night of sleep passed, but no dreams came.

As he sat by the still glowing embers of the campfire the morning of his fourth day, he opened his hands and lifted them to the heavens while looking to the east. The haze danced around him, but this time he opened his eyes wide and spoke aloud, pleading for a vision to come.

Rays of sunshine separated the mist, and warm sensations radiated through the half-blood's body. Knowing this was the sign he had been seeking, Custer reached for his knife and held it up, his arms outstretched to the heavens.

"My ancestors sacrificed their flesh to show the importance of their vision quests. I do this now for Sue Ann. Please take notice, Great Spirit, and give me a sign for my one true love."

Custer sliced off the tip of his index finger on his right hand, his dominant hand, without flinching. Then he reached into his pouch and pulled out the locks of hair, his and Sue Ann's, braided together, entwined and inseparable as their lives had been these last few years. He held the fingertip, with the braid, up higher and waited for a sign directing his next move.

Sunbeams grew brighter and blinded Custer, causing him to shield his eyes with one hand. But the rays of hope quickly changed direction, to a large boulder that stood a few feet outside Custer's circle. He approached the boulder and placed the piece of flesh and the braid on the flat surface. The mist cleared, and Custer returned to the circle to sit, wait, and watch.

An eagle circled overhead, and Custer watched, consumed by the giant wingspread of what was in past visions his own animal spirit. The eagle dipped and circled, coming closer and closer, casting a ghostly shadow over the boulder. But before the eagle could take the offering, a tiny chickadee landed on the surface and hopped around, casting quick glances at the flesh and the braid. His little wings fluttered with excitement.

Custer was mesmerized by the tiny creature as its black cap bobbed up and down as if trying to decide if the offering was there for him. Custer knew that even though the animal was tiny, its oversized head contained a highly intelligent brain. The bird had excellent long-term memory, and its little brain was able to erase the obsolete and replace it with new and more important information, even new song lyrics.

The eagle flew down and circled the boulder and the tiny bird, but the chickadee was not frightened, even though it knew it was no match for the bird of prey. Within seconds, the chickadee pecked at the flesh. The eagle perched itself on the other side of the offering. The two eyed each other and then began taking turns pecking at the fingertip, quick pecks that seemed like more of a tease than an actual attempt to seize the flesh.

Soon the mist covered the boulder and the scene ended. Custer stood, not knowing if the quest was over or if, perhaps, there was more. Once again, he smoked his pipe, prayed, and waited. Custer knew this was an important part of his vision but could not understand its meaning. He knew that often interpretation comes later, sometimes in a dream or in a follow-up quest.

When the mist cleared, the birds were gone and so were the fingertip and the braid. Custer rose from where he had been sitting and walked to the boulder. Two feathers lay in the spot where he had placed his offering, a white tail feather from the eagle and a tiny black feather from the chickadee's cap. Custer took the feathers and went back to his campsite. He cut a piece from the moose hide and placed the feathers inside along with ashes of the burned sweet grass and cedar and with tobacco from his pipe. Custer then tied the medicine bag closed with a long thin strip he had cut from the hide, and hung the bag around his neck. The fourth day, the traditional length of a vision quest, had yielded a vision, and Custer felt it was time to leave.

The mist was gone and so was Custer's exhilaration in thinking answers would be given and understood on this quest. He scattered the ashes of his cold campfire and returned the sage that had formed the circle to the edge of the trees. At the beginning of the trail he had followed four days ago, he stopped and once again purified himself with a sweat bath. Then he dismantled the sweat lodge and returned this site to its natural state. Once again, he put on the clothing of his modern life and began the trek home.

As he left the spot where his vision began, he noticed the raven watching him from the top of a nearby tree.

"Raven...not now! No tricks allowed. Sue Ann needs answers."

Custer spoke aloud, and as if acknowledging his

plea, the raven left his perch and spread his black wings, casting an oversized shadow over Custer as he disappeared into the mountains.

Custer did not understand what the Great Spirit had told him but trusted he would know in time. As he trudged down the mountain, heading for the old log cabin at the base of the Beartooth Mountains and to his love Sue Ann, he could not help but feel a little disheartened. Sue Ann would ask questions, and he knew he would not be able to give her answers. But he would be still and wait.

As he reached the trail that led to the cabin, he heard a shrill call from overhead. Custer cupped his hand over his eyes and looked up. An eagle, possibly the same eagle, was circling, probably readying itself to claim the carcass of a dying animal, its next scavenged meal. For some reason, Custer could not continue as he'd intended. He turned into the woods away from the trail, drawn to see what prey was in the eagle's sight.

He pushed through branches but stopped as he heard a different sound. He slowed, hoping not to scare the animal. Its bleat was faint, as if death were stalking it. Custer heard movement and stopped again, standing silent and still. His right hand clutched his knife in case it was a bear trying to beat the eagle to the dying animal.

His gaze soon made contact with a small set of eyes that stood fearless in his path. A fawn stared up at him. Then, as if the animal wanted him to follow, it tripped back through the woods. Custer hastened after the fawn, knowing this was not a usual occurrence. The bleating became louder, and Custer moved faster. Soon the fawn stopped and allowed Custer to pass beside him to enter a small clearing.

There, just a few yards away, a different fawn stood watch. Her mother had fallen into a sinkhole and was lying at the bottom of the death trap, panting, making soft distress calls. As Custer looked down into the hole, the doe raised her soft brown eyes to him as if pleading, "Help me!"

Custer knew any wild animal in distress could be dangerous but did not hesitate to help her. He cut long branches from nearby aspens, leaving the leaves intact, and put them down into the hole, propping them against the side to form a makeshift ladder or ramp. Holding to the side of the hole, he lowered himself, talking softly to the deer.

"Easy, girl. I'm going to help you get back to your babies. They need their mama."

The deer looked frightened but did not try to get up. Her legs were tangled in roots. Custer carefully removed each leg from the roots and then lifted her enough to move her away from the roots and toward the tree limbs. She did not fight him. Once she found her footing on the ramp, she fought her way to the top with Custer pushing her from behind to prevent her from sliding back.

The fawn at the top bleated encouragement to her mother, and, within seconds, she was beside her fawn, licking her face to assure her baby was all right. The doe shook herself, getting the blood back to normal circulation through her body, then turned away from her rescuer and limped into the woods with her baby beside her.

At the top of the hole, Custer found tufts of fur from the doe and the fawn. He retraced his steps to the edge of the woods, but the other fawn, who had led him to the spot, had disappeared. Here he found another tuft of fur. He placed these tufts with the other amulets in the pouch and headed home to Sue Ann.

Book I

The Woods Colt

Dr. Sue Clifton

Chapter One

Montana

Hawk found the small lump after they made love. But this was Betsy's body, and to Hawk it might as well have been a boulder. The nightmare was almost more than he could handle, the terror something he could not hide.

Married for almost three years, the two lovers still felt as if they were on their honeymoon. The ten months of hell, magnified by the trauma and tragedy life put them through before allowing their forever, made Hawk and Betsy treasure each other. But if their marriage was cake, Trapper, their three-year-old adopted son, was the icing.

The boy was the product of Betsy's deceased ex-husband's affair with a young secretary killed in the same tragic accident that later claimed his life. But Trapper and Betsy were joined in a deeper bond than biology could provide, the boy born from his mother's soul rather than her womb. The young Crow father, too, held a significant place in the child's life. Hawk's vision five years before he met mother and son had predestined the outcome, enabling him to wait for Betsy and sealing his own role in Trapper's life.

Summertime had come to the Beartooths, and with it came the outfitting job that took Hawk away from his family for days at a time. When allowed to be with them even for short periods, Hawk found his wife and son competing to see who could secure the most attention from the handsome half-blood head of the family. Usually, Trapper won, at least until the lights went out.

But on this night, the little cowboy was not willing to give in even though it was well past his bedtime. Hawk put his son to bed for the second time, told him a story about cowboys, kissed him goodnight, and headed anxiously in to his wife.

But before they could get in even one warm, wet kiss, the little boy in clown pajamas—accented by cowboy boots on the wrong feet that kicked his dad in the face as the boy climbed over—claimed a place between his parents, who could do nothing but laugh. The little cowboy grabbed each of them around the neck, pulling them to him with the smile neither parent could refuse.

"How much do you love me, Son?" It was Hawk's everyday question.

"One thousand!" The answer was always the same, the biggest number in existence to Trapper.

"And Mommy?" Hawk asked as he combed his fingers through his son's dark hair.

"One thousand!" Trapper's yelled response bounced off the ceiling.

"And I love you one thousand, Trapper, and you, too, Daddy." Reaching across the boy, the couple kissed, only to have their faces pulled down again to include their son's pucker that consumed his face.

With no choice but to give in, the threesome slept until Hawk awoke and carried the sleeping boy back into his own bedroom. Quietly closing his door, he tiptoed back to Betsy and found her awake, smiling in anticipation. Pulling off his boxers, Hawk disclosed just how anxious he was.

"Finally! Damn, I've missed you, sweetheart! I wish I hadn't told Jake I'd outfit this summer. It's torture being away from you and Trapper." Hawk pulled Betsy to him in a bear hug.

"You don't have to outfit, Hawk. We have money, if you'd let us use some from selling the construction company. Even the interest off the money would be enough to pay off our land and house, with more than enough left for Trapper's college."

"We've had this discussion before. Patrick left that money to you and Trapper. You and Trapper are my family now, and I'll take care of you."

Pulling her to him, he consumed her mouth, their tongues seeking out each other in their dance of passion. Continuing his kissing ritual down her neck, he stripped off her nightgown, worn only because of the little intruder who often sneaked into their bed in the middle of the night.

The next stop in his trail of passion was her breasts, followed by the belly button ring that could still arouse him with one tiny sparkle. As his head slipped beneath the covers, she raised herself to kiss the top of his head and lock her fingers through his thick black hair, tightening her grip each time he found her most sensual spots.

With bodies ablaze, Hawk entered her, driving repeatedly at her beckoning until the moment of exhilaration demanded he empty into her. Holding their bodies taut, he overflowed into her, liquid passion long overdue in its demand for release.

As always after making love, he cuddled her, stroking her breast, kissing her repeatedly as if there was no climax to his passion for her. It was then that he discovered it under her right breast.

"Baby, did you bump yourself?"

"Not that I know of. Why?"

"There's something here." Hawk turned on the bedside lamp. "Give me your hand." Taking her fingers, Hawk showed her what he was feeling.

" It's a lump. I can't believe I didn't know that was there." Betsy continued to feel under her breast as she responded to her husband's worried stare.

"Is it sore?"

"Just a tiny bit, Hawk. Or maybe that's because you keep fooling with it."

"I'm sorry, sweetheart!" Hawk scrutinized the lump, touching it gently. Betsy could see the terror in his eyes.

"It's probably nothing, Hawk. Don't look so worried."

"You've got to see about it. Tomorrow. Okay?"

Betsy reached across her husband and turned off the light before nestling into his arms, laying her head on his chest.

"I don't even have a doctor here, other than Doc Harris. Who will I see?"

"We'll find you one. We're not messing around with this, Betsy. It's too damn scary. If you can't get in to see somebody, we'll go to the reservation. You can see Adam. We were best friends as kids. He's an ob-gyn, and he'll see you on the side even though you're not Crow."

Betsy called every specialist in Billings the next morning, but the earliest appointment she could get was two weeks away. Hawk was not willing to wait that long and called his friend.

"Adam can see you late this afternoon. Call your mom to keep Trapper for us?"

"I think you're overreacting, Hawk. Why don't we just wait for the appointment in Billings?"

"No way! It's too risky." Hawk began pacing but stopped in front of Betsy. He took her in his arms and pressed her head to his chest.

"Please, Betsy. Don't fight me on this. I'm scared to death."

Hearing the fright in her husband's voice, she took his face in her hands, smiled, and kissed him.

"Okay, my darling. You win. But I'm telling you, it's nothing to be worried about. Women have cysts like this all the time. Call your mom and talk to her. Being a nurse, she'll tell you the same thing, I'm sure."

"Have you ever had one, a cyst?" Hawk stared into Betsy's eyes, waiting for her reply.

"No, but there's always the first time."

Hawk called his mother later. Just as Betsy had said, her mother-in-law mentioned cysts but also said with Betsy's history of cancer the prudent thing to do was to see a doctor as soon as possible.

When Betsy told her mother, Sue Ann was just as alarmed as Hawk but tried not to show it in front of her daughter.

"I'm sure it's nothing, but call me on your cell phone, Betsy, and let me know what Adam says. I need to know what he says before you get here to pick up Trapper."

****

"So you're the woman that tamed the infamous Hawk Larson! Finally, I get to meet you." Adam hugged Betsy when he entered the examination room before reaching for his old friend's hand.

"Well, I don't know that taming is possible, but he is my husband." Betsy smiled at Hawk as she answered Adam.

"She likes me wild, Adam." Hawk put his arm around Betsy, hugging her close. Even with the teasing and the small talk, Adam could sense how scared Hawk was by the way he kept rubbing his thigh with his left hand, a habit Adam remembered from their childhood on the reservation, where the two boys had earned renegade status by staying in nearly constant trouble.

"Hawk, you need to wait in my office while I examine Betsy. Besides, you're making me nervous, so I can imagine what you're doing to her." Reluctantly, Hawk left the room to pace the hall.

"You must be special, Betsy. I've never seen Hawk like this. He's a wreck. I'm used to him being the cool, tough guy."

"He's scared. I had cancer seven years ago—before I knew him. I had a hysterectomy."

"Oh?" Adam questioned as he continued to examine Betsy. "Hawk told me you two have a three-year-old."

"Our son, Trapper. He's almost four years old, but it's a long story. Trapper is our adopted son, but with his dark hair and eyes, he looks just like Hawk. Acts like him, too. You'd swear he was part Crow if you could see him galloping his pony."

After finishing the examination, Adam told Betsy

to get dressed and he'd talk to her and Hawk together.

"I'm sending you to see a surgeon in Billings, Betsy. With your history of cancer, I'm sure he'll want to do a biopsy. He's a good friend of mine, so I called him on his cell phone. Interrupted his golf game, but he owes me one. I've got you an appointment Wednesday morning."

"No damn way, Adam! This can't wait! Get your surgeon friend back on the phone and tell him he's got to see her sooner," Hawk demanded, giving Adam a frustrated look.

"Today is Friday, for God's sake! Don't go freaking out on us, Hawk. Jack Hopkins is the best in the field, specializes in breast surgery. He's the surgeon I'd want for my wife, if I still had one, but he can't see Betsy till Wednesday. He's on vacation. You know doctors have to have some time off, too, if they're going to stay alert and focused."

"Yeah, well, it won't hurt him to miss a fucking round or two of golf." Hawk stood, his face and posture showing the anger he felt.

"Hawk! I can't believe you said that!" Surprised at her husband's choice of words, Betsy tried a subtle reprimand to let Adam know this was unusual even for Hawk. Adam seemed unshaken by his friend's remark. He knew Hawk and understood his frustration.

"What if it's cancer, Betsy? Time is crucial. Adam, do something." Hawk walked to the window, running his hands through his hair.

"Hawk, sweetheart, I know you're terrified of all of this, but really it's okay. Remember, I've been here before." Betsy left her chair to stand beside Hawk, rubbing his back. "I can't believe how fast Adam got me an appointment. Be grateful and trust Adam on this one. Besides, even if it turns out to be cancer, it doesn't necessarily mean I'm going to die."

"Don't use that word, Betsy!" Hawk raised his voice. "Not even in that context." Hawk sat back down and rubbed his leg harder, never taking his eyes off Betsy.

"Hawk, she's right. I know you want this taken care of yesterday, when you two found the lump, but getting an appointment with Dr. Hopkins this quickly is unheard of. It usually takes a month or longer. Be thankful."

Adam rubbed his chin and stared at Hawk. "Since patience doesn't seem to be one of your virtues, I need to warn you. This process is not going to be instant. You could have a lot of waiting before you know for sure if it's malignant or not. With Betsy's history of cancer, I'm sure Dr. Hopkins will be very thorough and will possibly do additional tests. If he does a biopsy, and that is likely, he will be careful in analyzing results and may seek other opinions to be sure." Adam noticed the look of panic on Hawk's face.

"You need to keep a positive attitude, Hawk. Ninety per cent of lumps turn out to be nothing. True, it feels irregular around the edges, which is suspect, but even with that, chances are it's benign."

"But what if it's not benign, Adam? What then? A mastectomy? Chemo? How foolproof is all that? I need to know what we're up against."

Adam noticed Hawk's hands were shaking.

"Take a breath, man! The surgeon will answer all your questions on Wednesday. Damn, Betsy! How can you stand being married to him? I think I like the cool, tough Hawk better than the doting husband." Adam took out a prescription pad and scribbled on it before handing it to Betsy.

"What's that for?" Hawk looked over Betsy's shoulder at the prescription. "Is it pain pills? Does it hurt, baby?" Hawk put his hand on Betsy's back and rubbed her neck. He locked his eyes on hers, waiting for her answer.

"Hawk!" Adam raised his voice to get Hawk's attention. "The prescription is for you. It's a low dose of something to calm you down some, so you're tolerable at least, and so you don't rub your leg raw. Damn! You still do that just like when we were kids." Adam smiled and looked at Betsy. "My mom could tell when Hawk was lying about something we'd done, just by his rubbing that leg."

Hooking his fingertips in his pockets, Hawk stood defiant. "Keep your damn prescription, Adam! I'm not taking that shit. I'm fine!"

"Yeah, well, I'll let Betsy be the judge of that. She's the one who has to put up with her condition and have a lunatic for a husband at the same time." Adam looked at Betsy and motioned to the prescription. "Don't let him talk you out of getting that filled, Betsy."

Betsy laughed as they left Adam's office. She had whisked Hawk out to keep him from asking any more questions or going off on Adam again.

"This is not funny, Betsy. It's serious."

"It is what it is, Hawk, and you getting all upset is not going to change it one bit. Give me the keys. I'm driving. Look at your hands." Taking his hands, she held them up so he could see. "I've never seen you this nervous."

Hawk jerked his hands from her, putting them in his pockets.

"I'm perfectly capable of driving, thank you. And I'm not taking those damn pills. I just need a cigarette." Hawk looked away from Betsy as he made the remark.

"Hawk, you haven't smoked in years!"

"I know. It's just when I'm nervous." Hawk looked back at Betsy and smiled. "And sometimes after we've had really good sex."

"Oh? Let me know the next time you want a cigarette in the middle of the night. I'd like to know what gets the 'really good sex' rating."

This remark broke the tension, and Hawk laughed, giving Betsy the relief she was seeking. Putting his arm around her, he stopped in the doorway of the medical building and kissed her, disregarding the stares of the people in the waiting room.

****

The appointment with the surgeon went much better than the one with Adam, thanks to the pill Betsy forced her husband to take in addition to giving him a serious warning to "act civil." But the pills did not remove the alarm and helplessness Hawk felt at not being able to protect his wife from this potential enemy.

Betsy was sent down the hall for a mammogram and then for an ultrasound to determine if the lump was solid or fluid. Then, just as Adam had warned, there was more waiting to hear from the surgeon what the next step would be. With confirmation that the lump was solid, a biopsy was scheduled for a week later.

One night a couple of days before her surgery, Betsy awoke to find her husband's side of the bed vacant, something that had happened frequently since finding the lump. Leaving their bed, she put on Hawk's shirt that hung on the bedpost and headed for the big chair where she knew she would find him looking out their bedroom window at the moonlit mountains.

"Care if I join you in your mountain gazing?"

"Please." He looked up at her and smiled, patting his lap.

Betsy took her place in Hawk's lap, locked her arms around his neck, and kissed him tenderly as she combed her fingers through his hair.

"I'm sorry, sweetheart. I didn't mean to wake you."

"Then make sure you're always beside me and I won't wake up." Betsy played with Hawk's hair, twisting it in her fingers as she smiled into his eyes.

Noticing she had only buttoned one button on his shirt, he reached to button the one below it.

"You know, Betsy, it doesn't matter what you put on, this is still my favorite outfit. Remember the first morning we woke up together in your mom's cabin, and you put on my shirt? You were talking on your cell phone, madder than hell at what's-her-name for calling you, and you were pacing and trying to contain that long mass of blonde curls that kept falling in your face. I laid on that sofa and watched, hypnotized, amazed at how beautiful you were and how lucky I was to finally have a chance with you."

"Oh, yes! I remember. We made love so many times that first two days, I think even Guinness would be shocked."

Betsy moved her arms and cuddled against Hawk's chest as he played with her hair, caressing it and twisting her long curls around his fingers. Several minutes passed before either said anything, but even in the silence Betsy could sense the anxiety in her husband.

"Hawk. We need to talk. I know you don't want to talk about this, but we need to."

"No, Betsy!" Hawk spoke loudly. "Don't go there! I can't handle it!" He held her out from him and stared into her eyes almost in a rage as his eyes became transparent.

"I can't protect you from this, and I don't know how to deal with it. And I can't live without you. I won't! Do you understand me?"

His voice cracked, as if this was the release he had been seeking, and he wrapped his arms around his wife as she held his head to her chest. Even though he was silent, she felt his tears on her breasts and held him tighter, as if he were a child needing comfort in the dark.

"How did I get so lucky?" Pulling his face up to kiss him, she wiped his eyes with the sleeve of his shirt.

"Lucky? Yeah, you're real damn lucky to have a wimp for a husband." Hawk pulled away from her, leaving the chair and heading for the bathroom, where he hoped cold water would help him regain a little manliness. She met him at the bathroom door and put her arms around his waist, looking up at him.

"Yeah, a wimp who dragged himself to the top of a mountain with three cracked ribs and a bullet hole in his side, over three years ago, to save my butt. And just as important, a man not afraid to show emotion where his wife is concerned. You're right, Hawk. I'm real damn lucky to have you love me, and should something happen to me, you'll live because you are a man; you're

my man and you have to. A big part of me
with you, depending on you."

Taking him by the hand, she led him ac
to their son's room. The little boy slept with his cowboy
teddy bear nestled under one arm. A picture of him with
his mom and dad on their wedding day stood on his
bedside table, keeping watch over him as he slept.

They sat on the foot of the bed, watching him
sleep, for several minutes before leaving his room.
Hawk kissed the boy, took off the cowboy boots he had
sneaked on after lights out, and replaced the covers he
had kicked off.

Stopping in the hall, Hawk faced his wife, putting
his hands on her shoulders.

"Okay. When you're right, you're right, but just
don't feel you have to prove it. And please, Betsy, let's
not talk about it anymore. If things go wrong, there'll
be time to talk then. Right now, I just want you in my
shirt, at least for a couple of minutes, next to me in our
bed."

Smiling, she held tight to his hand as he led her
back to their bedroom.

****

The day before the surgery, Betsy put on her
walking clothes and grabbed her Winston fly fishing
cap.

"Where you going, sweetheart? Surely you're not
walking?"

"Hawk, I need to get away for a few minutes. I feel
fine. Besides, after my surgery tomorrow, it'll be a few
days before I get to walk again."

Taking down the prescription bottle from the
cabinet, she handed a pill to Hawk with a glass of

water. Each time she noticed his nerves becoming frayed, Betsy pulled out the prescription bottle.

"Here, Hawk, take this. You get Trapper to sleep while I'm gone, and try to get some rest yourself. Every time I woke up last night, you were awake, staring at the ceiling. If I'd had a pack of cigarettes, I swear I would have made you smoke."

After groaning in protest, Hawk took the pill.

"You won't be gone long, will you, Betsy?"

"You know how long it takes me to walk six miles. Here, I'll take my cell phone." Betsy picked up the phone from the table and put it in her pocket. "Now, can I just pretend this is a normal afternoon?"

Walking her to the porch, he kissed her.

"I love you, Betsy."

"I love you, too, sweetheart. Now get that pint-sized cowboy of yours to sleep, and you rest, too."

When Betsy got back to the cabin, Hawk was snoring on the sofa, on his back, with Trapper stretched out across his stomach and chest. She sat in the chair and watched them for a long time, feeling very lucky, even with her present state of affairs, to have these two guys in her life. Closing her eyes, she prayed.

****

In her remote cabin in the Beartooths, Sue Ann also prayed. She had moved to the porch, where she could look at the mountains and count her blessings while replaying her daughter's tragedies and joys. Try as she might, she could not stop herself from thinking the worst was possible. Custer had sensed she needed space and time alone and had walked to his old cabin in the aspen grove "to check on things."

As she looked up at Six Rocks, she replayed all the

bargains that had been made in these mountains. A seriously wounded Hawk bargained with God, begging for the strength to save Betsy from her would-be killers almost four years ago. Custer, too, bargained with the Great One that day to delay his heart attack in order to protect Hawk and Betsy. And Betsy bargained almost a year later, promising it would be her last time to love if God would give her one more chance with Hawk.

"Okay, God, it's my turn." Sue Ann's eyes filled as she searched the mountain peaks. "You've been here for my family forever, but it took a lot of convincing to get us to acknowledge you. And now here I sit, about to try my hand at bargaining, something I was taught as a child growing up in Mississippi that we shouldn't do. But I know you better than that.

"Decades ago, you gave me twins, Betsy and Tobi, and even though I was unwed and undeserving, you allowed me to keep one of them. I thought you had punished me by taking Tobi, but the truth was, you blessed me by letting me have Betsy, and I thank you.

"You blessed me again by letting her survive cancer and giving her so much happiness with Hawk and Trapper. And you even gave me Custer after I denied him so many times." Sue Ann wiped her tears and searched the peaks again.

"Now here I am again, begging. Please, God. If one of us has to have cancer, let it be me and not my daughter. You'll never hear me complain. Just let her live to love and be loved for a lot longer."

****

That night, Betsy cuddled in Hawk's lap as he sat in the big easy chair he loved, his legs outstretched on the ottoman. Neither of them desired to move, not wanting to rush morning. Jealous, Trapper climbed onto the ottoman.

"I wanna hold you, Mommy."

"Well, climb up here and hold me, Little Big Man."

Minutes later, Trapper was asleep with his legs around his mother's waist and his head on her chest. As she played with her son's hair and kissed him, she wondered how long she would be able to feel him against her breasts. As they sat nestled three deep in the big chair, they slept, exhausted from worry and thinking, until Isabel, Hawk's mother who had come to watch Trapper, took the boy from his mother's arms without waking her.

"I'll put him to bed, Son. Don't you think you two should go, too? You've got a long day ahead of you tomorrow."

"Thanks, Mom. We'll sit here a while longer. I just want to hold her." Kissing his wife's forehead, he rubbed his cheek on her head and locked his arms around her tighter.

Isabel patted her son's shoulder before leaving. Carrying her sleeping grandson, she turned out the light as she left the room.

****

"You want to get some coffee downstairs, Hawk? It'll probably be a while before they tell you anything." Custer watched his nephew pace in the waiting room at the hospital.

"No, Unk. I'm not leaving till this is over for Betsy. Dr. Hopkins said it wouldn't take long to remove the lump." The leg rubbing had begun, and Custer and Sue Ann could only watch as the young husband further

16

exacerbated his misery.

"Why don't you just bring us all a cup, Custer? I'll wait with Hawk." Sue Ann moved to sit beside Hawk.

"I don't know why we have to wait three days to get a pathology report." Hawk remarked to Sue Ann. "Seems like they ought to be able to tell as soon as they look at it if it's cancer or not. I should have asked the surgeon more questions, but Betsy wouldn't let me. I kind of acted like an ass the day we saw Adam." Hawk started pacing and stopped the leg rubbing.

"You and Adam must have been really good friends growing up. That was nice of him to be here for Betsy's surgery. I know it makes you feel better." Sue Ann tried to ease her son-in-law's worries.

"Yeah. Adam's a good guy. We were talking this morning about the last time he saw Custer. Back when we were seniors in high school, Unk sneaked bags of pot out of our backpacks and burned them in the campfire when we were passed out in our tent. We thought we were being so slick, taking our pot and heading for the mountains, but somehow he found out. Didn't even know he was there till we woke up the next morning. He still won't tell me how he knew. Says he can never divulge his sources."

"He sees all...he knows all, at least where you're concerned, Hawk. I hope you know how much he loves you."

"Yeah, Sue Ann. I know, and I'm grateful. He's always been more father than uncle." Back in the uncomfortable chair, the cowboy began rubbing his leg again but stopped when he noticed Sue Ann watching him. He picked up an outdated *Field and Stream* and turned pages without seeing anything.

Minutes seemed like hours, but Sue Ann knew it really had not been that long when Adam came into the waiting room.

Adam put his hand on Hawk's shoulder.

"She's doing fine. John removed the lump with no problems and sent it to the lab."

"What does he think? He must have some idea." Hawk stood to face Adam.

"If he did, he wouldn't say. He's an excellent surgeon but cautious. The pathologist will make the call on whether it's malignant or not. I wish I could tell you more, Hawk, but you've got some more waiting." Seeing the tension in his friend, he put his hand back on his shoulder. "Hang in there, man. You'll know soon."

"Oh, Adam," Hawk yelled to Adam to stop him as he turned away. "I never thanked you for helping us out. And I'm really sorry for being such a jerk that day in your office. I got a real lecture for using the"—Hawk cleared his throat and looked at Sue Ann—"the F word."

"It's okay, Hawk. I understood."

Adam crossed to Sue Ann and extended his hand. "Well, there's no guessing who you are. Betsy looks just like you."

"We hear that a lot." Sue Ann held to Adam's hand. "Thank you, Adam, for being here with Betsy today. It means a great deal to us."

"No problem. I was glad Dr. Hopkins asked me to assist."

Seeing Custer enter the waiting room, Adam walked toward him smiling.

Custer put the cups of coffee on the table and grabbed Adam's hand. They both glanced at Hawk, who was back to pacing.

"Can't you control Hawk, Custer?"

"Couldn't when you guys were young and can't now." Custer gave Adam a pat on the back. "You did good, Adam. Knew you had it in you. We're all proud of you."

"Thanks, Custer." Adam looked at Hawk, who now stood looking out the window. "Well, at least you've given your leg a reprieve. Where are those pills, Hawk? Don't you think you need to take one before you pass out on us?"

"Hell, no! I don't need a pill. I need my wife to be okay." Hawk didn't turn around as he spoke.

"You know, after losing my ass in my divorce, I didn't think I'd ever marry again. But if I could have what you and Betsy have, I believe I'd be willing to try one more time."

A few minutes later, Dr. Hopkins came into the waiting room.

"Mr. Larson, your wife is doing just fine. You'll be able to take her home as soon as the anesthesia wears off."

"Will you call us as soon as you get the report from the lab?" Hawk asked.

"Yes. As soon as I get all the results, I'll call. I promise."

****

The next two days seemed endless, and Betsy made Hawk take Trapper on a fishing trip to Keyser Brown the second day, just to give herself a reprieve from her husband's restlessness. But on the third day after her biopsy, there was no convincing him to leave the cabin for any reason. Knowing how anxious Betsy and Hawk were, Custer and Sue Ann took Trapper to spend the day and night with them.

Every time the phone rang, Hawk stood waiting for Betsy to answer it. Finally, late in the afternoon, the call came.

"This is she. Yes, I'll hold." Turning to Hawk, she smiled, trying to reassure him as he walked to her. He put his hand on her shoulder, rubbing it gently.

"Yes, Dr. Hopkins, this is Betsy." She listened attentively, knowing Hawk's heart was racing.

"Yes, I understand, Dr. Hopkins. Thank you for calling, and for everything."

When she turned to her husband, a big grin covered her face, and she grabbed him around the neck.

"It's benign, Hawk. No cancer!"

As they hugged, both began to laugh and cry at the same time.

Chapter Two

"Well, if it isn't Hawk and Hawk, Jr.! Just the man I wanted to see!"

Darlene left from behind the counter at the post office and came around to hug Hawk and to peek under the oversized black cowboy hat covering the eyes at Hawk's knees.

"Is there a cowboy under there somewhere?"

Pushing back his hat, Trapper smiled up at the woman. "It's me! It's Trapper, Dar-Ling."

"Oh, so it is, and how is your mommy doing?"

"Mommy's not in the hospital no more. Daddy bringed her home. She gots a Band-Aid right here." Trapper pointed to his chest.

"I'm so glad she's home, Trapper. You tell her Dar-Ling said hello."

"Okay." Trapper looked up from under his hat. "Daddy, tell Mommy Dar-Ling said hi."

"I'll do it, Son. Don't you let me forget, now." Trapper immediately headed for the copy machine to push buttons.

"She's good, Darlene, but she sure scared the hell out of me."

"Yeah, she scared us all. Tell her she even had big Mack on his knees. Don't know if it got higher than the handlebars on his Harley, but he prayed. We all did."

"Yeah. God sure smiled down on the Larson

family." Hawk propped his arm on the counter. "Any mail?"

"Gosh darn, I almost forgot!" A big smile covered Darlene's face. "It came, Hawk!"

"From her publisher?" Hawk stood straight and smiled. "Really?"

"Yep! Two boxes. I've had them for two days waiting for you to come in. Could hardly contain myself but knew you guys were pretty busy with more pressing matters."

Leaving the counter, Darlene headed for the back room. After two trips, two boxes sat on the counter.

"I can't believe it!" Hawk read the return address on the boxes. "The timing couldn't be any better. Don't tell anybody, Darlene. Sue Ann and I are planning a surprise celebration for her. You and Mack are invited. Could be Saturday. Can you make it?"

"Wouldn't miss it for the world. I better have a copy in there. Lord, we've all been waiting so long for this book. Everyone in Red Lodge is excited."

"Yeah, well, I might be a little red-faced for a few weeks when you read it, but I'm really proud of Betsy. She writes like her mom and can be pretty graphic."

"Hawk Larson, red-faced? Now I really can't wait!" The postmaster threw back her head and gave the hearty laugh she was famous for.

Hawk loaded the boxes into his truck but did not head home. Instead, he delivered them to Sue Ann and Custer's cabin, where the plotting began.

****

"Are you ready, Betsy?"

"Just about. I still can't believe Mom and Custer are throwing a party. Guess they must have really been worried about me."

"They didn't invite many people. Sue Ann just wanted to thank them for all the prayers and good wishes they sent when you had your scare."

Pulling onto the forestry road, Betsy couldn't believe the vehicles. "Didn't invite many people? How on earth will they fit all these people in the cabin?"

"Actually, I think they're having it outside. Custer's been barbecuing all day, from what I've heard. I offered to help, but he wouldn't let me."

While Betsy waited for Hawk to take Trapper out of his car seat, several people walked toward them. Overwhelmed with hugs and well wishes, she couldn't help but feel they were making way too big a deal over one small lump. As they moved to the side of the cabin where tables were set up, cheers rose from the crowd and a banner was raised.

Red Lodge Proudly Presents:
THE HAWK AND THE DEER
by
Elizabeth Parish Larson

Betsy stared at the banner as Hawk put his arm around her waist.

"Congratulations, sweetheart. Your book has arrived." Betsy looked up at Hawk and grabbed him around the neck and kissed him.

"You didn't open the boxes?"

"Nope. Saved the honors for you."

Moving to the table that held the two big boxes, Betsy smiled at her mom, who stood by them.

"Are you ready, Betsy?" Sue Ann held up a box cutter.

Hugging her mom and then Custer, she took the

cutter.

"I'm too nervous. Help me, honey. I'll slice myself." Handing the cutter to Hawk, she waited anxiously while he cut the tape loose.

"Okay, Betsy. She's all yours." Hawk moved back.

As Betsy held up the first copy, the crowd chanted, "Speech!"

Hawk lifted her up to stand on the bench by the table, and the crowd became quiet.

"I feel like I'm accepting an award or something. Well, let's see. How about the first copy goes to the person I dedicated the book to." After opening the book, she cleared her throat.

"To Hawk, my fly-fishing partner, my lover..." Betsy stopped here to direct a wink and a grin at her husband, who beamed as the crowd laughed. "My husband, my best friend. I love you."

Handing the book to her husband, she put her arms around him and kissed him like they were alone in the dark instead of surrounded by a multitude of well-wishers. Once again the crowd applauded.

"The second copy goes to my mom, Dr. Sue Ann Parish, my inspiration, the source of any gift of writing I might have. I love you, Mom." She presented the book with a hug, and Sue Ann took the book and held it proudly to her chest.

By the end of the celebration, many had already read parts of the book, some aloud, much to Hawk's pretend embarrassment as he assured everyone that he'd taught Betsy everything she knew. After the last of the guests left, Betsy and Hawk sat on the sofa in front of the fire. Hawk put his arm around his author wife and hugged her tight. He was glad the mountain air had provided a chill, the perfect ambiance for the occasion, just as it had been that summer they first met and first made love in the old cabin.

"Are you ready, Custer? We better get Tonto home to bed." Trapper was asleep on the floor in front of the fireplace. He was still wearing the headband Custer had made for him.

"Where are you going?" Betsy looked at her mother and Custer, who had picked the sleeping boy up and headed for the door.

"Oh, something Custer, Hawk, and I planned. You two have the cabin for the weekend. Custer and I will keep Trapper at your place. We figured you two might want to replay some of those scenes from *The Hawk and the Deer*."

Betsy looked at Hawk, who raised his open palms and gave a mischievous look like he had no idea any of this was planned.

"What?" he asked, smiling.

"You guys! As if the whole night wasn't enough! Thanks, Mom, Custer! I love you." Betsy hugged them again and kissed Trapper goodnight as they headed out the door.

As the car headlights pulled away from the yard, Hawk looked at Betsy, giving her his most roguish grin. Reaching under the sofa, he pulled out a small box and handed it to her.

"What's this?" Inside the box was a gold charm—a book, engraved with *The Hawk and the Deer* by Elizabeth Parish Larson.

"Oh, Hawk, it's beautiful! I can't wait to add it to my bracelet."

"There's something else underneath."

"There's more?" Pulling up the cardboard, Betsy gasped. A diamond belly button ring with two big diamonds, one at each end of the bar, sparkled up at her.

"Hawk, this is beautiful, but it's too expensive. I don't want you outfitting anymore this summer just to make extra money to pay for this."

"I've been saving for this since the day you finally submitted your book to the publisher. It's paid for. You might never get anything else this nice, but it's important to me that you have it now. After all, it's how you attracted me in the first place."

"Oh, yeah? So you're telling me if I put this on right now, I can expect more, maybe even new material for my next novel?"

"I don't know. Is there anything we haven't done?" Noting her look of disbelief, Hawk recanted.

"Guess not! Let me rephrase that. Is there anything we did here that you'd like to replay?"

At the same time, they both looked across the room to the bearskin rug.

After undressing her, he began the voluptuous kisses he was famous for as she leaned back on the sofa, supple and eager. Handing her the box containing his new jewel, she put it on as he undressed, leaving his shirt nearby, the outfit he planned for her to wear the next day as she read their love story aloud to him.

"This is so beautiful, darling. Thank you."

After they had ravaged every inch of each other's bodies, bringing them both almost to the point of no return, Hawk lifted his wife and started across the room. With her legs wrapped tightly around his waist, she smiled in eager anticipation as her handsome half-blood carried her to the bearskin rug. Tenderly, but with the unbridled passion she longed for and expected from her lover and husband, Hawk made love to her surrounded by the deep softness of the old grizzly—the rapture temporarily over, the ecstasy complete once again.

****

A few weeks after the celebration, Betsy received her first report from her agent about the sales of her novel. Excited and surprised with how well it was doing already, she headed to her mother's cabin, knowing her mom would be just as thrilled. She found her sitting on the porch, looking soberly at the mountains.

"Mom, you look so sad. Is something wrong?"

Smiling at her daughter, she motioned for Betsy to sit in the other rocker. "Oh, I have a little something on my mind, but you first. I know you've got some good news by that smile you were wearing when you got out of your Jeep."

"Unofficial sales report. Look!" Betsy handed the paper to her mother.

"Oh, Betsy, this is wonderful! I knew it would be a best seller." Sue Ann smiled through her tears. "So what now, Daughter? Got another one in the works?"

"Not yet, but it'll happen. Didn't you tell me not to stew over ideas? You said they'll just come to you, sometimes in the middle of the night, or when you least expect them."

"Yes, I did, and they will." Sue Ann's somberness returned as she gazed again at Six Rocks.

"Betsy, I hate to put a damper on your joy, but there is something I need to tell you. Try not to be upset." She reached over and patted her daughter's

27

hand. "It's important to me that you stay focused on your life and your joys, because your joys are my joys."

"Mom, you're scaring me." Betsy folded the report and dropped it in her backpack, giving her mother her full attention. "You're not moving back to Alaska, are you?"

"I wish it were that simple. No, I'm not moving from this cabin or from Custer. My life is complete now. I have no regrets, and having you and Hawk and my precious grandson close by is pure gold."

"Then what is it, Mom?" Betsy's gaze was glued to her mother's, and she scooted her rocker closer.

"You know last week, when Custer and I spent a few days in Billings?"

"Yes. You said you needed to do some shopping."

"That was only partially true, Betsy. I was in the hospital, getting some tests run." Sue Ann looked at her daughter and saw the alarm in her eyes. "I know. I should have told you, but I just didn't want to worry you. You've had enough worries of your own."

"Mom, please. Now I'm really scared. Tell me."

"Well, you know the breast cancer you didn't have? Your mom is not quite as lucky."

"No! This is not happening!" Betsy jumped from the rocker and stood in front of her mother. "Is it a lump? How do you know it's not benign like mine?" Betsy put her hand to her heart.

"It's not just a lump, Betsy. It's much bigger, and it is malignant. I start chemo at the end of the week and have opted for a double mastectomy as soon as they think they have the tumor shrunk enough."

Betsy began sobbing out of control and fell to her knees, burying her head in her mother's lap.

"Don't cry, Betsy. I need you to be strong for me. It doesn't mean I'm going to die. It just means I'm going to be very uncomfortable and, well, less attractive for a few months. I just hope Trapper will recognize me without my braid."

"You'll lose your hair?" Betsy reached and caressed her mother's thick, curly braid that hung over her shoulder and reached almost to her waist.

"Only the rare cases don't. In fact, Custer and I are both getting our hair cut short. That way it won't be quite as drastic when it starts coming out. We'll donate our hair to 'Locks of Love.' He insists on cutting his braids, too, but I told him he is not getting his head shaved, like so many mates do to show support. I want some hair next to me to run my fingers through."

"Just get your hair made into a wig, Mom, and you wear it. That way it will still be yours."

"No. Vanity has never been a major part of me, Betsy. I'd rather some woman have it who is really concerned about her appearance. Besides, I'll just recuperate sitting here looking at our mountains. Most women with breast cancer aren't this lucky." Sue Ann stared at the mountains and smiled, trying to comfort Betsy.

"When did you find out, Mom?"

"For sure, yesterday. I wanted to pick a good time to tell you, but there is no good time for news like this." Sue Ann reached and took her daughter's hand. "There is something I want you to help me with, Betsy."

"What, Mom? Anything you want, I'll do. You were there for me when I had cancer, and I'll be here for you."

"It's sort of a project, something my publisher has

been asking me to do for a while, and now seems the perfect time. I need to write my story like you did for you and Hawk. Actually, it's more than one story."

"Will you write your love story with Custer?"

"Custer has been part of many stories in my life, since we've been in love for so many years. I just finally realized how important he was to me, so I've made our being together full time. I won't end my story with Custer, because I want it to go on and on." Sue Ann reached for Betsy's hand. "Will you help me, Betsy? There will be times when I'm too weak to write, but I can tell you, and you can put it into beautiful words like you did *The Hawk and the Deer*. This will be the last I'll write—not meaning I think I'm dying, but I just want to spend time enjoying Custer, you and Hawk, and most of all my grandson. I've been fortunate and am leaving a legacy already, not to mention having a daughter who writes even better than I do. We'll author this first book as a mother/daughter team. Will you do it?"

"Yes, Mom. When do we start?"

"As soon as you're ready." Sue Ann smiled.

"Where will you begin?"

"At the beginning. In Mississippi when I was a child growing up in that turbulent era of the '50s and '60s that made no sense at all to me. We'll start with my taboo friendship with Elizabeth and end the first book with the birth of you and Tobi. I already have a title—*The Gully Path*. There will be one more book to follow, one that tells Shade's and my story in Alaska. And I already have the title for it. It could only be *Under Northern Lights*. We'll take it one day at a time, one book at a time."

"Does this mean you'll finally tell me about my father—that ghostly shadow you refused to talk about except for telling me he died in Vietnam?" Betsy looked deep into her mother's eyes.

"Yes, Betsy. You will know more than you care to know about him, and you will have some misconceptions cleared up." Sue Ann paused and looked at the mountains again as if searching for words. "No, let's be truthful." She redirected her eyes to Betsy's. "They were outright lies. I haven't been honest with you, my daughter. Promise me that you won't judge him or me too harshly for the way things turned out." Sue Ann put her hand to Betsy's cheek. "I must warn you, Betsy. You may be hurt."

"Can it be any worse than the news you just gave me?"

"Probably not. I just wanted you to be aware that what you will learn might shock you." Both were silent again and used their silence to search the mountain peaks for solace. Betsy was first to break the silence.

"Does Hawk know about your...?"

"It's cancer, Betsy. Call it what it is."

"Cancer, then. Does he know?"

"Custer is telling him as we speak. They took Trapper and went for a ride up to Keyser Brown. Custer is going into the wilderness for a few days, seeking visions of reassurance. He's pretty devastated by this whole thing but doesn't have that tender expressiveness that Hawk does."

"I'm glad Hawk decided not to outfit anymore this summer. He can take care of Trapper while we write. Mom, promise me one thing."

"Anything, Betsy."

"Don't give up. Don't ever give up until you take your last breath. I need you, Mom."

"I promise."

Mother and daughter embraced as the snow-peaked mountains looked down on them with promises, or hopes, of tomorrows.

Chapter Three

Seattle

His outward demeanor and expression was that of a humbled and apologetic man as he walked through the gates of the Washington State Prison, a free man again, but he was laughing inside. His incarceration for involuntary manslaughter was over for the model prisoner who "found Jesus" during his stay, reading his Bible for hours daily and greeting his fellow inmates with, "Smile, Jesus loves you," just like the prison chaplain who helped win him an early release.

Four years had passed, four years of punishment for driving under the influence of alcohol and cocaine and running down an old lady as she crossed the street in Seattle, an old lady who had the misfortune of looking like the abusive grandmother who raised him and his older brother Billy. The old lady in the street was one in a long line of victims and was the easiest kill of all—an act by a crazed man who impulsively forgot there would be no monetary gain.

Maltese Townsend, "Malty" for short, had no respect for women other than for what temporary sexual pleasure they could give him, and this was often the last act of "kindness" he provided just before carrying out a contract on a beautiful woman. But he had been careful with those jobs, leaving no clues, not even so much as a hairpin drop of semen in women who had provided more than just pay.

"Rule Number One: Semen is deadlier than a fingerprint," Billy had told Malty. Malty had idolized Billy and copied everything his older brother did, always following his advice and training.

The smile left Malty's face as thoughts of Billy came back to him. There would be no brother to welcome him home. In fact, most people thought Malty had no family, having grown up in and out of foster care after the untimely death of his mother, except for the miserable period he lived with his grandmother. Later this despised grandmother had died in a "mysterious" house fire. One personal kill was left for Malty, and it would be the most important job of his life even though he would receive no pay for this one, either.

He drove out of the high security parking lot, shifting gears in the Porsche his brother had hidden from authorities during Malty's years in prison. Gunning the accelerator, he fed off the rush of speed and the feeling of total freedom. The car had been a present from Billy when his little brother turned thirty, right before he ran the old woman down.

Malty's mind plotted, fueled by what had kept him going the last three years in prison—revenge. But first he needed an accomplice, someone dispensable, a woman to feed his sexual hunger after years of deprivation but who could also help disguise his identity as he visited Julia, Billy's partner, in the women's federal prison in Seattle.

Turning onto the Pacific Highway South, the International Boulevard strip, the ex-con drove the

Porsche slowly, looking for the perfect accessory to complete the identity he planned for his visit to the prison. Seeing the expensive sports car, every hooker left her post, each flaunting her wares in an attempt to flag down the obviously wealthy driver. All looked cheap and hard, but Malty, like his brother, could see past the façades.

And there she was, sauntering gracefully back and forth under the light, looking like someone's sister made up to give out candy on Halloween. Her hair was brown, spiked just a little with the usual red highlights that looked as if she had taken a paintbrush to her hair. Even though she was dressed like a hooker, in a short black vinyl skirt, a low-cut, tight purple spandex shirt, and high heels, she didn't carry herself like one. Malty thought she'd be perfect but took the precautions taught him by his brother, just in case the girl was a decoy, an undercover cop trying to bust desperate men and women who patronized prostitutes.

"Wave or smile at her, or ask if she needs a ride, but don't mention sex or money. And never use words like 'date' or 'work' until she gets in the car. Decoys don't get in the car with johns. If she gets in of her own free will, she's fair game, and your ass won't end up in jail for ninety days with a heavy fine to boot."

After pulling to the curb, he rolled the window down and smiled at the girl without saying anything. Just as his brother had said would happen, the girl walked to the sports car, opened the door, and slid in, looking comfortable with her career choice.

"Hi! I'm Malty." He gave the prostitute his most charming smile.

"I'm Rose. What's your pleasure, Malty?" She

eyed him up and down, returning the smile.

Holding tight to the steering wheel, making sure he stayed within the speed limit, Malty turned the Porsche toward the motel on the other side of the city, as far away from Prostitute Alley as he could get. Reaching down with his right hand, he unzipped his pants, exposing himself.

"That'll be fifty bucks for starters—registration fee, if you will." Rose held out her open hand and smiled at Malty before casting her eyes down to where Malty wanted her attention.

This girl was all business, just like Malty. He liked her. Maybe he'd keep her, if she worked out, and she could become his partner like Julia had been to Billy.

"I'll make a deal with you. Be mine for two nights and a day, starting right now, and I'll pay you a thousand bucks. But no keeping tabs. You do what I want when I want it, but I'll warn you: I'm starving." Reaching across the console, he ran his hand under her skirt.

"Make it twelve hundred and it's a deal, but nothing too kinky, and when we have sex, you use a condom." Rose pulled her skirt a little higher.

Malty smiled, thinking of "Rule Number One."

"You drive a hard bargain, Rose. It's a deal." Rose released her seatbelt, draped herself over the console and began earning her pay.

****

"A nurse's uniform? You're kidding, right?"

Rose sat naked on the foot of the bed the next morning, staring at the white uniform he had laid beside her. Her mascara had run, blackening her eyes, tarnishing an otherwise pretty face. Malty was a rough and demanding client, causing even one who was experienced with hard sex to sweat profusely.

"I've played some fantasy roles before—been spanked more times than I care to recall, and even laid across the desk in a headmaster's office once, dressed in a plaid school uniform, just so he could prick me like the child molester he wanted to be. But I've never been asked to play a nurse. This could be fun. Maybe you can just do me with the white stockings on and nothing else." Rose pulled the white hose over her tanned hand and arm.

"You're not wearing it for sex. Least not till we get back. First thing is, I need you to act like a nurse and push me in a wheelchair when I go to visit someone."

"Act like a nurse? Push you in a wheelchair?" Rose cocked her head. "For real?"

"Yeah. You'll see, when I get this makeup on."

Rose watched, fascinated, as Malty transformed himself from a muscular, oversexed, thirty-something-year-old to a decrepit, crippled invalid with deep wrinkles and gray hair.

"Now! How do I look, Miss Rose?" Malty asked in a crackly voice suited to an elderly man.

"Ugly! Really ugly!" Rose answered without hesitation as she stared in the mirror at Malty's reflection.

"Now for you. First thing, hit the shower and scrape off every bit of that awful makeup. You have to look like wholesome young RN Rose Atwood. I'll get your new ID ready while you're getting cleaned up."

A couple of hours later, Rose pushed Malty in his wheelchair into the prison checkpoint, playing her part like a pro, stopping to make sure her patient's legs were covered with the blanket in his lap.

"Paul Bailey, here to visit my daughter, Julia Robinson. Rose, would you get my ID from my jacket pocket, please. My hands don't work too well anymore. Arthritis." In his feeble voice, Malty directed his comments to the guard, who seemed alert to everything going on around him.

"Let's see, Mr. Bailey. Yes, you're listed as one of the approved visitors for Inmate Robinson. I'm sorry, sir, but we will have to search you. If you'll just step—I mean, if you'd just push him over to that area, Nurse." As Rose pushed the wheelchair away from the check-in, the guard called her back.

"I need to see your ID, too, miss." The guard looked at the ID and then at the computer screen. "You can push him into the visitor's room, but you'll have to stand next to the guard at the door. You're not on the inmate's list of approved visitors."

Rose watched from the door as Malty waited at a table for his pretend daughter to enter the room. After only a few minutes, a guard ushered in a woman who was attractive even in a prison uniform.

"Dad, I'm so glad to see you!" Taking his hands that lay on the table, the inmate smiled at him. After the guard left, she dropped his hands and the two began to talk quietly across the table, both with serious looks. At one point, Julia became visibly angry and began crying.

****

Rose wondered what this woman was to Malty and why she was in prison. Rose looked away, not daring to act the least bit curious. She was already uneasy at being at the beck and call of a man who had a friend in federal prison, a friend he had to visit disguised as someone else. The woman cast several glances at her and seemed to be talking about her to her visitor, adding to Rose's discomfort.

****

After helping Malty into the rented van and putting the wheelchair in the back, Rose drove away from the prison.

"Well, that was interesting! Got any other capers for me, or will we just do what I do best for the rest of the day and tonight?" She asked the question jokingly but was uncomfortable with the silence that had surrounded Malty ever since they left the prison.

"Oh, I'll try to make it interesting, but we'll just wear out the sheets at the motel for a while." Malty answered as he traced Rose's white hose up her thigh.

Later, that night, Malty told Rose to get dressed and they'd go for a ride in the Porsche.

"Tell you what, Malty. I'll settle for the thousand, and you can take me back to the strip. My regular clients will be wondering where I am." Rose grew tense as they headed out of the city on a highway that she knew was mountainous and desolate.

"No. I owe you for that act you performed today. When we finish, I'll pay you what I promised and let you go early."

Malty sped up, taking the curves much faster than he should have, and Rose tightened her grip on the door.

"You're scaring me, Malty! Can you slow down a little?"

He said nothing but stared straight ahead until slowing down to turn onto a narrow side road, one that led to a scenic overlook.

"You gotta see this view, Rose." He stopped the car and put the top down. The stars were out by the millions, but Rose sensed all was not right in God's world. Malty pushed the button releasing her seatbelt.

"Come on, Rose." Malty walked to her side of the car and opened the door.

"No, Malty." Rose gripped the seat refusing to get out. "I don't like heights. Just take me back to the strip. Please!" she begged, showing the fear she felt.

"Just one look and I'll take you back."

Grabbing her arm, he pulled her out of the car. Trying to change his focus, Rose moved against Malty, using her hands to divert his attention.

"Oh, you can't get enough, huh?"

Grabbing her and spinning her around, he shoved her face down hard on the hood of the car as he began jerking at her skirt. Sensing her fear only added to his adrenaline rush, and he forgot Billy's "Rule Number One." When he finished with Rose, he turned her to face him and put a hand on either side of her face. Thinking he was going to kiss her, she closed her eyes.

Malty's hands moved to the girl's throat. Gasping for breath, she pulled at his arms, but she was unable to pry loose his strong hands. Remembering what she had learned from a cop "friend," she kneed him hard in the groin.

As he grabbed himself, groaning, she ran down the road, kicking off her high heels to enable her to run faster, but it was no use. He tackled her, knocking her to the pavement, and with one fist across her face her struggle ended.

Malty carried her to the edge of the cliff and stood looking down into the darkness. The ocean waves beat against the rocky shoreline, and he knew the tide would take her body far away. No one would ever know what happened to Rose, if that was indeed her name, and no one would care. With only a slight sense of remorse, he heaved the girl over the cliff and walked back to his sports car.

Too bad about Rose, but Julia was right. Billy would have told me the same thing. Rose knew too much. From now on, I'll go it alone.

Malty put all thoughts of Rose behind him as he headed the car back to the motel to load up his things. There was no need to wait until tomorrow. He'd hit the interstate, head east, and be in Montana by tomorrow night. He had a date with Hawk Larson but would take his time and plan with care. No rushing ahead. Julia had given him all the information necessary, but he still needed to do reconnaissance, just to make sure everything would go as planned.

"No mistakes this time," Malty thought. "I'm on my own."

Chapter Four

Montana

Betsy was nearing the end of the stack of pages of the manuscript. She had been reading aloud for hours, but her mother would not let her stop until the final chapter was read. Betsy took a sip of her bottled water.

"Here it comes, Mom. The last chapter of your story, or I should say 'our story.' " Betsy reached across and patted her mother's hand. "Are you ready?"

Sue Ann nodded her head to indicate she was, and Betsy began reading aloud the final chapter of *The Gully Path*:

The Promise

COFO disbanded, and Tate finally gave in to the demands of his parents, leaving Mississippi and me in the spring of 1965. This was incomprehensible to me, ever the optimist, believing forever was actually attainable.

We spent several wonderful months together from that turbulent August in 1964 until he left. The last four months, we hid from our families and Mississippi on a lake, in a small isolated cabin that I rented, out from Paxton, while I did my student teaching.

But it was more than just a shabby cabin. It was a haven, our utopia, a place where Tate and I could play house and pretend our lives and loves would go on for eternity in our world filled only with love, void of racial hatred, violence, and misunderstanding. We lived and loved each day like it was our last, with no thought of a reality-based tomorrow.

Tate taught me to fly fish that spring, and when we weren't making love and playing like an old married couple, we were fishing for bream in the lake, listening for the magical explosion as the fish hit our popping bugs, followed by the dance across the glassy water.

At night, we cuddled before the wood-burning stove, our only source of heat, but we needed little warmth, being capable of producing quite enough on our own. Our passion never waned, and to make the cabin reminiscent of the one where we first made love, Tate carved "T.P. Decimbur 1862" on the baseboard beside our bed. It was in this cabin on the lake, with Tobi casting shadows beside us, where we loved unabated and often carelessly.

On one evening in particular, we sat wrapped in a blanket before the wood stove, mesmerized by the amber glow and the red-hot crackles and pops created by the green wood we were forced to burn, being at the end of our winter supply. As usual, Tate had his arm around me, playing with my hair, twisting my curls around his fingers, his main entertainment other than when we fondled each other's bodies.

"Can you imagine the hair our kids will have, Sue Ann, both of us with these blonde curly mops? They'll hate us for it."

"Is that a prospective proposal, Mr. Douglas?"

"Just thinking, wishing ahead a few years. We both have to finish college first."

"Well, I'm ahead of you there. I graduate in a few

weeks. Remember?"

"Yeah! I've got some catching up to do."

Tate became quiet and reflective. I thought he was just enjoying the atmosphere created by the fire.

"There's something I need to tell you, Sue Ann. It's not something we've wanted to think about, but it's happening."

I left his arms and looked into his face, noticing for the first time his serious expression.

"You're scaring me, Tate. What is it?"

"COFO is disbanding. I'll be leaving at the end of the month. Going back to New York, back to my parents and college."

"Oh, I see."

But I didn't see. I had assumed we would stay like this forever and would eventually get married and live happily, somewhere other than Mississippi where "ever after" was possible.

"I can't take you with me right away, Sue Ann, but I promise I'll come back for you. Will you wait for me?"

"Why do I have to wait? I could go with you, get a job teaching and support us while you go to college."

"No. I want everything perfect for us. No wife of mine is going to be the breadwinner. You didn't answer my question. Will you wait for me?"

"How long are we talking here? Years? Decades? Have you been just stringing me along, Tate? Maybe I should have listened to Daddy the first time he told me to stay away from you."

Furious and hurt, I left the blanket and stormed to the door. As I opened it, Tate reached around, slamming it and turning me to face him.

"Don't say that, Sue Ann. I love you. I'll always love you, and you know it. I just want things to be right for us when we make that move. Two years, max, and I'll see you every chance I get. Don't be upset. Please tell me you'll wait for me."

As always, I gave in to Tate's affections and promises of love. We vowed to each other to make every moment we had left unforgettable and sealed it with our usual passion.

Tate left at the end of March, assuring me he loved me and would come back to me soon. I never heard from him again.

When I found out I was pregnant, two months later, I called his parents' house and was told Tate was at a going-away party at the home of his fiancée. Tate had been drafted and would, no doubt, be sent to Vietnam to fight in the war that he hated. I did not leave my name or number but only told his mother I was an old friend from COFO and that I wished him well.

As I paraded in the Chain of Magnolias procession to receive my college degree, I looked down at my parents' adoring faces, looked hard into my mother's pride, and knew she was engraving this moment in her mind forever as she witnessed the accomplishment of the first Taylor to graduate from college. The flutter I felt in my newly protruding belly secretly warned her to savor the moment, for it would be short-lived, to be overshadowed by a mother's worst nightmare, an unwed mother for a daughter.

My secret remained with me until I was unable to hide the inevitable any longer. When I confessed my sin to stunned parents, my daddy sat silent, as if in trauma, with eyes full of fear and pity. Mama reacted just as I knew she would, with ranting and sermons and "How could you do this to me?" The more she demanded I tell her who the "s.o.b." was who was responsible, the more determined I was to remain silent.

After all, I had kept Tate a secret from my parents, at least from my mother, and from my community during those volatile months in the summer of 1964. I vowed to keep him a secret all the way to the delivery room and even to the grave if necessary.

Mama, furious with my silence, took matters into her own hands. Regardless of what I wanted to do, or not do, she found a doctor who performed illegal abortions in Tennessee. Within the week we were heading north up Highway 51.

"Sue Ann, it's going to be just like normal. You'll see. I'm going home and bake us a chocolate pie. You want fried chicken? We'll have a good supper, and all this will be behind us. I bet church will be packed tomorrow. It's fifth Sunday, you know. I better think about what I'm carrying to the church for dinner. Maybe I'll make two chocolate pies. You know there's never a piece of my pie or any of my cooking left over after our fifth Sunday dinners."

Mama rambled on and on as if this was just any day rather than the end of my life. Daddy drove in silence, but I felt him looking in the mirror at me as I sat frozen in time.

"Watch where you're going, Zeke! You almost ran off the road."

Mama had obviously noticed Daddy's constant gaze in his rearview mirror and purported to put a stop to it, probably afraid we would start some of our silent talking to each other and he might turn around and head back to Parrish Oaks, where they both knew I wanted to go.

"Speed up, Zeke! My lord, you drive like you're sixty. The speed limit is 55, not 40."

"You all right back there, Sudi?" Daddy asked into the mirror, letting Mama know he was ignoring her orders.

"Of course she's all right. You just concentrate on driving."

I sat motionless, stoned by guilt and trepidation, indifferent to the conversation from the front seat. My emerald-green eyes, Mama's eyes, stared at the trees passing too fast at the side of the two-lane highway.

Why wouldn't she let me make the decision I wanted to? After all, I was almost twenty-one. But in 1965, parents had more control over their children, and a person couldn't get an abortion just anywhere. Mama was determined this would not ruin my, or rather our, life, and had found a doctor who would "rid the Taylor family of this blight."

We pulled up to a rundown, faded green, concrete building in Dyersburg, Tennessee, four hours from home but the nearest place Mama could find that committed such atrocities. The clinic fit well into the shabby section of town, and my stomach, our stomach, curled into a knot in anticipation of the horror that awaited me.

Minutes later, I lay on a cold metal table in a plain room that, though clean, reeked of disease and crime. The only décor was a calendar, a gift from a propane company probably owned by a deacon in the First Baptist Church.

The calendar had two angelic children on top, a

boy and a girl dressed in their Sunday finest, each holding the hand of a parent, a mother and father also dressed for church. Over the picture was written, "Don't send your children to church, take them." I tried to concentrate on the picture and pretend I was somewhere other than on this slab about to commit murder.

The doctor, a thin man with graying hair, did not look like a murderer as he examined me for ten daylong minutes. My body trembled with cold terror.

"Be still, please," the doctor demanded sharply.

"Be still, Sue Ann," Mama repeated. "It will be over soon."

"She's too far along." The doctor looked up from the table. "It will be more complicated than I thought."

"You mean it will cost more than you said," interpreted Daddy from across the room with a frown on his face.

"At least a hundred more." The doctor directed his statement to Mama, perhaps sensing that she was the one in control and who would not hesitate to pay the extra money just to end the nightmare.

"We'll pay it," assured Mama. "Just get this over with."

Daddy looked at Mama with anger as he approached. He looked down at my sweat-soaked, pale face, all that was showing from under the tent sheet the doctor had draped over me and the stirrups to protect the abominable transgression he was about to perform from the watchful gaze of my distraught parents. This was obviously a scene the doctor had become accustomed to, a scene for which he had developed emotional immunity.

"It ain't our decision!" Daddy said emphatically, more to Mama with a look that told her to be quiet than to the doctor.

"Sue Ann, do you want to go through with this?"

"No, Daddy, I don't," came my tearful reply.

"Then let's get the hell out of here."

I was whisked away to wait out my pregnancy with an uncle in Arkansas. Mama told the lie that I had run off and got married, moving away with my fantasy husband. I went along with the story to pacify Mama and took it one step further, changing my last name to Parish so that my baby could grow up in dishonest acceptance in a South that shunned bastards.

Elizabeth had Andy do the legal papers to make the change and helped me decide on Parish as a name, much to Mama's disagreement. She was sure this would make the story unbelievable to the locals, since our house was named Parrish Oaks. I would not budge on the issue but dropped one "r" to appease her.

Endless days were spent in Arkansas as I holed up away from outsiders. The only exception was the graduate classes I took at the small college nearby. I had only occasional visits from Mama and Daddy.

Mama further embellished the story in the House of Style by telling how I had to divorce my husband soon after our marriage because he had a "bad problem with alcohol and was even abusive when drinking." Her clients all sympathized with my plight of being the young expectant mother without the support of a husband.

I passed my time reading and looking at the children's section of the Sears and Roebuck Catalog, trying to envision what my child, who I was sure would *be a boy, would look like. But I was not to have the satisfaction of knowing how close my imagination was. There would be no woods colt, an old southern name which my grandmother, being gentle and unlike most southern women who were notorious for gossip, preferred to the usual "bastard." There would be no little towheaded, curly-haired boy who walked on his tiptoes for this degenerate daughter of Mississippi.*

I buried my son, Tobias Ezekiel Parish, next to Old Ma, beneath the biggest, most beautiful cedar tree in Liberty Creek Cemetery. Daddy cried more than I did. I guess, for the one short day of Tobi's life, Daddy felt God had finally given him a boy, only to snatch the precious gift back before he could even feel his little boy's heart beat as he held him in his arms for the first and last time.

My grief was overshadowed by my guilt, and I was sure Tobi's death was a punishment from God for my having strayed from what I knew was right, for allowing passion and love of a man to supersede my Christian values and strength.

But in that last instant before God carried out this great retribution, He had a change of heart and decided perhaps the penalty was too harsh, especially for one who had been so faithful for twenty years of life in practicing virtue and, in the last few years of growing in maturation, keeping virginity intact. In that last moment of predetermination, he relinquished his pride, giving me a healthy baby girl, a living part of twins. I named her Elizabeth Ann Taylor Parish after Liz Bess and me, but from her first day of life she was my Betsy.

As I held her in my arms in the back seat of my parents' car on our way home from the hospital, I made a vow to myself, one that I would never break.

"I am Sue Ann Taylor Parish, daughter of a new Mississippi. Nothing can prevent me from being what I want to be. I will not tolerate condemnation and will not stop until I have made a name for myself, a name Betsy can be proud of. With God's help, all is possible.

"Tomorrow will be a brilliant forever, Baby Girl. No regrets."

The End

Betsy wiped her nose for what seemed the millionth time as she finished reading. She turned the last page of the manuscript face down on top of the others, folded her hands, and looked across the table at her mother.

"Well, that's done. What do you think, Mom? Is it the way you would have written it?" Betsy gathered up the pile of tissues in front of her mother and put them in the trashcan beside the table.

"No. It's better than I could have written it, Betsy. Your way with words is a true gift. You took my story as I told it to you and were able to describe my thoughts and emotions as if you were me." Sue Ann reached across the table and patted her daughter's hand. Her own hand shook as it had since her last treatment, but it was getting better.

"You look tired. I think you need to lie down for a while."

Betsy brushed her mother's face with her hand, trying not to stare. It was hard to believe this was the same beautiful woman who, only a few months ago, was sitting on the porch telling her daughter to "be brave."

"Mom, Trapper keeps asking where you are. He

misses you. Can't I call Hawk and tell him to bring your grandson out to see you?"

Sue Ann slowly lifted herself out of her chair, holding to the table as she made her way to the sofa. She stopped to look in the mirror that hung over the buffet and rubbed her hand over her head. Her long thick graying curls had been replaced with short sprigs of new hair. Her eyes looked sunken in her thin face, a sight that she had purposely hidden from herself in the last few weeks of chemo by never stopping in front of this mirror.

Betsy stood beside her mother and put her arms around her. "With every breath you take, my dear mother, you become more and more beautiful. Trapper will know you. You are thinner; you no longer have your long braids; but you are still his Sudi, and he loves you unconditionally."

"Give me a little longer, Betsy. I am getting stronger every day. I miss my little man so much but just could not bear it if he was frightened of me. My last treatment was a doozie, and with the mastectomy— well, it will just take a little time to recover fully." She turned away from the mirror to face Betsy. "Does Trapper know I've been sick and that's why I haven't been able to see him?"

"Yes. Hawk and I both tell him every time he asks for you, but he doesn't understand why he can't come out here. To a three-year-old, being sick means you have a tummy ache."

"Then I'll will myself to get better so I can see my grandson soon. I promise." Sue Ann went past the sofa and headed for the porch. Betsy followed her but stopped to retrieve a quilt that was always ready for whoever needed its warmth or its palette of colorful memories.

Sue Ann held onto the wall and eased herself into the rocking chair.

"Here, Mom. Let's get you covered up. There's a chill in the air."

The two sat in the rockers, gazing at the mountains without speaking for several minutes.

"What is it about us and mountains, Mom? I never tire of looking at those peaks. They are so…so uplifting, even in the most difficult of times. And it doesn't matter if the mountains are in Alaska or in Montana, you and I thrive when we live near them."

"Yes. I know what you mean, Betsy. I feel so very blessed to be able to sit here and look at those mountains, but they make me think about Shade sometimes. I've been thinking about him a lot lately, especially on my bad days, when I feel like I'm nearing death." A few more minutes of silence passed.

"Do you remember the picture I had hanging in my bedroom at Parrish Oaks, the one of the little cabin by the lake with the mountains looming over?"

" 'My heaven!' That's what you called it. I remember looking at it with Annie and telling her that this was our heaven, mine and yours."

"That's right. One day I overheard you asking Annie if she wanted to go to our heaven with us. I decided I'd overstressed the beauty of it."

"Just don't go getting any ideas. Heaven on earth is here in the Beartooths, and this is where you need to be for a long, long time. Shade knew it, and that's why he left it for you to enjoy, and he'd want you to think only about living, never dying. He died so you and I could live, and by golly, that's what we will do, Mom."

"You are so right, Betsy, but I'm not afraid, and I don't want you to be, either. However, Custer says it's not my time, if that's any consolation."

"Really? What did he mean by that? I think I need to hear this."

"Remember when I first found out I had breast cancer, and Custer went into the wilderness area on a vision quest?"

"I do remember. What did he see?" Betsy leaned up in her chair, anxious for any positive revelation Custer had received.

"He won't tell me but said he would when the time was right. He takes care of me but won't let me give in to my weaknesses—forces me to be as independent as possible. He says there is much ahead of me worth living for but I have to fight for it."

"That Custer. He is really a mystery man, but somehow he is always right. I agree with Hawk. Custer should have been a shaman."

"I believe him, too, Betsy. I think I will beat this, but there is never any guarantee that it won't come back. But I don't have to tell you about the fear one lives with after having cancer."

"But the happier we are, the less stress and the more chance of survival."

"So true, my daughter. So true."

Just as Betsy was thinking she should be leaving, she caught movement from the corner of her eye. A doe stood at the edge of the woods and stared at them. Betsy pointed so that her mother would see her, and just as Sue Ann got a glimpse, the doe turned and headed into the woods with a fawn trailing behind her.

"Did you see them, Mom? It was a doe and a fawn, just like I saw on my first morning here. It was just like in Hawk's vision years before he met me, and it even included Trapper as a little fawn." Betsy smiled at her mom. "I believed in my man's vision, and you should believe in Custer's."

"Yes, Betsy, I, too, believe our men have connections with 'the Great Spirit' as Custer refers to Him. And I saw the doe, but she had two fawns. One remained hidden in the edge of the woods. I'll know in time what Custer's vision was and what it meant. He has assured me of this."

As if they needed any reassurance that it was a sign, a raven dipped its wings overhead and called to the two of them.

Chapter Five

"Mom, I never thought I'd like you with short hair, but I swear you look ten years younger."

"Really? I think I look like Leonia, even though I'm not African American. Do you remember Elizabeth's aunt? She had that close-cropped curly Afro—the 'natural look' was what Elizabeth called it."

"Yes, I remember Leonia. Maybe it looks a little like hers, but I'm just glad it's growing back curly. You were so afraid it would be straight after the chemo. Don't get me wrong. Even though I think it's cute, I still want you to let it grow so we'll look alike with our braids. If I even thought about cutting my hair short, Hawk would be devastated."

"I have to agree with Hawk. That braid is definitely you, Daughter. And it's me. I'll have one again some day. You know how fast my hair grows, or it did at one time. Right now, I'm proud of every fuzzy strand that grows and reminds me that the chemo and, hopefully, cancer are in my past. Custer says we'll take it one day at a time and be grateful for each sunrise and sunset that I remain cancer-free."

"Have you heard anything from your agent yet on *The Gully Path*?"

"Nothing since last week. But she says we'll be getting the galleys soon. My publisher wants it on the shelves by spring."

"When do you want to start *Under Northern Lights*?"

Sue Ann leaned her head back on the rocker and cast her eyes sideways at Betsy.

"Will you be okay remembering how it was in Alaska that year, Betsy? I can write it myself, in time, if it will bother you."

Betsy put her head back in her own rocker and waited a few seconds before answering.

"That year was very traumatic, but I want to help you write it. I owe it to Shade, and it's time I talked about it. Besides, it seems danger follows me wherever I go, but so far, I'm a survivor." Betsy looked toward her mother. "So when do we start?"

"Soon, but there are parts I need to write on my own."

"The love scenes." Betsy rolled her head toward her mom and smiled. "Movie-star good-looking!"

"Yes, he was, but oh, my, how he could make a girl feel like she was the special one, the only woman on his planet!" Sue Ann smiled, remembering. "I'll write this one in third person rather than first. It is not as much of an autobiography as *The Gully Path*, since it is only one year in my life, and I want to be able to describe Shade as the unique, strong warrior that he was." Sue Ann raised her head and looked at Betsy, who had a big smile on her face as if knowing what her mother was about to say. "And to describe without embarrassment the way he made love to me. If it's in third person, my readers will think it's fiction, but I'll be able to write it as the truth according to Shade."

"I, for one, cannot wait to read those scenes even though I never slept quite as soundly as I led you to believe in my little room across the hall from yours and Shade's. I think he knew it, and that's why he built the new bedroom on the other end of the cabin."

"Well, there's no rush to write it, so you, my dear, will just have to wait. Besides, I'm thinking about going to visit Elizabeth and Parrish Oaks, if I can convince Custer to go with me. So far, he's balking at the idea. Says Mississippi fire ants and humidity are not his idea of a vacation. Elizabeth is so dear to me after what we went through in the sixties just to be friends, since blacks and whites, even children, did not mix back in those days. I really miss her, and I want her to meet Custer." Sue Ann smiled thinking of Elizabeth. "I've got something I've been meaning to do anyway and just haven't gotten around to it."

"What's that, Mom?"

"Before Mama died, she had Rita Jean box up things for me and had them shipped to Parrish Oaks. I had told her I didn't want anything when Daddy died and to will her house, possessions, and everything to my sisters. They were both still upset that I got Parrish Oaks and the land way before our parents died. Mama sent the boxes five years ago, and I've never gone through any of them. They just sit there filling up the attic room."

"How could you stand not knowing what was in them? You should have had them sent here, Mom."

"I'm talking five big boxes, Betsy. Where would I put them here? This cabin is already overflowing. But I would like to go through them and see what Mama thought should be important to me. I guess I'm just getting old and nostalgic." Sue Ann laughed.

"Nostalgic? Probably. Old? Not my mother. You

should have Elizabeth help you. I bet she'd love that."

"Yes, she would. I'm sure it would be a long trip down memory lane. She says my family history is like the history she never had, not knowing the identity of her father until it was too late. Elizabeth loved my daddy. She cried and cried when he and Mama moved to south Mississippi, and she was devastated when Daddy died." Sue Ann paused, reminiscing. "You should see what Elizabeth has done with Nagalee's quilt I kept all those years. It is repaired and is displayed as a wall hanging in her library. She sent me pictures. Elizabeth always said family history was the most important type of history, and her philosophy is exemplified in her grandmother's quilt."

"I can help you start the book before you go, if you want."

"There will be plenty of time to write when we get back. I say 'we' assuming I can convince Custer to escort me. Regardless, I won't be staying in Mississippi that long."

"Well, I'll be here every day to check on the cabin anyway, and we can start *Under Northern Lights* as soon as you get back. I'm so glad Hawk took the counseling job in Red Lodge, so we didn't have to move back to the reservation for the school year."

"I hope it was what he really wanted to do, Betsy, and not just that he didn't want to take you away from me while I was finishing my treatment."

"Actually, he likes it at the high school, and he has more time to work on the courses he's taking online. Hawk really wants that degree in clinical psychology so he can open his own office and maybe do some testing and consultancy with several of the school districts. The superintendent on the reservation told Hawk he will always have a job there if he wants it, but I don't think he'll leave Red Lodge."

"You still can't convince him to buy that ranch he's always wanted and leave counseling completely?"

"He's just too proud and flatly refuses to use the money Patrick left to Trapper and me. I did get him to agree that if I become financially successful with my writing, he'll consider the ranch then."

"He has a lot of Custer in him. And there could be much worse things than being like his uncle—or his clan father, as Hawk and Custer put it."

Sue Ann and Betsy sat on the porch of the old cabin, watching Trapper gallop his stick horse Custer had made for him, complete with a carved wood head and black mane. Behind the boy, the Beartooths stood watch, bathed in the colors of early autumn. Mother and daughter became quiet, obsessed with mountain gazing.

"Mom, do you think he's still alive?"

"I assume you're talking about your father. I wondered when you'd bring the subject up and had about decided you wouldn't, since it's been so long since we finished *The Gully Path*."

"I figured you had enough on your plate without worrying about me going hunting for a phantom. But I can't help but wonder about him."

"I don't know if he's alive or not, Betsy. For me, Tate Douglas died in Vietnam, but I never tried to find out, not wanting verification of the real reason I never heard from him again after he left Mississippi. Pretending he was dead was easier than finding out he married someone else. As cruel as it sounds, his pretend death was kinder than his betrayal." Sue Ann searched the mountain peaks with an intense look on her face.

"I know you'll think this is a silly question, Betsy, but does it bother you to find out I was an unwed mother and that your last name, Parish, was made up along with the story of my pretend marriage?"

"No, it doesn't bother me, but I wish you had told me the truth. Being a bastard child is no big deal in today's world. Besides, I've been blessed with the best mother imaginable."

"Oh, Betsy, please don't use the 'bastard' word. Remember I told you about my grandmother that you never got to know? She was the kindest person I've ever known, and I much prefer her term 'woods colt' for a child born out of wedlock."

"Yes, I think I prefer it, too, but it really doesn't matter, Mom."

They both became quiet again. Betsy broke the silence.

"You know, we could do a people search on the Internet and see if Tate Douglas is still alive. It's really easy."

"And what would you do with the information if you found out your father is alive?"

"I don't know, Mom. I want to hate him for what he did to you, for leaving you with the idea that he would come back for you. He betrayed you, and that is inexcusable." Betsy looked at her mother to see how she was reacting. The one thing Betsy did not want to do was to upset her mother after what she had gone through.

"But then there's this curious part of me that wonders what he's like. Do I look like him? Do I have any half brothers and sisters? Mostly, would he want to know me at all? Those kinds of haunting questions."

"Well, all those haunting questions are what made me keep these secrets all your life, but I don't want you to hate him. I just thought it would be easier on you and me if you thought he was dead. I've given you the information, Betsy. How you deal with it is up to you, but be careful. I don't want you hurt any more than the truth has already hurt you. Think it through before you make a decision to go looking for him."

Chapter Six

Denver

In the police station after his work hours ended, the detective typed out his resignation. Without even proofing the letter, he folded it, put it in an envelope addressed to his superior, and placed it in the inner office mail.

His desk was cleaned out except for one photograph he found in the back of the drawer, a snapshot of his family taken three years ago when he had received a citation for bravery. His superior officer had called his actions "stupid but gutsy." The detective had shot his way into an abandoned building and past three armed suspects, without backup, to save a fallen comrade.

Holding the picture, he ran his finger over his ex-wife, giving her a good thump on her gorgeous face as he moved to his thirteen-year-old daughter. Carrie was beautiful, looked like him, especially with her blonde curls cut short. And she had his outgoing personality, not the somber, bitchy persona of her mother, thank goodness. The girl wanted to live with him, but the judge agreed with her mother that a teenage girl needed her mom more than her dad. Carrie was the only reason he hated to leave the city.

Standing between Carrie and him in the photograph

was his grandmother, who had raised him after he lost both parents in an automobile accident when he was fourteen. His grandmother had done a good job of raising him, working endless hours as a nurse and saving for his college so he could get a degree in law enforcement. His dream was to be a cop like his father had been. But his grandmother, too, had left him—just a month ago, after Alzheimer's ate away her mind and her will to live.

"Family. Yeah, right!"

Not realizing he had spoken aloud, he tore the picture to pieces and threw it in the trashcan along with numerous certificates of merit he had earned during his fifteen years with the force. Leaving the office he had so proudly occupied after his promotion to detective five years prior, he turned out the light without looking back.

Before he left Denver, he stopped by the Vision Center to pick up his contact lenses. He had ordered a large supply, since he was leaving for good. Wearing contacts, something he had always hated, would come in handy now that he needed a new look.

"Your eyes are such a beautiful color, I don't know why you want to change them."

The girl who waited on him was flirting as she watched the handsome ex-cop put in a pair of the new contacts. He didn't try to explain, thinking it was none of her business anyway, and just ignored the comment and left.

The back of his truck was loaded with a few boxes, everything that was meaningful to him at this point. At the last minute, he had included his weightlifting equipment even though his heart was not interested in physical fitness at the moment. His mental wellbeing was his major concern.

As he reached the outskirts of the city where he had spent most of his life, he looked in the mirror. A brown-eyed stranger with short-cropped hair hidden by his Denver Broncos cap looked back at him. Reaching beside him, he picked up the book and turned to the back where the author's picture was located.

"Now all I have to do is find you, Elizabeth Parish Larson."

Chapter Seven

Montana

It was raining and cold when he drove into Red Lodge late at night. Tired from driving most of the day and from way too much thinking, he pulled in at the first motel he came to.

"Just for one night?" the desk clerk asked as he took the guest's credit card.

"Could be several nights, if you have a vacancy. I'd like to keep the room until I tell you different."

"No problem. It's slow right now, especially with the pass still closed from the rockslide. We have continental breakfast ready at 6:30 each morning, if you're interested."

After putting away his credit card, the guest turned from the desk and noticed a book display off to the side. Picking up a book, he pretended to read the jacket cover.

"That's a book written by one of our local authors, Elizabeth Larson. We all know her as Betsy. It's darn good, but don't tell anybody I've read it. It's more of a romance for women, although the hero in it is our own Hawk Larson, Betsy's husband."

"Really? That's interesting." The stranger continued to survey the book.

"They're for sale all over Red Lodge. Heard she's

already made a bestseller list. Maybe they'll make a movie and shoot it here. We need some publicity, with what that damn rockslide has done to the tourist industry in the last few months. Anyway, if you want to buy a copy, you can get it signed next week. Betsy's doing a signing down at the bookstore on Main Street, donating the bulk of it to Casting for Recovery."

"What's that?"

"They take women who have had breast cancer on fly fishing outings free of charge. It's good therapy, physically and mentally. Betsy's mother, Sue Ann Parish, is recovering from breast cancer and she's quite a fly fisher herself, and so is Betsy. In fact, Betsy is about the best caster in this part of the Beartooths, or so Hawk says. He outfits in the summer."

"Are you talking about Dr. Sue Ann Parish, the romance writer?"

"Yep, that's her. You know about her?"

"My grandmother read every book she ever wrote, but I never read any of them, needless to say." The man smiled at the clerk, hoping he wouldn't take the remark personally. He turned to put the book back on the display.

"Yeah! I know what you mean. I heard Sue Ann and Betsy have written a new book together, but it's not out yet."

Hearing this, he turned quickly to face the clerk.

"Dr. Parish lives here? I thought she lived in Alaska, or that's what my grandmother said."

"No. She's been back a little over three years. Lives out from Red Lodge on the old Lake Fork Forestry Road, her and Custer Larson. Now, there's a story!"

A few minutes later, he got his bag from his truck, but not before picking up the copy of *The Hawk and the Deer* from the passenger seat and tucking it into his duffel.

Timothy Harden, ex-cop from Denver, did not make it to breakfast the next morning. He was still sleeping after reading all night.

****

The next afternoon, Timothy found himself at the trailhead on his way to a point that overlooked Lake Fork Forestry Road. He knew he should be able to see her cabin from there, but he had to be careful. No way did he want them to know he was watching. If things worked out, they'd know soon enough.

Digging his pack out of the back of his truck, he checked his camera to make sure it was loaded with film and made sure his high-powered lens was attached properly before starting up the steep trail. Even though it was cool in the mountains, Timothy found himself sweating as he hiked.

"Next time I'll wear shorts instead of these jeans," he told himself as he removed his jacket and tied it to the outside of his pack. Even though he was muscle-bound from a daily regimen of weightlifting, he knew he would also need aerobics to keep his mind and body in shape. He'd remedy that with hiking and running.

A few minutes up the trail, he saw the cabin. It looked like something out of an old western movie, and he was intrigued. He moved to a better position higher up the trail in the edge of the woods and got out his binoculars. Then he noticed her sitting on the porch. Even though she did not have the long braid she was pictured with on the back cover of her books, he knew it was Dr. Parish. His heart skipped wildly as he focused the camera and began clicking away.

Sue Ann soaked up the morning sun with her head back against the rocker and her eyes closed. She had always enjoyed drinking her first cup of coffee on the porch, but after her battle with cancer, each morning seemed more enjoyable than the morning before. As she sat content in her rocker, Custer joined her, stopping to kiss her and tuck her blanket around her before heading down the trail that ran beside the cabin.

Timothy continued to take pictures, smiling periodically. As he stopped to change film, a Suburban pulled into the front yard. And there she was, Elizabeth Parish Larson, in the flesh, and with her was a small boy in an oversized cowboy hat. Focusing the camera on the mother as she sat on the edge of the porch holding the boy, he clicked the camera repeatedly.

After reloading, Timothy sat watching the threesome through the lens for a long time without shooting. He had taken enough pictures but was unable to make himself leave his watchtower. Betsy's blonde braid sparkled in the sunlight. He had never seen a more beautiful woman. He wanted more than anything to hold her tight in his arms. Intent on his own watching, he did not notice the other man, whose binoculars were fixed on him.

****

"Who the hell is that?"

Malty hid behind a boulder overlooking the cabin from the opposite side and, like Timothy, had been watching the three for several minutes. The reflection of the sun in the camera lens had caught Malty's attention, making him refocus his binoculars on the trail straight across. He ducked behind the boulder and then withdrew to the trail behind him, being careful not to be seen by his rival watcher.

Making his way to the trailhead, he saw the big 4x4 Dodge truck with Colorado license plates and knew it belonged to the other man, since the only other vehicles there were the used Trailblazer he had bought in Billings and an old beat-up truck pulling a horse trailer. He decided to hang around and follow the guy and check out who he was and why he was trespassing on his territory.

Timothy noticed the brown Trailblazer pull out behind him as he left the trailhead but didn't think anything about it until it pulled in beside him at the motel.

"Is this a decent place to stay?" The man had parked beside him in the parking lot and yelled from his rolled-down window.

"It's comfortable and reasonable, if you're planning on staying any length of time." Timothy answered before getting out of the truck.

"Thanks. I believe I'll check it out." Malty walked to the front of Timothy's truck and stopped. "Didn't I just see you at the trailhead?"

"Maybe. Doing a little hiking while I'm here." Timothy turned away from the man, getting his pack from the back, not wanting to make conversation.

"Oh, sorry. Name's Mal Cagle." Malty held out his hand to Timothy.

"Timothy Harden." Reluctantly, Timothy gave the man's hand one quick shake before hurrying into the motel. "Got things to do. See you around."

Even though Malty had rented an old isolated

house outside Billings, he checked into the motel. He intended to find out who this man was and why he was watching the cabin. Nothing would be allowed to interfere with his plans.

****

"Mr. Larson is in one of the ninth-grade classrooms, Betsy, but you can wait in his office. He should be finished in about ten minutes."

"Thank you, Jean."

Going to her husband's office at the high school was something Betsy seldom did, but she loved it when she could find an excuse to go. She had helped Hawk decorate using rustic western furniture and Remington and Russell prints like the ones in their home. The only thing that made it look like a regular counselor's office was his desk.

Hawk had insisted that she and Trapper have their pictures taken professionally, to hang behind his desk. Hawk had gotten sick of flirty high school girls when he was a counselor on the reservation and had asked to be transferred to the junior high. He did not want this to happen in Red Lodge.

"I want a big picture of my gorgeous wife and my beautiful son, so there'll be no doubt that I am a happily married man."

And that was just what he got. Betsy was almost embarrassed by the picture of herself hanging in her husband's office. In it, she was leaning against the porch post of her mom's old cabin, dressed in her tight, low-rise, destroyed jeans with her short, Scully-beaded and fringed western suede jacket and boots. At Hawk's insistence, she wore her hair long, her curls cascading over one shoulder. Regardless of how hard her husband tried to convince her, Betsy refused to show her belly button ring, but did take one in that pose just for his wallet.

Trapper's picture looked like a miniature Hawk as he stood beside his pony. The small boy was dressed in his black cowboy hat, boots, and jeans worn with a light blue, monogrammed button-down shirt just like his daddy wore. His Montana Silversmiths buckle was almost as big as he was.

"Hi, baby! What's up?" Hawk was surprised to see Betsy in his office and as always kissed her, hugging her tight even though a student stood behind him in the door, watching in embarrassment.

"Uh, I'll come back later, Mr. Larson." The boy grinned and turned away from the door.

"I'll see you after lunch, Ben." After closing the door, Hawk returned to his wife and smiled.

"Now. Where were we?" Wrapping his arms around her and pulling her close, he kissed her long and passionately like they were in their bedroom instead of his office.

"Hey, I like this attention. I think I'll visit you at work more often."

"Are you saying I've been remiss in showing affection to my wife at home?" Hawk held her at arm's length, waiting for her reply.

"No. Well, yes, now that you mention it. You have been pretty busy with all those classes you're taking. In case you haven't noticed, Trapper and I fight over you every time you leave that damn computer screen."

"I'm sorry, sweetheart. I didn't realize it was going to consume so much of my time. I'll try to do better. Promise. Now, I'd like to think you just couldn't stand being away from me, but I know you wouldn't be here if you didn't have something on your mind. Shoot." Sitting in the chair behind his desk, Hawk pulled Betsy onto his lap. As always, she began playing with his hair that hung to his collar.

"Mom and Custer are leaving for Mississippi next week, and I kind of thought we might take advantage of some free babysitting before they go. I'd like to spend some time just you and me."

Hawk smiled. "I like the sound of that. What do you have in mind? You want to go somewhere special, or just spend the weekend in bed?" Hawk moved his hand under his wife's shirt, fingering the belly button ring that sat just above the waistband of her low-rise jeans.

"Whoa, baby! I better quit or I'll embarrass myself when I walk out of here. Maybe the lap isn't such a good idea, either."

Betsy smiled and left her husband's lap and sat on the edge of his desk.

"Mom offered for her and Custer to keep Trapper at our place. She knows how I love autumn up there in the old cabin in the mountains. And maybe we can hike up to Keyser Brown. It won't be long before the snow will block the trail."

"Yeah. Sounds good to me. Just you and me, the fireplace, and the old grizzly rug!" Hawk left his chair and walked to the window pulling at his jeans.

"Damn, Betsy! I have been spending too much time at that computer."

"Yes, you have. In fact, I've considered taking a nude picture of myself and doing a pop-up for your screen, just to remind you of your responsibilities at home."

Laughing, Hawk walked back to his wife and took her in his arms again.

"And what stopped you?"

"Afraid it might somehow get transferred to your laptop and end up at school. Now, that would be a lesson for these kids!"

"You keep talking and I'll have to take the rest of the day off. By the way, where's my son?"

"With Mom and Custer. You want to meet me at Mom's after school? I'll cook you a big T-bone." Betsy put her hands on his chest, fingering the buttons on his shirt. Her emerald eyes met his brown ones as she gave her most flirtatious smile.

"That's not the first thing I want when I get there. Can you arrange that?" Hawk began caressing Betsy's hips.

"Oh, yeah! You know how I like having dessert first, Neopolitan Man." Betsy had a flashback to the first time she had seen Hawk naked as he showered in the waterfall after a day of guiding. It had been only her second encounter with the handsome half-blood who would become her husband.

"Betsy, you've got to stop! You're killing me!" Hawk held her at arm's length, giving her a serious look as if reprimanding her. "You know comparing your man to ice cream just because he happened to be sunburned in spots and tanned in others the first time you saw him naked would not be considered a compliment by most men."

"Did I mention I crave vanilla?" Betsy gave Hawk her most seductive look, parting her lips and running her tongue over her bottom lip.

"Oh, what the hell!" Pulling her back to him, he kissed her, his kisses quickly moving down her neck. A knock on the door stopped him from going further.

"Mr. Larson, I hate to interrupt you, but don't forget you're due at the district office for a lunch meeting with the board in ten minutes."

The secretary spoke without opening the door, possibly afraid of what she might expose to the students waiting in the outer office.

"Thanks, Jean. I'll be right out," he replied. "Shit, Betsy! Now see what you've got me into?"

"I'll leave, sweetheart, so you can get ready for your meeting. I'll see you at Mom's place after school."

Giving him a quick kiss and a pop on the butt, Betsy left his office smiling.

Chapter Eight

Rose, the girl Malty said no one would care about or miss, remained in a coma in Charity Hospital in Seattle. Beside her bed sat a young nineteen-year-old man, a young man who came every day between his classes at the university and his night shift at the pizza parlor just to hold the girl's hand and promise he'd make whoever did this pay.

Just after daylight a week earlier, some fishermen had spotted her body hanging on a narrow ledge, halfway between the overlook and the ocean below. The girl's back was broken, and severe head injuries caused her brain to swell and keep her in a coma, but she was still alive. It would be two days later before a name would be attached to the victim. After filing a missing person's report with the Seattle police, her brother identified the girl as his older sister, Janine Berryhill.

The police guessed the girl's profession from the way she was dressed and from the excessive amount of semen found in and on her body. Their first thoughts were of the Green River murders of the '80s and '90s, and the police feared a copycat replay of those terrible years. Then one of the girl's peers from the strip told police she saw Rose get into a Porsche three nights before she was found on the rocky ledge. None of this fit the old crimes, and the police were relieved.

****

Betsy sat swaddled in her husband's arms, overlooking a double kaleidoscope of yellow with a hint of red as the trees swayed in the cool fall breeze and reflected in the lake at Keyser Brown.

"I don't want this weekend to end. It's been perfect, Hawk. Thank you for spending it with me."

"My pleasure, sweetheart. And I could sit here and hold you forever, but I think there's a little boy who might be getting a little antsy by now, thinking his mom and dad have deserted him after two days."

"Oh, that's right! We do have a son, don't we?"

"Yes, we do, and it might be time to relieve his grandparents." Hawk stood and held out his hand to Betsy.

"Are you sure you're not just anxious to get back to that research paper you're writing?" Betsy took Hawk's hand but was reluctant to leave the beautiful scene.

"I told you. I'm yours for the weekend, and that includes the rest of the day. Maybe we can stop back by the cabin for a little while longer before we pick up Trapper?" Hawk kissed her again, letting his tongue reinforce what was on his mind.

Hawk held Betsy to him, unaware of the high-powered rifle that had its site set on them. The shot echoed off the canyon walls, intentionally hitting a few feet beside them. Instinctively, Hawk threw Betsy to the ground, covering her with his body.

"Stay down, Betsy!"

"No, Hawk! We have to find cover!" Betsy struggled to move from under him.

"When I stand, you run for the trees! I'll be right

behind you!" Hawk yelled.

Jumping to a standing position, Hawk pulled Betsy up, pushing her ahead of him as a second shot hit just below where they had been lying.

"What the hell? Betsy, we've got to get out of here!" Grabbing her hand, Hawk ran away from the trail and through the thick trees. After several minutes, they reached the trail again, much farther down from where they had started. Hawk stopped to allow Betsy to catch her breath.

"Are you okay, baby? God, you're all scratched up!" Using his shirtsleeve, Hawk wiped the blood from Betsy's cheek and over her eye.

"I'm okay, Hawk. We need to go!"

"Listen to me, Betsy. I want you to run ahead to the cabin and call for help. Whoever was shooting was high up on the mountain, and there's only one way down unless he's some kind of mountain man and knows these woods better than most. I'm going back and find out who the hell he is."

"No, Hawk! I'm not leaving you! Come with me!" Betsy grabbed Hawk's arm.

"Do what I say, Betsy! There's no time for arguing!"

"No! I won't leave you!"

"You are so damn stubborn, Betsy!"

"That may be, but the only way I'm going is if you're with me."

Knowing he'd be wasting his breath, Hawk grabbed Betsy's hand and started running down the trail toward the cabin.

****

"Hawk, I think it was probably just a hunter with a

wild shot. I know there's been some in that area. Whoever it was didn't use the main trail. He headed out through the woods on the other side, probably used that old logging road." The sheriff reported back to Hawk after he and his men searched the area, looking for the shooter but finding nothing.

"One shot maybe, but two shots that close to us? I'm not convinced." Hawk shook his head in disagreement with the sheriff's theory.

****

On Monday morning, Hawk shut the alarm clock off and turned to cuddle his wife.

"You're going to be late, Hawk."

"I'm not going to work today." Hawk kept his arm around Betsy and made no effort to get up.

"Hawk, I know what you're thinking. I don't think you slept any last night. You can't stay here to protect Trapper and me. You have a job. The sheriff was probably right, and it was just a hunter."

"All I can think about is three years ago. What if Rosanna Cavalera contracted someone else from prison? I'm going to see the sheriff and get him to check into it. I have to know, Betsy. I don't want you here by yourself."

"And what will you do when tomorrow and the next day roll around? Are you going to quit your job just because you're afraid for us?"

"I'll do whatever I have to. Do you think you could convince your mom to hold off on the trip to Mississippi? At least, for a few days?"

"Hawk. I told you I don't want Mom to know about this at all. They're leaving tomorrow, and I don't want her worrying. You promised you wouldn't tell her."

"Yeah, but I didn't promise not to tell Uncle Custer. He won't leave if he thinks you and Trapper need him."

"That's not fair, and you know it. Mom needs him more, and she deserves this trip after what she's been through."

"Stop being so damn selfless, Betsy!" Leaving the bed, Hawk walked to the window, stopping to stare at the mountains.

"Honey, please, don't do this to yourself. There is no contract out on me. Why would Rosanna wait this long? Besides, Patrick is dead. There's no reason."

"I guess you're right, but it scares the hell out of me. For once, I wish we lived right in the middle of town instead of so far out. See, if you'd done what I asked you to, I'd know who fired those shots, hunter or otherwise, and there wouldn't be all this concern."

"You are so bossy when you're in your protector role. No way would I let you go back there, and we don't live in town by choice. We're not going to live our lives looking over our shoulders constantly. Now, get dressed and go to work. Besides, I know where the rifle is, and I can use it if I have to. Remember?"

"Now who's getting bossy? I'm not going to work today, Betsy, and that's final. Maybe if I have a day to think about all this, I can feel better about leaving you tomorrow."

Crossing the room, he took her in his arms, moving his hands under her gown, pulling her next to him, massaging her cheeks.

"How about we go back to bed for a little while before Trapper wakes up?"

****

"And who does this go to?" Betsy looked up as the man placed the book in front of her.

"You don't have to put anything. Just signing it is enough." His eyes caught hers, and for a few seconds they stared at each other.

"Do I know you? You look so familiar." Betsy could not help but stare at the good-looking guy.

"No. I'm new to town. My name is Timothy Harden. I'm from Denver."

"Well, it's nice meeting you, Timothy." Betsy shook Timothy's hand and smiled, but sensed he was uneasy. She also sensed he did not want to leave. He continued to hold her hand and smile at her.

"Thank you for buying my book. Is there anything else I can do for you?"

"Oh! Sorry." Timothy dropped her hand and picked up the book. He turned to leave and then stopped. "Thanks for signing it, Betsy. It's a good book."

As Timothy left the bookstore, he noticed Mal sitting on the bench outside. He was beginning to think he was being stalked.

"So have you become a reader of romances since you got to Red Lodge?"

"Maybe. Got a problem with it?" Timothy did not like this guy but didn't know why. Being a cop, an ex-cop, he had a sixth sense about people and felt this guy was nosing around too much, especially where he was concerned.

"No problem at all. Read it myself, in fact. You know, just trying to learn a little about the locals."

"And why is that? Thought you were just passing

through, a tourist like myself." Timothy stared at the man, waiting for his reply.

"It's kind of a quaint little place, in a cowboy sort of way. I might stick around a while. How about you?" The man asked the question with a smirk on his face.

"Don't know yet. What's it to you?"

"Nothing. Just wondering." He glanced back to the bookstore. "Elizabeth Parish Larson is a real knockout. That Hawk Larson is a lucky man, don't you think?" His smirk grew more pronounced.

Timothy did not reply as he turned to walk away.

"Yeah, wouldn't mind taking her to bed myself, if you know what I mean." Mal left the bench and moved beside Timothy, nudging him with his arm like his remark was a joking matter.

Timothy gave the man a glare that said how reprehensible he found him and moved in front of him, where he could respond eye to eye.

"You'll keep your filthy thoughts to yourself, if you know what's good for you." Timothy's face glowed red with anger.

"Oh, I didn't mean anything by it. Just guy talk. You know her or something?" Mal sensed he had hit a nerve.

"No. Just don't like disrespectful bastards like you." With these words, Timothy walked away knowing he had shown Mal too much of his emotion and his business.

Mal smiled as he watched Timothy get in his truck and speed away. This guy had an obvious interest in Betsy Larson, and Mal wondered just what it was.

****

The day after the book signing, Betsy went to

check on her mom's cabin as she had promised. As she stepped onto the porch, she noticed someone coming down the trail from Custer's place. She immediately recognized the man as the one from the book signing and became a little apprehensive, wondering what this stranger was doing out this far.

"Hello, Betsy. You probably don't remember me." He stopped several feet from the porch, not wanting to make her uneasy.

"Timothy Harden from Denver. Yes, I remember you." Trapper had run to the hitching post to get his stick horse.

"Cute kid. He must be about three or four. I remember when my daughter, Carrie, was that age. Full of piss and vinegar, as my grandmother used to say."

"I haven't heard that expression since I left Mississippi. Your grandmother must be from the South." Betsy smiled as she remembered her grandfather Zeke using that saying to describe her as a gully-climbing, imaginative child.

"Yes. Tennessee, actually."

"What are you doing way out here, Timothy? This is a good ways off the main trail."

"Oh, I'm sorry. I guess I'm trespassing. This is your property, right?"

"Actually, it's my mom's place. Down that path is Mom's friend Custer's cabin. Well, he's a lot more than a friend, but they haven't chosen to get married as yet."

"The old cabin in the aspen grove?" Timothy asked as he pointed down the trail.

"Yes. Did you see it?" Betsy moved to the porch and sat in a rocker.

"I did. I was hiking the other day on the trail to

Keyser Brown, and I saw your mom's cabin. It's like something out of a western movie. I just had to get a closer look. Guess I should have asked first." Timothy moved to the porch and propped a hiking boot on the bottom step. "I wanted to see where the trail beside the cabin went and found the small cabin. Would it be for rent? I'm looking for a place."

"Custer lives here with my mom, but they're in Mississippi right now. I don't know if he'd want to rent it or not, but I'll ask the next time I talk to him. What brings you to Red Lodge, Timothy?"

"Just needed a break from city life. Always wanted to come here, and it's everything I thought it would be. Being from Denver, I'm a mountain lover. I'm thinking about staying here a while."

"What did you do in Denver, if I may ask?" Betsy kept her eyes on Timothy.

"I was a cop, a detective with Denver Police Department. It's a pretty stressful job, and I decided I had to have a break. I resigned last week. If you want, I can give you some references."

"That would be helpful. I'm sure if Custer decided to rent to you he'd want to know something about you."

"Tell you what, Betsy. Here are the names of a couple of people that I worked with. You can call them." Timothy opened his pack and pulled out a pad. After writing on it, he handed the paper to Betsy.

"You know, there's no running water at Custer's place. He hauls it from the stream that's in back of the cabin, but it needs to be filtered before drinking it." Betsy paused. "And there's an outhouse."

"No problem. I'm up for the challenge. Peace and quiet always come with a price, and I'm willing to pay." Timothy took a step back. "Well, I better go. I'm staying at Red Lodge Inn. If Custer says he'll rent to me, just leave a message at the desk, or you can call me on my cell if I'm in range." He reached back in his pack and pulled out a card. "Here's my old card from the police department. It has my cell number on it."

As he reached the edge of the yard, Timothy stopped to talk to Trapper and admire his horse. Trapper immediately galloped to show off for his new friend as Timothy laughed at the boy's antics.

****

Betsy noticed how muscular Timothy Harden was. He wasn't very tall, but every inch of his height was well developed, the product of a disciplined regimen of weight training, probably. Even with his admirable physique, he walked on his tiptoes like a little boy. When he reached the steep incline on the trail going up, the muscles in the backs of his legs protruded even more. With his Broncos cap pulled down on his head so tight it made his ears stick out, he looked more boyish than ever. Betsy liked Timothy Harden for some reason but had no clue why, since she had just met him.

Later, she told Hawk about Timothy wanting to rent Custer's cabin. Hawk was not convinced it was a good idea.

"Who is this guy anyway?" Hawk drew his eyebrows together in a scowl of disapproval.

"Timothy Harden. He was a police detective in Denver. His references checked out. In fact, his old boss said for me to tell him he's still pissed at him for leaving without telling him in advance that he was resigning. Wants him to call ASAP."

"I don't know, Betsy. You and Trapper go to your

mom's almost every day, and I'm a little concerned about some stranger being so close, especially after being shot at the other day." Hawk arched his brows as if in deep thought. "I need to meet this guy before any deal is made."

"He's really likeable, Hawk. You might even feel better knowing there's a man close by to help look after the place, especially an ex-cop. That's what Mom and Custer thought, too."

"You like him, huh? Should I be jealous?" Hawk pulled Betsy to him.

"I hope you're kidding. But he is really fit and muscular like you used to be before you got so attached to your computer." The twinkle took over Betsy's eyes.

"Used to be?" Hawk pulled away from Betsy and stared at her. "What's that supposed to mean?"

Betsy moved close to him and patted his stomach. "What size jeans did you have me buy for you the other day?"

"That does it! If you want to see me before dinner from now on, you'll have to come to the tack room in the barn. I'm starting my weightlifting again—just as soon as I send in this last assignment. Used to be? I can't believe you said that, Betsy!" Hawk walked out of the room grumbling, sucking in his stomach as he felt around his sides.

Chapter Nine

He broke into the cabin at night, searching the house for something to use to divert attention should he need it later. On the table downstairs, he found a box containing a manuscript titled *The Gully Path* written by Dr. Parish and Betsy.

"Should be interesting reading, a sneak preview before publication." Giving a sadistic smile, he put it in his backpack and headed for the stairs to have a look around.

Malty stayed up late scanning the manuscript and reading parts he thought might be useful. When he finished, he knew a lot more about Sue Ann Parish and Betsy, but he was still puzzled about where Timothy Harden fit in. Of what value any of his new knowledge would be, he did not know. Billy had taught him that the more he knew about a job, the easier it would be to accomplish and the less chance there'd be of a screw-up. He knew what he'd do with the stolen item when the time was right.

The next afternoon, he watched from the woods at the top of the hill as the doting couple and their son rode horses across the pasture at their place out from Red Lodge. The little boy trotted his pony ahead of his dad and mom. All were laughing and having a good time. At one point, Hawk rode close beside his wife, reached over and kissed her, grabbing her hand and holding it as they rode watching their son.

It was then that Malty decided how best to make Hawk Larson pay. He'd take away his family just like Hawk had done to him when he killed Billy. Hawk Larson would want to die, but he'd let him live to suffer alone.

Later, as he entered Red Lodge, he saw Timothy going into a restaurant on Main Street. Timothy looked directly at him, but Malty was sure Harden didn't recognize him in the old truck. Seizing the opportunity, he headed for the forestry road that would take him as close to the cabin Timothy had rented as possible. After hiding the old truck behind a clump of trees, Malty followed the trail that led past the Parish cabin to the small cabin in the aspens.

The door was locked, as he knew it would be with a city person living in it, but with one swipe of a credit card, it opened. Inside, it was easy to distinguish the renter's belongings from the half-breed's as he turned over clothes in drawers and went through cupboards, being careful to replace everything as it had been. Three cardboard boxes were stacked in the corner, all unopened except for one that proved to be interesting.

The box was filled with books, all written by Dr. Sue Ann Parish, all yellowed with age. Lying on top of the books was a large envelope filled with recent pictures of Dr. Parish, Betsy, and the little boy, some recognizable as shots taken the first day he saw Timothy on the trail above the big cabin.

Taking the manuscript out of his pack, he placed it in the box of books and put the envelope of pictures back on top. Everything was set.

"Just a little while longer, Hawk Larson, and your

world will collapse around you," Malty thought aloud as he relocked the door to the cabin.

****

Two days later, Malty waited. He had watched and knew what time Betsy always left her house, heading for her mother's cabin, and right on schedule she pulled out of her driveway. Keeping a distance behind her, he could see the black cowboy hat in the back seat of the Jeep and knew the boy was with her. Checking in his rearview mirror, he saw the highway was empty and knew it was time to act.

****

Betsy saw the old truck coming fast behind her and sped up, but there was no way she could go fast enough in the Jeep to get out of his way. In her mirror, she saw the bearded man glaring down at her as he rode her bumper. Speeding up again, she reached for her cell phone and hit redial.

"Damn it! Answer, Hawk!" Betsy screamed at the phone.

"Hey, babe." Hawk answered as he opened the door to his office.

"Hawk, someone is right on my tail! He's trying to run me off the road!" Betsy screamed into the phone in a panic as she felt the truck hit her bumper.

"Where are you, Betsy?" Hawk stopped and headed back toward the outer office door.

"A few miles from the house. Oh, God! He's gonna bump me again, Hawk! I'm scared!"

"I'm coming, baby! Hold on! What's he driving?" Hawk could hear Trapper crying in the background, having sensed his mother's fear.

"An old blue truck, a Ford! He's coming up on my

side, Hawk! Oh, God! Hold on, Trapper!" Betsy dropped the phone and clutched the steering wheel tightly with both hands.

The next sound Hawk heard was Betsy's scream and the screeching of tires, a sound that would haunt him the rest of his life. The sounds became muffled but he could hear Trapper crying in the background.

"Betsy! Betsy! Can you hear me?" Hawk yelled into the phone as he ran from the office as students and office staff stared.

Betsy tried to keep the Jeep on the road, but it was no good. The mad man was determined to run her off the road. As her right tires hit the shoulder again, she lost all control, going down an embankment and through a fence, spinning around and stopping headed in the opposite direction. But as the car stopped, she knew her fears were just beginning.

Before she could lock her door, the mad man jerked it open and snatched her out. She fought him as Trapper watched and cried, "Mommy," from his car seat, but his mother was no match for the big man.

Using the butt of the gun he held, he hit her across the forehead, knocking her unconscious. After jerking the back door open, he took the boy from his car seat as he screamed and cried.

"It's okay, Buddy. We're going some place fun." Malty held the kicking boy to him, talking softly in an effort to calm him.

After buckling him into the front seat of the truck, Malty grabbed the gas can from the back and headed back to the Jeep. He picked Betsy up and shoved her limp body back inside. Seeing her cell phone on the floor, he grabbed it and shoved it in his pocket, knowing he could retrieve Hawk's number from it.

Malty could see a truck coming over the hill in the distance and knew he had to hurry. Sprinkling gas on the ground, he stood back and struck a match.

"Partial revenge, Billy, but there's no time to put a smile on this beautiful woman. Now to kick Hawk Larson in the balls one more time."

The pickup sped away as the flames leapt from the ground to the Jeep.

****

Hawk met the truck as he tore down the highway, but all he could see was the driver, and Hawk's priority was to get to his wife and son. He saw the smoke before he saw the Jeep. A truck was stopped a few feet away and David West, a local rancher and neighbor, was spraying the vehicle with a fire extinguisher.

Leaping from the Suburban, he ran toward the smoke.

"Betsy!"

The rancher grabbed him as he tried to get close to the Jeep.

"She's okay, Hawk! I got her out. She's over there by my truck with Jackie. The ambulance is on its way."

"My son! Where's my boy?"

"Trapper wasn't with her, Hawk. It was just Betsy!"

"Yes, he was. I talked to Betsy just before she was run off the road. I heard Trapper crying." Running to his wife, he cradled her bleeding head in his arms, calling to her.

"Betsy! Betsy! Can you hear me, sweetheart? Where's Trapper, Betsy?"

The rancher's wife handed him a wet rag, and he

began wiping the blood from her face. Slowly, she began coming around.

"Hawk! Is Trapper all right?" Betsy tried to sit up but couldn't.

"He's not here, Betsy! He's not in the Jeep!"

"No, Hawk!" Hawk had to restrain her as she tried to get up again.

"That man must have him! You've got to get to Trapper! He's so scared!" Losing consciousness again, she fell back against her husband.

"David, did you see a an old blue pickup when you got here?"

"Yeah! We wondered why he left in such a hurry and didn't try to get Betsy out."

"I don't know who he is, but he ran her off the road and took Trapper. If he gets away, I may never find our boy."

"The ambulance should be here any minute. We'll take care of Betsy, Hawk. Go after your son," David said, urging Hawk to leave Betsy.

A few miles from Red Lodge, Hawk saw the truck sitting on a side road. Before he came to a stop behind it, he knew it would be empty. All that was in it was Trapper's black cowboy hat lying on the front seat. Taking it, he crumpled it in his hands, holding it tightly to his chest as he fell to his knees screaming, "No!"

Chapter Ten

Seattle

Janine Berryhill regained consciousness after two weeks in a coma, and the police were called immediately. With her brother holding her hand, she told of her ordeal with Malty and the visit to the prison. But questioning Julia Bailey proved fruitless for the police. She refused to give any information or to identify the visitor that had been with Nurse Rose at the prison. But the police already had something to identify her attacker, and the semen he'd left in Rose's body was already in the crime lab ready to be tested for DNA.

****

Montana

Hawk told the sheriff everything he knew as he paced in his wife's room at the hospital. Betsy kept slipping in and out of consciousness but would be all right. She had a concussion but was mostly in shock knowing Trapper had been kidnapped. Hawk called Sue Ann and Custer, and they were at the airport in Memphis waiting on a flight back to Montana.

The sheriff issued an Amber alert, and immediately Trapper's picture was broadcast all over the state. No description of the kidnapper was known except that he had a beard and drove a blue truck at the time of the abduction. As Hawk paced, Darlene came into the room.

"I just heard, Hawk. What can I do?"

"Stay close, Darlene. If there's any information on Trapper, I might have to leave, and I need somebody here with Betsy. She's in shock. They're keeping her sedated."

"I'm here as long as you need me." As Darlene sat in the chair by Betsy's bed, Hawk's cell phone rang.

"Find your boy yet?" A man laughed on the other end.

"Who the hell is this? Where's my son?" Hawk paced as he held the cell phone tight to his ear.

"You should be more careful about who you rent to, Hawk." The voice warned.

"Timothy Harden has him?" Hawk yelled the question into the phone as the caller hung up.

"Who was that, Hawk?" Darlene was standing, a look of panic on her face.

"I don't know, but I'm going to Custer's cabin. Can you stay, Darlene?"

"Don't you worry about Betsy. Just go find Trapper."

Hawk was out of breath by the time he reached the cabin, but he had not stopped for a breath. He knew Timothy Harden was around, since his truck was parked at the head of the forestry road. Finding the door locked, Hawk kicked it open, but Timothy was not inside. Hawk ransacked drawers and cupboards and, finding nothing, moved to the boxes stacked in the corner.

The open box was full of Sue Ann's romance novels, and he assumed these belonged to Custer. He almost pushed the box aside but noticed the big envelope and a smaller box on top of the novels. He opened the smaller box and found the manuscript and knew Betsy had left it at Sue Ann's cabin. Next he opened the envelope and found it full of recent pictures of Betsy and Trapper. Now he knew Timothy Harden had something to do with Betsy's accident and Trapper's abduction. As he stood holding the pictures, he heard someone on the porch.

"Hawk? What are you doing here?" Timothy asked as he entered the cabin, but he was not given time to close the door.

"You son-of-a-bitch! Where's my son?" Hawk grabbed Timothy by the front of his shirt and threw him hard against the cabin wall, pinning him there.

"Trapper? I haven't seen Trapper in days!" Timothy held his hands up to ward off Hawk's fist that was coming at him, but it did no good.

Hawk's punch knocked Timothy to the floor, and Hawk held him there with a knee to the chest. Timothy coughed and tried to reason with Hawk.

"Stop, Hawk!" Timothy wheezed from the pressure on his chest. "Tell me what you're talking about!" Timothy wiped the blood from his lip but did not fight back.

Hawk grabbed the pictures he had dropped and shoved them in Timothy's face as he lay on the floor. "Why do you have these pictures of my wife and son?" Hawk grabbed Timothy by the shirt again and pulled him up from the floor, raised his fist and started to hit him again, but Timothy pushed Hawk back against the table and raised both his hands.

"I can explain, Hawk! Just let me talk."

Hawk grabbed Timothy and shoved him into a chair. "You better explain fast, or I swear to God I'll kill you!" Hawk kept his fist in Timothy's face. "Now start talking."

"You'd find out sooner or later, and it better be sooner if I want to save my ass." Jerking the bandana from his head, he wiped the blood that gushed from his lip and nose. Then he pulled each eyelid open and popped out his contacts.

"Look at me, Hawk!" Timothy ran his hand through his hair, a mass of short blond curls.

"Forget the crap, Timothy! I need to know why you tried to kill Betsy and where you took my son."

"Somebody tried to kill Betsy? And took Trapper?" Timothy stood up with a terrified look on his face. Hawk knocked him back in the chair and drew back his fist to hit him again, still holding him by the shirt with his left hand.

"Damn it, Hawk! Stop!" Timothy threw up his hands to ward off Hawk's next blow. "Look at me! Look at my hair. Look at my eyes. For God's sake! Who do I look like, Hawk?"

Hawk stared at the man sitting in the chair and released his shirt, taking a step back.

"Who the hell are you? I know who you look like, but it doesn't make sense. Why did you steal the manuscript from Sue Ann's cabin? And why would I get a call saying you know where Trapper is, if you didn't take him? You better give me some answers and fast, or I'll still beat the hell out of you."

"I don't know anything about a manuscript, and I would never hurt Betsy or Trapper. And you'll have no trouble beating the hell out of me because I won't hit

Betsy's husband—no matter what." Timothy wiped at the blood coming from his lip again without taking his eyes off Hawk.

"My God!" Hawk took another step back, still staring at Timothy. "How the...?"

"I'll explain later, but you need to tell me about Betsy and Trapper. I'm an ex-cop, a detective, and a damn good one. I can help. Besides, Betsy and Trapper are important to me, too. They just don't know it."

Walking to the closet, Timothy reached on the shelf and took down a holster with a 9-millimeter handgun.

"Oh, and I think I'll go back to my old contacts now that my eyes can be green again." Popping in the clear contacts, Timothy looked at Hawk.

"Sure giveaway, isn't it? Not many people have eyes this color. When I saw Betsy's picture in the back of her book, I knew I'd have to disguise my eyes."

Hawk stared at the man and couldn't believe what he was seeing. Why he hadn't identified himself right off would have to wait.

"Now, let's go visit the sheriff. You can tell me what happened on the way. We need to find Trapper." Timothy grabbed his truck keys and headed out the door ahead of Hawk.

Chapter Eleven

"Rosanna Cavalera hasn't had a visitor or any mail in over a year, according to prison officials. I think we can rule her out." The sheriff quickly read the report that he had just taken off the fax and relayed the information about the woman who had hired people to kill Betsy and her ex-husband Patrick over three years ago.

"What about the guy Hawk killed in the canyon, that contract killer Cavalera hired who was after Betsy? And what about that female accomplice of the killer? Isn't she in prison?" Timothy had taken an active role in the investigation, and the sheriff welcomed his expertise.

"Julia Robinson? I know she's serving a long sentence in prison, but we haven't checked on her. I'll get someone to get right on it."

"Sheriff, if you don't mind, I can call Denver and get some information pretty fast." Timothy took out his cell phone ready to make the call at the sheriff's okay.

"No, I don't mind at all. The quicker the better, where a child abduction is concerned, especially when you're dealing with a criminal like this one."

Hawk had gone back to the hospital to check on Betsy and found her still sleeping. He hoped they would keep her sedated so she wouldn't know the danger their little boy was in. Darlene agreed to stay until Sue Ann and Custer returned home later that night. When he got back to the sheriff's office, Timothy met him at the door.

"Hawk, I think we've identified the kidnapper. As soon as I called, my old boss got busy. Turns out William Townsend had a younger brother, Maltese Townsend. And get this. He was recently released from prison and is already wanted for attempted murder of a young prostitute in Seattle. Seems he paid a visit to Julia at the prison right after he was released, disguised as an old man, and had this girl pose as his nurse. Guess he didn't need the girl anymore, so he threw her off a cliff that overlooked the ocean. He thought he had gotten rid of a witness, but she lived. We should be getting a faxed picture of Maltese Townsend any minute."

"God! I can't believe Trapper is in the hands of a killer like that. We've got to find my boy, Timothy. What next?" Hawk started pacing but stopped when a deputy delivered the fax they had been waiting on and handed it to Timothy.

"Well, this is our guy all right. He even stayed at the motel where I stayed when I first came to town. Called himself Mal Cagle. I didn't like him from the start. Should know by now to trust my gut. In fact, I saw him a couple of days ago in an old beat-up truck and wondered what he did with the brown Trailblazer he'd been driving."

"Let me guess. A blue Ford truck."

"Yes. You know him, too?" Timothy arched his eyebrows and handed the fax to Hawk.

"No. That's the truck he abandoned after he ran Betsy off the road and took Trapper." Hawk stood and began pacing as he stared at the picture of Townsend. "We've got to do something. I can't just sit here while my son…" Hawk stopped and looked at Timothy.

"We'll get Trapper back, Hawk." Timothy put his hand on Hawk's shoulder and then turned to the sheriff. "We need to alert law enforcement all over Montana to be on the lookout for a brown Trailblazer. He must have just bought it, because it had one of those drive-out dealer tags, no regular license plates. Can you get that information out, Sheriff?" Timothy asked the question but knew the sheriff would agree.

"Consider it done. I wonder how many other vehicles he has access to," the sheriff replied as he headed for an officer sitting at a computer.

"Let's see. The report from Seattle said he picked the prostitute up in a red Porsche." Timothy looked over the notes the deputy had given him. "That ought to be easy to spot. Let's get a license plate, Sheriff."

Timothy noticed Hawk's hands were shaking as he stared again at Maltese Townsend's picture.

"Hawk, we're doing everything we can. Why don't you go stay with Betsy? I'll call you the minute we hear anything."

"I can't, Timothy. I'm terrified Betsy will wake up and want Trapper, and I won't have him for her." Hawk sat down and began nervously rubbing his thigh. "A father ought to be able to protect his son, and I've failed miserably. I should have known something was wrong the day Betsy and I were shot at when we were at Keyser Brown. I should never have left them alone." Hawk put his head in his hands.

"Don't be so hard on yourself. You had no way of knowing. This Townsend guy is slick." Timothy put his hand on Hawk's shoulder. "We'll find Trapper, Hawk."

"What do we do now that we know who the kidnapper is? Do we go on TV with his picture and hope someone identifies him? Or would that push him to hurt Trapper? What do we do? Timothy? Sheriff?" Hawk stood casting worried glances from one to the other.

Before either of them could answer, Hawk's cell phone rang.

"Someone wants to talk you, Hawk." It was the voice Hawk feared and hated.

"Daddy, I want you. Come get me, Daddy." Trapper began whimpering.

"Trapper? Are you all right? I'll come for you, Son. I promise."

"That's real sweet. But you'll never see him again, Hawk—at least, not alive." Townsend gave a demonic laugh.

"Please! Don't hurt him. He's just a little boy. It's me you want, not him. Tell me where to meet you and take me instead."

"Touching. Real damn touching, but you'll hurt more this way." With these words, he hung up.

"Check your caller log, Hawk."

"It's no use. I tried that the first time he called. It's blocked." Hawk's hands were shaking more now, and Timothy could feel his panic.

"I think it's time we got the news media involved, Sheriff." Timothy looked from the sheriff to Hawk. "Get his picture on TV with the heading 'Wanted for attempted murder and kidnapping.' Describe the Trailblazer but hold off on the Porsche. Maybe we can push him to try to leave in the sports car thinking no one knows about it. It'd be hard for a man to leave a Porsche behind."

Knowing the bulletin would be breaking on TV shortly, Hawk called to warn Darlene.

"Is she awake yet, Darlene?"

"No. The doctor came in and said they're going to keep her sedated today. Any word on Trapper?"

"We know who has him. Whatever you do, don't turn the TV on. I don't want to risk Betsy hearing any of this. It's William Townsend's brother."

"Oh, no, Hawk!" Darlene clutched the phone and lowered her voice to a whisper as Betsy stirred. "What do you want me to do?"

"Wait with Betsy and pray." Hawk put his cell phone away and sat down with his face in his hands.

****

"I want my daddy."

"Stop whining and eat your pizza. You're a cowboy, not a baby. Here, let's find something on TV." Malty started flicking through channels on the TV and stopped when he saw his own face plastered across the screen, followed by a picture of Trapper.

"How the hell did they find out?" As he clicked the volume louder, a picture of Rose came across the screen giving the details of her attempted murder.

"That little bitch is alive! Damn!" A furious Malty swiped the pizza off the table before redirecting his gaze to the TV.

"You said a bad word! You're a bad man! You hurt my mommy! I don't like you!" Trapper screamed the words as he slid out of his seat at the table. He folded his arms, poked his lip out, and stomped his foot.

"Shut up, kid, and eat!" Malty picked up the little

boy and shoved him hard into the chair. After picking up a piece of pizza from the floor, he put it in front of Trapper, who began to cry. Malty turned the TV up as loud as it would go and stood in front of it.

Maltese Townsend was last seen driving a brown 2004 Trailblazer. If you see this man, contact the police immediately. Do not try to apprehend. He is considered armed and dangerous.

"Okay, cowboy. It's time you and me took a ride in some real horsepower."

"Are you…taking me…to Daddy?" Trapper asked between sobs.

"Not yet. But we are going to stop and get something to make you feel better." Malty bent down and softened his voice. "What kind of candy do you like?"

"I don't want candy. I want Daddy." Trapper poked his bottom lip out and began to whimper again.

"Well, if you're a good boy, maybe I'll take you to your daddy later." Malty picked up Trapper and headed out the door.

Malty stopped at a convenience store and filled the Porsche with gas. He made sure the boy's seatbelt held him tight while he went inside to pay for the gas and to pick up some over-the-counter nighttime adult cold medicine. As he picked up the bag to leave, he heard a little voice behind him.

"I want ice cream." Trapper stood with his lip poked out.

"How did you get out of that seatbelt? Kids are just too damn smart these days." He directed his comment to the young cashier. "Okay, what kind do you want? Chocolate or vanilla?"

"Manilla." Malty headed for the small freezer containing ice cream.

"Hi, little cutie. What's your name?" The girl smiled down at the boy as Malty grabbed an ice cream from the freezer and threw it on the counter.

"Trap…" Malty put his hand over the boy's mouth. He dropped a five-dollar bill on the counter to pay for the ice cream and picked up Trapper.

"Sorry, about that. I thought he was about to tell you to 'fuck off,' something his older brother taught him thinking it would be real cute. Keep the change." Malty hurried out the door.

As he sped away, he yelled at the boy.

"You get out of this car again, and I'll spank you! You hear me, brat?" Malty grabbed Trapper's arm.

Trapper tried to pull his arm away but couldn't, so he stuck his lip out and yelled back at the man like the brave little cowboy in his favorite book his daddy always read to him. "My mommy and daddy don't spank me. They put me in time out," Trapper yelled and crossed his arms.

"Feisty little devil, aren't you?" Malty laughed at the little daredevil. "I'll fix that."

Pulling into a parking lot, Malty took out the medicine and poured the plastic measuring cup full, an adult-size dose.

"No! I don't like it!" Trapper pressed his lips closed and covered his face with his hands.

"You don't get your ice cream until you take this medicine." Malty shoved the medicine cup to Trapper's lips and held his mouth open.

Reluctantly, the boy took the medicine, shivering at its sickly sweet taste. Before he could finish his ice cream, his head was already bobbing.

****

In Red Lodge, the deputy answered the call.

"Sheriff, you better take this one." The deputy shoved the phone toward the sheriff.

"This is Sheriff Donaldson.…A Food Mart on the other side of Billings?…Fifteen minutes ago?…Red Porsche, huh? That's our man all right.…We're on our way."

Turning to Hawk, the sheriff smiled. "He's in Billings, heading west on I-90. A cashier recognized Trapper. He was okay fifteen minutes ago. Let's go, Timothy. We'll try to head him off."

"I'm going, too, Sheriff. I need to be where my son is." Hawk headed for the door, and the sheriff knew there would be no stopping him.

"Hawk and I will follow you in my truck. Let's go, Hawk. You're in no condition to drive." Timothy led Hawk through the door at a fast pace.

"Here, take this radio so you'll hear the reports we get." The sheriff handed Timothy a radio and then turned to Hawk. "Hawk, under no circumstances are you to come anywhere near Townsend when we catch him. See to it he keeps his distance, Timothy. You don't know Hawk Larson like I do."

"Believe me, I know his temper. Got the sore nose and jaw to prove it." Timothy rubbed his jaw as he stretched it open.

"Sorry about that, Timothy. Damn good thing you look like you do, or you might be dead by now." Hawk climbed into the truck with Timothy.

The sheriff, with Timothy and Hawk behind him, sped down the two-lane, paved road with sirens blazing.

Two deputy cars followed Timothy's truck.

"Suspect is heading west on I-90, at Exit 426. Pursue from a distance and wait for instructions," the radio blared, and Timothy floor-boarded the accelerator to keep pace with the sheriff, who had sped up considerably.

"We're almost to I-90, Hawk."

"Step on it, Timothy!" Hawk grabbed the door and leaned forward as if trying to help the truck along.

"You want me to run over the sheriff? We've been hauling ass the whole way."

"Sorry, Timothy. Damn, I'm nervous!" Hawk could hardly sit still in the truck.

"Understandably so. We'll get him, Hawk. I've been chasing criminals for fifteen years."

"You don't think he's heading back to Red Lodge, do you?"

"Only if he's a bigger fool than I think he is. He's a caught man, and he knows it if he's watched any TV at all this afternoon. Hopefully, he'll think about that and turn himself in peacefully without hurting Trapper."

Just as Timothy reached I-90, Hawk's cell phone rang. The two men looked at each other. Timothy turned the radio down in case it was Townsend.

"Hello."

"So you know who I am, Hawk. Wondered why you said it was you I wanted and not the kid."

"Please don't hurt my son, Townsend. Turn yourself in before you get in any deeper." Hawk glanced at Timothy, and Timothy motioned for him to keep Townsend talking.

"I like it when you beg. Did my brother beg for his life before you killed him?"

"He was unconscious. Never knew what happened to him. I had to do it to protect Betsy. You should understand that."

"I don't give a shit about your wife or your kid!" Townsend's voice was loud and angry. "Billy was all the family I had. I owe it to him to make you pay."

"Not with my son. You can have me. I killed Billy. I'll make it easy for you. Just don't hurt my son."

"That's it. Keep begging, Hawk. Makes me know you'll suffer like I'm suffering. I don't mind dying, knowing I got revenge for Billy. Got no family and nothing to live for. I'd let you say goodbye to your little cowboy, but he's asleep. I gave him some adult cold medicine. It's better that he doesn't know what's about to happen. See, I'm not as heartless as you think. Have a happy life, Hawk."

"No, don't hang up!" Hawk yelled into the phone, but no one was on the other end. "He's gonna do it, Timothy! He's gonna kill Trapper! Do something!" Hawk's voice ricocheted off the top of the truck.

Timothy picked up the radio and pushed the button.

"Sheriff Donaldson. Hawk just had a call from Townsend. He's talking about killing Trapper soon. You've got to move in." He paused to listen. "Okay. I'm right behind you." Turning onto the ramp with tires screaming, Timothy headed westbound on I-90.

"Suspect just passed Exit 408. Prepare to overtake," the radio blared.

"This is it, Hawk! Hang on!" Timothy stomped the accelerator, passing the sheriff's car.

"Sorry, Sheriff, but you are too damn slow!"

Within seconds, the red Porsche was in view, traveling fast. From out of nowhere, state troopers appeared on both sides of the interstate. Up ahead, blue lights flashed as patrol cars waited on the shoulder to cut off the Porsche as it approached. Townsend saw the lights, too, and cut across the median without breaking his speed.

"He's on the eastbound side. Hold on, Hawk! We're cutting him off!"

Turning sharply to the left, the big truck bumped and spun its way across the median and pulled across the interstate. Two cars and a truck came to screeching halts, blocking both lanes, and just behind them was the red Porsche.

"Stop, Hawk!" Timothy reached for Hawk as he opened the truck door, but it was too late.

Hawk jumped from the truck and ran toward the Porsche. As he got closer, Townsend got out of the car, holding the sleeping boy, and ran to the shoulder of the road where he knew there was nothing behind him. He stopped with his gun pointed at the boy's head. Immediately, everyone standing outside their vehicles ducked for cover. Only Hawk remained facing the gunman.

"Don't, Townsend! For God's sake, don't do this!" Hawk stopped and held his hands up to show he was unarmed.

"I like this better, Larson. You get to see your kid die." As he cocked the gun and held the barrel to Trapper's face, Hawk plunged toward him, yelling.

"No!"

Two shots rang out. Townsend fell to the ground with Trapper on top of him.

Hawk grabbed his son from the fallen man and backed away. Trapper was covered in blood.

Trembling, Hawk fell to his knees, hugging the limp boy to him, sobbing aloud. Timothy ran to his side and squatted beside him with his gun still directed at Townsend.

"Daddy? I want Daddy…"

Hearing the sleepy little voice, Hawk held the boy out from him and wiped the blood from his eyes. "I'm here, Son. I've got you. He's alive, Timothy! My boy's alive." As Hawk hugged the boy tight, Trapper began to squirm.

"You're squeezing me, Daddy."

Laughing, Hawk loosened his grip and continued wiping away the blood, Townsend's blood, from his son's face.

"I'm sorry, Son. I'm just so glad to see you." Hawk's voice cracked as he stood holding Trapper to him.

"I want Mommy." The boy mumbled his words as he fell back asleep with his head against his daddy's chest.

"We'll go see her, Trapper. When you wake up good, you'll see Mommy. I promise." Hawk hugged his son again as his tears fell on his little boy's face.

"I've never wanted to be as sure of a shot in my life, Hawk, but I couldn't take the time to aim like I wanted to." Timothy put one hand on Hawk's shoulder and the other on Trapper's head. "When he cocked that gun, it was then or never. Thank God I hit him and not Trapper."

"I heard two shots, didn't I?" Hawk asked.

"Townsend's gun went off as he fell, but the bullet went wild."

"Thank goodness, you're all alive!" The sheriff ran

up with his gun drawn and stood in front of Hawk. "Should have known Hawk couldn't be controlled in this situation."

"If you can take it from here, Sheriff, I need to get Hawk and this little man to Betsy." Timothy looked past the sheriff at the line of blue lights driving up the median. "It looks like you've got plenty of backup, but I don't think you'll be needing it for Townsend."

"I've got it, Timothy. And thanks." The sheriff began issuing orders as Timothy turned to Hawk.

"Let's go see Betsy, Hawk. I've got a lot of catching up to do, and I think there's a sleepy little boy who'll be a welcome sight. But we might ought to clean him up a little first."

Chapter Twelve

"Go on, Hawk. I'll be up in a minute. Just need to check in with the sheriff one more time."

Hawk knew Timothy was giving him a chance to be alone with Betsy when he took Trapper to her hospital room. He also knew Timothy was nervous about the disclosure he had to make. Darlene was waiting for Hawk and hugged him when he came into the room carrying a very sleepy Trapper.

"The doctor didn't order her another sedative after you called. I told him the good news. She's been waking up off and on asking for you and Trapper." Darlene kissed the sleeping boy, hugged Hawk, and left the room.

"Betsy? Sweetheart? Somebody wants to see you. Trapper, wake up. It's Mommy." As he laid the boy beside his mother, Hawk kissed each of them. Betsy drowsily opened her eyes and looked up at Hawk.

"Hi, honey. What time is it?" Betsy was still groggy.

"Time for this little boy to cuddle up to his mom."

Rolling over, Betsy smiled and put her arm around her son.

"Hey, Little Big Man. Where you been?"

"I wanna hold you, Mommy," Trapper mumbled.

"Well, cuddle up here and hold me, baby."

"You, Daddy." Trapper reached back for him, but

his limp arm fell to the bed as his eyes rolled, unable to wake up.

Scooting his son over close to his mother, Hawk lay beside him and reached across to caress his wife's hair. Overcome with relief and exhaustion, he fell asleep nestling his son and wife.

****

When Hawk awoke early the next morning, Sue Ann and Custer were sitting in the room. Both had dozed off. As he moved off the bed, he groaned from the crick he had gotten in his neck trying to hold on to his family and to hang on to the edge of the narrow hospital bed. Trapper and Betsy were still wrapped in each other's arms, sleeping soundly.

"Hawk, come give your mother-in-law a hug and promise you'll remind me of all this the next time I get a wild hair to go to Mississippi." After hugging Sue Ann, he noticed Custer stirring.

"What time did you two get here? I never even heard you come in."

"About two this morning. No way would we wake you. You three looked like you'd been in a battle zone. The nurses told me that was pretty much what it was. I don't even want to know why you and Trapper have blood all over your shirts." Sue Ann put her hand to her trembling lip.

"It was pretty terrifying, Sue Ann, but Trapper and Betsy are safe now. God looked with favor on the Larson family again. Don't know why he's so good to us, but at some point, we better start showing more appreciation."

"You look like you could stand some coffee, Son." Custer was awake now as he stood to hug his nephew.

"Don't think I've ever been happier to see anybody in my life than when we walked in this room and saw the three of you asleep in that bed."

"A lot happened while you were gone. A lot more than you'll ever imagine." Hawk looked from Custer to Sue Ann.

"Well, I want to hear about it all eventually, but right now, I want to get to a motel room, take a shower, and come back later to visit my daughter and grandson when they're awake." Sue Ann stood and headed for the door, and Custer followed her.

"I'll wait here and see what the doctor says about Betsy. I'm hoping he'll let me take her home later today. Unk, do you think you could spare one of your shirts?" Hawk held his shirt out, looking down at the bloodstains, blood that belonged to a monster.

Hawk walked into the hall following Sue Ann and Custer, but Sue Ann had stopped. She stared down the hall, her gaze on the approaching stranger.

The stranger walked in a bounce, stretching each step full length from heel to toe, pausing to balance on his toes like young children often do when first learning to walk, probably an attempt to make himself appear taller. His head was covered in thick, blond ringlets, and he never looked up until he was almost to Betsy's room. When he saw the older version of Betsy just a few feet away, he stopped. Their green eyes met and neither could break the magnetizing spell of unexplained familiarity. Hawk broke the silence.

"Sue Ann, this is someone you need to know. Let's go back in the room." He took her arm, but she refused to look away or to move. Hawk released her arm as she began walking toward the man. She stopped directly in front of him and put her hand gently on his cheek, looking deep into his emerald green eyes, her eyes.

"Tobi?" Her voice cracked as she continued to stare, her hand still on his cheek.

"Yes, Mom. It's me."

Tobi caught her as she collapsed, and carried her into the hospital room.

****

A family reunion like no other took place at Betsy and Hawk's cabin the next day. Tobi brought the box full of yellowed romances that his grandmother had saved for him, and he brought the small box with a letter she wrote when she found out she had Alzheimer's.

"She never gave me any hint about what she had done, and I'm sure my mother, the woman who raised me, was not aware Grandmother had made the switch. Betsy, would you read the letter out loud so everyone will hear it at the same time? I know what she did was unconscionable, but Grandmother really was a kind and loving person."

After handing the letter to Betsy, Tobi sat beside Sue Ann to listen.

Dear Timothy,

Before this terrible disease eats away my mind, I have a confession that I need to make to you. It will be shocking, but I hope something good will come from it.

When your mother became pregnant for the last time, she was ecstatic. She had miscarried three babies and was told she could not have children. We were all so hopeful, especially after she carried this one almost full term.

The day she gave birth to a son was the most

wonderful day ever for our family. I was working in the nursery at Baptist Hospital in Memphis, where you were born, and was excited to get to care for my daughter's only child, my only grandchild.

In the room next to Nora was a young girl named Sue Ann Parish. She claimed to be divorced, but I overheard her talking to her mother and knew that really she was an unwed mother. On the same day, almost at the same time that your mother gave birth, Sue Ann gave birth to twins, a girl and a boy. She called the girl Elizabeth and the boy Tobi, but I never knew their full names. Both mothers were so blessed and were so very happy, but tragedy would change the lives of both forever.

Nora's baby boy, Timothy Wayne, died during his first two hours of life. I was the only one in the nursery, and I found him. I was grief stricken. As I held him in my arms with my tears falling on his little face, I asked God to forgive me for what I was about to do.

After removing his wristband, I switched him with Sue Ann's healthy baby boy. It just didn't seem right for this young mother, with no husband to support her, to have two healthy babies and my Nora to have none. God forgive me, but I never regretted the decision I made.

You were your parents' answer to a prayer, and their lives were complete until they were taken away from us when you were fourteen. I always felt losing Nora and Jim was God's punishment for my terrible sin.

By the time you read this, I will be gone. Please forgive me and know that what I did was out of love for my daughter.

You've brought me great joy all your life. Now it's time to find your real mother, Timothy, and your twin sister, and give them the opportunity to know and love you as we have.

I love you,

Grandmother

P.S. The books that gave me so much pleasure during the last years of my life were all written by your mother, Dr. Sue Ann Parish. Maybe if you read them, you will get to know her.

Opening the small box, Toby took out the two plastic wristbands that had been cut apart. On one was written Boy Harden, and on the other Boy Parish. Sue Ann took them, rubbing her fingers over them as her tears fell. Then she wiped her eyes, put the wristbands back in Timothy's box, looked up, and smiled at her son.

"Well, now. That's that. Let's get on with life, Tobias Ezekiel Parish. We have some catching up to do." Reaching for her son, she hugged him again. Tobi returned the hug like he would never let go.

"So now are you Tobi or Timothy?" Hawk asked the question again, for the last time.

"I'm Tobi, but I'll have to get my name changed to make it legal. While we're making introductions, I'd like to show you pictures of your granddaughter and niece." Opening his wallet, he removed a picture. "Her name is Carrie. She's thirteen, and she has blonde curly hair and green eyes, if you can imagine that."

"My granddaughter! How wonderful, Tobi. Now I have two grandchildren." Sue Ann smiled as she stared at the girl's picture.

"Oh, Tobi, she's beautiful." Betsy looked over her

mom's shoulder at the picture before it began making its way around the room. "I think she looks like me, don't you, Mom? When can we meet her, Tobi?"

"Soon. She won't believe all this, but she'll love the mountains and all of you. Especially you, little cowboy." Tobi reached for Trapper, and he crawled into his uncle's lap and pulled his uncle's arms tight around him as if he had known him forever.

"Thank goodness you're my brother-in-law, Tobi. I was getting a little jealous when Betsy started talking about your muscles." Hawk put his arm around his wife.

"Speaking of jealousy, there's something I've been wanting to do since I saw Betsy that first day through the telephoto lens of my camera. I want to hug my sister and see if that's what's been missing all these years. It was like something always gnawing at me that I couldn't explain—an extension of myself like a shadow that followed close but would never show itself fully."

"I know what you mean, Tobi. I've felt it, too. Come here, Brother." Betsy patted the sofa beside her.

As Tobi and Betsy hugged, the sun's last rays of the day streamed through the window of the cabin, lighting up the whole room. But the sunlight could not compare with the joy that radiated from the family within the log walls.

"I love you, Betsy." Tobi held tight to his sister's hand.

"I love you, too, Tobi. Twin love, the best kind." When they broke their embrace, Betsy put her hand on Tobi's cheek. "Now I know why you weren't kicking that walrus skull around behind the Northern Lights." Betsy laughed, knowing she would have to explain this one to her brother, and to her husband.

****

It had been a long, wonderful, but tiring day for Sue Ann, and Custer had to make her leave Betsy and Hawk's cabin, where Tobi would also be staying until he found a place of his own. She and Custer talked all the way back to their cabin about how things had turned out.

"I told you there was much to live for, Sue Ann. I just wasn't sure how it would all come together."

"Yes, I do have much to live for, but not just for my children. Oh, my! Children. That has a nice ring to it!" Sue Ann reached across and took Custer's right hand off the steering wheel and clutched it with both her hands.

"You, my darling, are still the sunshine in my life. You're my strength. I hope you know how much I love you, Custer."

Custer smiled at Sue Ann and squeezed her hands.

"Yes, I know. We have both come close to death, and maybe that is what made us appreciate our love for each other and to finally put in place our life together in the mountains."

"We have been blessed." Sue Ann released Custer's hand and stared ahead. They had turned onto the bumpy forestry road to the cabin, and she knew Custer needed two hands to control the truck. The mountain silhouettes loomed ahead of them, set against a brilliant backdrop of stars.

Custer opened his door, ready to help Sue Ann out and into the cabin. He knew she was tired. But before he could exit, Sue Ann placed her hand on his arm to stop him.

"Custer, I think it's time we made our union official." She looked at him, waiting for his reply.

"You mean get married?" Custer's voice sounded surprised.

"Of course. We've been together for almost four years now, and off and on for more than twenty years. Don't you think we've had enough time to know if we're right for each other?" Sue Ann gave Custer a serious look, waiting for an answer.

"I love you, Sue Ann, and I hope we have many more years of happiness together. But I need to think about this and make sure this is what should be."

"Your vision quest. There is more that you haven't told me—something else besides me with my two babies—fawns, as you will—when I was at the brink of death with one baby remaining aloof, hidden." Her eyes searched Custer's, and in the moonlight, she could tell he was contemplating his answer.

"Yes, but I don't know the meaning of the other part any more than I knew the meaning of the fawns and the doe. I just knew it was important enough for you to fight to live. As soon as I saw you put your hand on Tobi's cheek at the hospital, it all made sense. I knew the moment you knew it was Tobi standing before you."

"So you have no idea what the mystery part of your quest is?"

"No, but it will be shown just as Tobi was. I just feel we have to give it time to be disclosed before we make any great changes in our lives."

"And you won't share it with me until you know the interpretation?"

"You already know that is how it works, Sue Ann,

and we may know at exactly the same time, like we did with Tobi." Custer drew her close to him and kissed her with the passion of a young brave. "Now, let's get you to bed. You looked tired when we left Betsy and Hawk's, and I know you'll rise early, especially since they're all coming for breakfast."

****

An hour later, Custer was sitting on the porch, his thoughts embedded in mountain shadows. He was unable to sleep, thinking about the unanswered part of his vision quest. The second vision had come true, telling him it was only a matter of time before he would know the meaning of the first vision.

Just when he was about to go inside, he heard a flutter. A small bird had flown through the porch and perched on one of the rotten hitching posts at the edge of the yard. Custer had started to knock the old rotted post down the day before leaving for Mississippi, but Sue Ann had stopped him.

"I've seen a bird carrying twigs to that old hollowed-out post. I think maybe it's building a nest. Hopefully, we'll have some baby birds Trapper can watch hatch and grow." Custer had tried to convince her that it was way too late for birds to be building nests, since nesting season ended in July, but he could not convince her. The bird had become personified in Sue Ann's mind, and she had the idea that perhaps the site had been chosen by some female with a futuristic instinct, the nest to be used in the spring.

After retrieving a small flashlight from the cabin, Custer made his way to the post. The sound of a human approaching frightened the tiny bird, and it flew away. Being careful not to leave his human scent, Custer held his breath as he shined the light down into the hollow of the old post, and there it was...a nearly completed nest, but no eggs were inside.

Rabbit fur, mud, and twigs made up most of the nest, but one bit of material caught his eye. It was near the bottom where the construction was first begun. A braid of hair, Sue Ann's and his, was wound through the twigs, adding solidity to the nest.

The chickadee!

Custer turned off the light and stumbled through the silence and darkness back to the cabin—back to Sue Ann. Now he knew the meaning of the second vision, and his heart grew heavy.

Book II

The Chickadee

Dr. Sue Clifton

Chapter One

Tobi was packing up his things in Custer's cabin, preparing to move to the small cabin he had bought outside Red Lodge. Familiar whistling and then steps on the porch told him Custer had arrived. Next came a quick knock followed by the door opening.

"Looks like you've been busy." Custer stuck his head in the door.

"Come on in, Custer. I guess you're ready to get your cabin back—even though you don't live in it anymore." He cut his eyes at Custer and smiled.

"Thought you might need some help taking your stuff to the forestry road. I've got a couple of Hawk's packhorses outside." Custer scanned the few boxes stacked on the floor.

"Good idea. Thanks, Custer. Two miles is a good ways to be packing stuff in and out. I know, since I packed it all in." Tobi moved to the boxes and took a small box off the top. "This is the manuscript to *The Gully Path*. Maltese Townsend planted it here to convince Hawk I was Trapper's kidnapper." He handed the box to Custer. "I hope Mom doesn't mind, but I read it. I know a lot more about my family now than I did. Interesting reading."

"You are referring to your father, Tate Douglas, I assume." Custer put the box under his arm and looked at Tobi.

"Don't get me wrong, Custer. I am pleased Mom and you have each other. She obviously loves you very deeply, and I don't want her to be alone." Tobi walked back to his boxes and then stopped. "I'd be lying if I didn't admit to some curiosity about him, though. I haven't talked to Betsy or Mom about him yet. Just not a priority at the moment." Tobi went back to moving boxes.

"I understand, son. You don't have to apologize. It's natural to want to know if your father is alive and what he's like." Custer picked up a box and headed for the door.

"Custer, let me carry the boxes. You don't need to do that with your heart condition." Tobi took the box from Custer.

"My old clock is ticking pretty good at the moment." Custer put his hand to his heart and followed Tobi out the door to help put the box on the packhorse. "Must be all those egg whites Sue Ann puts in front of me."

"Just in front of you?"

"Yeah, but don't tell her. I sneak them in the garbage can when she's not looking." Custer chuckled. "So what are you going to do about your curiosity about Tate Douglas? Are you planning on using your detective expertise?" Custer held the door open as Tobi carried out another box.

"I don't know yet. I need to talk to Mom and Betsy. Tate Douglas has never been around, and Betsy is angry at him for betraying Mom like he did. Hawk told me that much."

After loading the last box on the horses, Custer led them tied one behind the other down the trail, with Tobi walking beside him so they could finish their conversation.

"What do you think, Custer?" Tobi kept his eyes on the trail.

Custer hesitated before answering.

"That is your decision. Sue Ann already gave Betsy the go-ahead but warned her she might be hurt more by finding him." Custer was silent for a few more seconds. "I have a saying, Tobi. Two sayings, actually. I want you to remember them."

"Okay. Let me hear them. I know Betsy and Hawk think you're the wisest man they've ever known, and so does Mom."

Custer shook his head and chuckled before going on. "The first is simply, 'Follow your heart.' Simple enough, and a bit of a cliché. The second one is probably more important."

"I agree with the first one. Now hit me with the second one."

"Don't play games with life, or life will come back and kick you in the ass." Custer glanced at Tobi to gauge his reaction.

"You think Betsy and I might get hurt by what I find?" Tobi stopped, and Custer stopped beside him.

"That I cannot answer, son." Custer started back down the trail. "I do know that if this gnaws at you long enough, you'll give in to it." Custer paused again. "Just be careful."

****

Tobi stared at his computer screen that night at the words he had typed in the search box, "Tate Douglas, New York, 1945-Present." Tobi rubbed his hands together, nervous with the prospect of finding something. He had several search engines at his disposal, most bootlegged from his old job, but he had decided to use the one that all the departments he'd worked with considered the best. If Tate Douglas was still in existence, his son would know in just a few seconds.

He looked at the family pictures he had unpacked and left on the table. New pictures covered the table: his mom, sister, and himself; a picture of Trapper on his pony; and a group picture with all of them, including Custer. In the middle, his favorite picture of Carrie peeked out, surrounded by the relatives she did not know. How he missed his daughter. He hoped she could come for a visit when she got a break from school, and he could not wait to share his newfound family with her.

If I find Tate Douglas, what will I do with the information? What if he wants to know us, Betsy and me? What will it mean to Mom, and will Custer be hurt?

Tobi continued to stare at the screen, his finger hovering over the Enter key as he continued to reason with himself.

But getting the information does not necessarily mean I will share it or act upon it.

With no more hesitation or thought, he hit "Enter."

Chapter Two

New York
May 30, 1965
Dear Sue Ann,
*This is the hardest letter I have ever tried to write.
In a few minutes I'll leave for months of training in the
military and then off to Vietnam. You know I oppose
this war, but now I find myself about to be sent into the
thick of it. Regardless of my feelings, I will fight for my
country to the best of my ability, the country I hope will
be better for all its people some day because of the
sacrifices made by people like Schwerner, Chaney, and
Goodman. But that is not what I'm writing to tell you.*

*I know I hurt you by not calling or writing, and I
don't deserve you. When you met me a year ago, I was
engaged to a girl in New York, an old high school
girlfriend. I never told you because I knew I would
never go through with the marriage. My joining COFO
was partially an escape from her. My mother always
wanted me to marry Cynthia, my fiancée, and I'm
afraid I let Mother control me too much in that respect.
When I got home to New York, I did not have the
courage to end the engagement immediately. My
mother was so insistent that I continue with wedding
plans that I played along to keep peace in the family,
but I was waiting for the right time to break the
engagement.*

5

When I received my draft classification of 1-A, everything changed. I joined the Marines, not because I have any delusions of being a tough guy, but because my dad was a Marine in World War II. I only hope I can make him proud. He, unlike my mother, only pushes me to be my best at whatever I decide to do with my life. Dad realized I did not love Cynthia and encouraged me with "follow your conscience and do the right thing before you leave for war."

I broke my engagement two days ago. I wish I could have come to see you to tell you all of this in person, but there was no time. And now, here I sit, as always, thinking of you and all we had together and wishing myself back in that little cabin in Paxton, sitting by the fire with my arms wrapped around you.

Remember the night I told you I was going back to New York? I was twisting your beautiful, silky, blonde curls while I held you in front of the fireplace. The green logs, the last of our wood supply, were popping, adding ambiance to what should have been the perfect romantic moment. But the moment was a façade of what was my reality. Even so, I knew then what I really wanted was in Mississippi, not New York.

This morning, I thought of that evening and how I talked of how our kids would hate you and me for giving them these blonde out-of-control curls we somehow share. In a short time, my curls will be gone as I prepare for my soldier life, a role I was not born to play. I'm sending you this lock of my hair, tied with a ribbon that you wore at the end of one of your braids. It was left in the safe house where you took me when I was transferred from Bartonville by COFO. I treasure this ribbon, the little bit of you I let myself carry from

Mississippi, the greatest self-imposed torture of my life. Maybe you are so angry with me that you'll just toss this lock of hair in the garbage, but I hope not. I only wish I had a lock of your hair to carry with me to comfort me in battle.

My time with you was the best part of my life, Sue Ann. I was being honest when I told you I love you and always will. My only hope is that you can find it in your heart to forgive me. When my time in this war is over, I will come back for you and hope you will have me. I carry your picture with me and will take it into battle and everywhere I go. If I don't make it back from Vietnam, just know you were with me, right over my heart, to the very end.

If you don't answer this letter, I will know you could not forgive me for betraying our love, and I will understand. I will continue to write to you even if you choose not to answer my letters, and pray that some day you will take me back into your heart. Hope is all I have at the moment, and I will not relinquish it without a fight. My prayer is that you will save these letters describing my time as a soldier in this war as a keepsake for the children I hope we share some day.

I love you,

Tate

P.S. If you choose to write me, send your letters to my dad's office address below. He has promised to get them to me wherever I end up. He knows all about you, but my mother does not. She is much like your mother, I'm afraid, and I can't deal with her at the present time.

Address: Robert Tatum Douglas, Esq.

1200 Brookvine Ave., Suite 35

New York, New York

Chapter Three

Custer was headed into Red Lodge to check the mail and pick up a few things at the grocery store when his cell phone rang. The caller ID showed it was a Mississippi number.

"Hello?" Custer answered in a question, wondering who would be calling him from Mississippi.

"Custer, it's Elizabeth."

"Oh, hello, Elizabeth. If you're calling to check on Sue Ann, she could not be better, especially with Tobi finding his way back to her."

"I know, Custer. It's the best miracle ever. I'm planning on coming soon so I can meet Tobi and share in my dear friend's joy." Elizabeth was silent for a few seconds, and Custer matched her silence, waiting.

"Custer, I'm calling you because I found something while going through Sue Ann's boxes in the attic of Parrish Oaks. You know—the ones her mother sent years ago, the ones you two didn't get finished going through with your quick departure?"

Custer pulled to the shoulder so he could listen and talk safely.

"That something must be a doozie, as Sue Ann says, since you called me and not her."

"It is, but I don't know what to do with it." Silence prevailed again on both ends. "I found some letters addressed to Sue Ann. I thought they were unimportant but decided I'd better glance at them to make sure it was not something Sue Ann might want to keep. You know she gave me carte blanche to throw away anything unimportant."

"Yes, I remember. She figured anything her mother thought was important would certainly not be something she felt was valuable. She and her mother were quite the opposites, from what Sue Ann has told me."

"That is an understatement." Elizabeth laughed. "But these are not silly letters from college friends." More silence followed.

"Are you going to keep me guessing, Elizabeth?" Custer, usually a patient man, could lose some of his coolness when Sue Ann was the concern.

"Yes. I am going to keep you in suspense, but not for long. I am mailing them to you. Not to Sue Ann, mind you. I want you to read them and determine for yourself what should be done with them. Just make sure you check the mail in the next few days. I don't want Sue Ann getting them first. She is doing so well with her recovery from cancer, and I just don't want anything to dampen her spirits or add stress to her life."

"All right, Elizabeth, but I can tell you I'm not so sure about reading someone else's mail, no matter how old it is. Seems unethical."

"She told me to look at everything, and now I'm asking you to look at these letters before she does. You are Sue Ann's heart and soul, Custer. Help her by making the decision if or when she should see these letters. They will be coming Priority in a document mailer. There aren't many, but believe me, there are enough."

9

Custer found an excuse to go to town every day in the next few days, until he received the package from Elizabeth. When he got back to the cabin, Sue Ann was napping, so he left her a note saying he was going to check on his old place.

He wasted no time, once inside his cabin, and pulled a chair up to the table. After putting on his glasses, actually Sue Ann's old glasses, he opened the mailer and pulled out a small stack of letters held together with a piece of yarn. Custer thumbed through the stack and saw no return address on any of them. The envelopes were old and yellowed and had been opened with a letter opener or a knife. The postmark of the first letter was New York. Custer's stomach began to churn.

Custer left the table and took the first letter out onto his porch, both as a delaying tactic and also to give him the courage and reassurance the mountain shadows cast over him like a protective mother. Behind him, the slow ripple of his mountain stream whispered, offering additional comfort.

After Custer finished reading the first letter, he reached into the envelope and pulled out the lock of hair that was curled, almost totally concealed, in the corner. The blonde curl was wrapped with a green ribbon, the same color ribbon Sue Ann had worn tied around her braids the first day he met her at her cabin in the Beartooths.

Custer started refolding the letter, but soon his anguish took control and he crumpled it in his fist. He looked to the mountain for consolation, but none came. Carefully, he straightened the letter out on his knee and refolded it as it had been.

This is Sue Ann's letter, and only she can decide

what to do with it.

As he placed it back in the envelope, a small bird began chirping from the end of the porch. A chickadee, its black head bobbing and almost turning full circle, hopped around on the rail. It stopped, stared at Custer, and then flew directly over him and off into the forest.

Custer took his medicine pouch from around his neck, opened it, and placed Tate's lock of hair inside with new locks of Sue Ann's and his own once again braided together. Also in the pouch were the feathers from his vision quest. The tufts of deer hair had been removed once that part of the quest had come to fruition with Tobi's arrival.

Custer stared at the letter, hating the thought of reading any more, but he knew it was important that he read all of the letters if he was to help Sue Ann deal with this and if he was the one to decide if she should be given the letters.

Is this my decision? Do I have the right to keep them from her?

Custer left his chair on the porch, looked at the mountains one more time, and reentered the cabin. He sat down at the table and took the next letter from the stack.

March 30, 1966
Dear Sue Ann,

I am sure you have received my letter of apology by now, since I wrote it months ago, but I have not received a letter in return and can only assume I killed your love. I have contemplated whether to continue writing you like I said I would but just cannot continue this life without you in silence. My months of training were brutal, giving me little time to think or to write, and maybe I should have left it at that. But now, with time on my hands, my thoughts return again and again to you.

I am in Vietnam awaiting my next orders, but the so-called "war" is nowhere to be found. The only battle we're fighting is with the mosquitoes. I thought Mississippi was hot until I got here. It's 100 degrees and the temperature is matched evenly with the humidity. I guzzle water but never seem to quench my thirst. The conditions are miserable, but not because of the war. My buddy from Texas, James, says this war was over before it began, and I tend to agree with him. Being here is a complete waste of time. I need to be stateside trying to win you back. The virtuous honor I felt in joining the Marines has been replaced with endless thoughts of "all for naught" and "how the hell can I get out of here?" We are all antsy. We want to ask when we will see action, but the Marines have a saying, one of hundreds: "Marines don't ask questions; they do." Since I'm here, I'm ready to "do" and get this over with.

The commander had a cookout for all the guys yesterday, complete with steaks and an endless supply of beer. We just sat around playing cards and getting drunk, the best cure for homesickness. The more the brass tries to make this place feel like home, the more miserable we all are and the more of a hellhole it is for most of us. Some of the guys, especially the Tennessee boys, put on a good front and appear to be having a good time. I think they enlisted together and were part of a country band at home. They play their guitars and get us all going when they sing, "Glory, glory, what a hell of a way to die." The camp barracks where I am assigned is more like a college dorm, one lacking any semblance of décor, comfort, or atmosphere for learning. The commander tries to reassure us that we are here for a purpose and tries to cheer us before we actually begin fighting the North Vietnamese.

The Vietnamese people are skinny little people, extremely impoverished, far worse than anything I saw in the black communities in Mississippi, but these people don't seem to know it. They are mostly rice farmers and have very little to live on. Their entire world revolves around their village.

The children are the bright spots here. We are given plenty of chewing gum and candy bars to dole out to them, our way of letting the people know we are here to help and protect. The kids act like they love us, but some of the people, especially the elderly, keep their distance, unsure of our intent, or, perhaps, afraid the VC will interpret their friendliness as betrayal and will punish or kill them.

One sergeant who has seen action told how the VC killed a Mama-san at his last assignment. He said the old lady was so helpful to the GIs, doing their laundry and all their grunge work, they openly acknowledged their appreciation and love for her with all kinds of gifts. Her favorite was a New York Yankees baseball cap, a gift from one of her "boys" whose favorite player was Roger Maris. Mama-san strutted around the village in her cap, and each time she would meet the GI who gave it to her, she would point to the cap, bow her head and say "Wa-juh." One day she did not come to work, something out of character for her, and during that night, a box was left outside the barracks. The commander ordered it to be opened, taking precautions

13

in case there was an explosive inside, but what was inside was far worse than explosives. Mama-san's head, with the blood splattered Yankees cap still attached, had been cut off, wrapped in an American flag, and stuffed in the box. I hope this is a lie, made up to make Sarge look bigger than life, or to scare the shit out of us "cherries," but I don't know for sure.

Who knew places like this existed? Who cared? I have to slap myself often for feeling sorrier for myself than for these pitifully poor, war-weary people we are sworn to protect. Can this be me talking? Where in the hell has Tate the Crusader gone? I don't think I would recognize him if he was standing in front of me.

I miss you, Sue Ann. I miss home. At the risk of sounding like a spoiled brat, all I can think about is the fun everybody is having back in the States, just living their lives normally while I sweat to death. Eating burgers, going to college, or doing nothing by choice will never be taken for granted when I get back. I just hope I am enjoying these things with you by my side.

We stand guard, ever vigilant in the pursuit of the enemy, but we have seen no enemy. We stare at the jungle day after day waiting for an attack that never comes. It's quiet here—so very quiet. I caught the commander asleep in his field office yesterday, and I just let him sleep. Maybe we should be happy that nothing is happening. My fear in coming to Vietnam was dying in war, but now I fear I will die from boredom before ever seeing any action.

I miss and love you,
Tate

Custer put the letter back with the others and secured the yarn around them. The other letters would be read in due time, but Custer needed time to absorb Tate's words from the first two. Once again, he must wait for the sunlight to pour through and dispel the mist that surrounds his heart.

Chapter Four

Custer left the post office in what should have been a jovial mood. He knew the package he had picked up would bring a smile to Sue Ann's face, something that brought him joy but that also instilled fear in his heart. Sue Ann's much-anticipated autobiography *The Gully Path* had arrived, the author's proofs for the books that would appear on bookshelves all over the United States in a matter of weeks. Once the books were available to the public, there was a good chance Tate Douglas, if he was alive, would see the book and know that Sue Ann had given birth to his daughter. If he decided to do further research, he would also find out he had a son. The *Billings Gazette* had done a big feature article on Sue Ann in the Sunday newspaper and included the story of Tobi showing up, announcing he was Sue Ann's twin boy—a "switched at birth" true story. Several TV shows had contacted Sue Ann, but she had turned down any more interviews, not wanting to commercialize her family's story.

Custer knew Sue Ann and Betsy were in Red Lodge so decided he would go by and see how Tobi was doing on the restoration of the old cabin he had bought. The cabin sat on the side of a mountain with a view that "inspired poetry, or the writing of music lyrics" as Sue Ann had announced when she saw it for the first time. Tobi had no idea what he would do for work in Red Lodge, but at the moment, he was financially sound with the inheritance left by his grandmother. The one thing he knew for sure was that he would never leave Red Lodge, not as long as his mother and sister were here.

Custer left his truck and headed in the direction of the loud banging that echoed off the woods surrounding the cabin and into the valley below, sounding like a crew of carpenters instead of one.

"Anybody home?" Custer called from the front door that stood slightly ajar.

"Beware, Custer. If you come in, I might hand you a hammer," Tobi yelled as he climbed down the ladder from the loft. His shirtsleeves were rolled up, his hair was contained in a do-rag, and he was wearing a tool belt.

"I'm actually pretty handy with a hammer. You know I restored that old cabin of mine and most of the furniture in it, what little there is." Custer reminded Tobi. "'Course that was a few years ago, say forty or so."

"How about a cup of coffee? I made a pot about thirty minutes ago and forgot to drink any of it." Tobi headed toward the kitchen end of the great room.

"You didn't have to stop work on my account. I could climb up there and talk while I watch you work." Custer smiled at the implication.

"Nah! I need a break. Besides, I have Carrie's loft room just about finished. Betsy is in charge of decorating, including picking out the color for the paint that she insists is needed to trim the room and make it 'girly.' " Tobi made the universal sign of quotation marks with his fingers. "As soon as I finish with the window frames, my sister will put her magical decorating touches on it."

The two drank their coffee in silence for several seconds.

"So, aren't you going to ask me?" Tobi smiled over his coffee cup.

"I don't have to ask. You'll tell me when you're ready." Custer added more cream to his coffee.

"You amaze me, Custer. You don't even ask what I'm talking about. Sometimes, I swear, you can read people's minds." Tobi shook his head and looked across the table at his guest, who was laughing at the "mind reader" description. "Maybe you should have been a shaman. Hawk and Betsy told me about you taking Hawk on a vision quest, the one where he saw Betsy years before he ever met her."

"The Bible says 'Seek and ye shall find.' " Custer paused to let this sink in. "I seek by watching and listening…" Custer paused. "And the truth finds me." Custer pointed up with a finger and then took a sip of his coffee. "Hmm. Maybe I could be a minister?"

"Mom told me about your vision with the doe and the fawns, too. When Carrie comes, would you tell her that one, Custer? I want her to hear it firsthand from you."

"When do we get to meet Carrie? We're all anxious, especially your mother." Custer took his cup to the sink, rinsed it out, and placed it in the drainer.

"She's coming this summer for a long visit. I can hardly wait for her to meet all of you and for you to meet my little queen, although she'd rather be sitting on a horse than a throne. Boy, will she fit in this family!" Tobi followed Custer's lead and rinsed out his cup.

"Well, I better let you get back to work. If you decide you can use some help, I'm available." Custer headed toward the door.

"I've hit a dead end, Custer." Tobi made the comment just as Custer opened the door.

"Oh?" Custer turned to face Tobi.

"I know he was a Marine and fought in the Vietnam War, was discharged in 1968 after being wounded." Tobi sat back down at the table. Custer took this as his cue and returned to the table and sat down also.

"But you don't know if he's alive?" Custer put his elbows on the table and gave Tobi his full attention.

"No. I know he was in a VA hospital in upstate New York for several months, but I don't know what happened to him after that. It's like he just vanished."

"What about his parents? Did you find them?"

"No. I know his dad was a lawyer, but he must have retired after Tate, my father, returned from Vietnam. I do know that Tate's mother died in 1975, but I could find no record of his dad dying. His name was Robert Tatum Douglas, so I guess his son was named for him, at least the Tatum part." Tobi left the table and walked to the hearth of the fireplace, where he had the mantel filled with family pictures, his newly found family plus many of Carrie at different ages.

"There is a hole in this parade of family pictures, Custer." Tobi stared at the row of photographs. "I think I'm supposed to fill it, but I'm not sure where to go from here."

When Custer got back to the cabin, Sue Ann was still not back. He didn't go inside but instead headed down the path to his old cabin.

Chapter Five

July 15, 1966
My Dearest Sue Ann,
I crouch here in a tunnel vacated by the VC, waiting to be rescued by what's left of my platoon. James is wounded, shot in the upper part of his leg. I got separated from my platoon when I pulled him to safety, if there is such a thing. We have been holed up for hours, ever since we began our early dawn jungle chase of the VC, a trap to get us deeper into the jungle. Little did we know the jungle was also full of NVA. James is propped against me and is whispering, a weak whisper, taunting me that he's going home and leaving me in this shithole. I am almost envious until I notice my boots and uniform are covered in his blood, too much blood, that spurts rather than runs and cannot be replenished until we are rescued. I remove my belt and tie it tightly around his leg, trying to stop the blood flow, and hope it will cover the wound enough that he can't see the volume of blood that puddles beneath our feet.

Search and destroy. Those were our orders, but it seems that all that is being destroyed is our hope of surviving this Godforsaken war. The enemy body count is much higher than ours, something the commander interprets as a victory, but for each one we kill, there seem to be more than a hundred to take his place.

Things have changed drastically, and I find myself praying for the boredom I so flippantly complained about in my last letter. Even though it is quiet for the moment, and over 100 degrees, I can't stop shaking. You may find my scribbling hard to read, but the only relief I get in hell is imagining you reading my letters and hoping, praying, for my safe return.

It's bad, Sue Ann! Real bad. Seeing men die is hard, but the worst thing about this war is the noise. Bullets crack around you incessantly; bombs land so close the noise itself tears at your guts, destroying every ounce of courage you once flaunted; artillery shells explode so close you expect immediate silence gained through ruptured eardrums. But the cacophony of sounds is a reprieve from the screams of the wounded and dying that lie soaked in mud and blood on the jungle ground. I try to grab sleep when I can, always during daylight, but when I do close my eyes, it is from sheer exhaustion and is a restless sleep interrupted constantly by nightmares of battle.

I've never been so close to death. When the attack began, we had zips in the wire. The VC overran the compound and killed two of our men. We killed about a dozen of them before they retreated into the jungle as we gave chase, following orders, and had no idea how badly we were outnumbered.

Reinforcements are desperately needed. Choppers have not been able to land because the LZ is too hot. Air attacks are out of the question; the enemy is too close to us. All we can do is obey the orders we are given and pray we will make it out.

I hate the Viet Cong even more than the NVA. The VC is everywhere and they are nowhere. They are the shadows that creep and crawl through jungle tunnels. They are the quiet villagers who tend their rice paddies by day and set land minds and punji pits by night. They are the children who take our gum and chocolate bars with a smile while hiding grenades in the baskets they carry on their heads. How can you kill an enemy you cannot identify? At least the regular army wears uniforms.

Many soldiers' bodies lie rotting. The jungle is no respecter of the dead. The stench of death is like nothing I have ever smelled. When even a slight breeze blows, the smell becomes unbearable. You can taste it in your mouth and feel it on your skin. But death is not the worst picture I can paint.

The VC managed to capture a young private the day of the first attack. He was outside the wire at the edge of the jungle when the attack started, and they snatched him. The devils tortured him periodically and used a loudspeaker to make sure we heard him. His screams pierced the jungle and bounced off every tree in all directions. We wished they would just put him out of his misery. It is mental torture for us, and we covered our ears each time it started. Andrew, the young soldier they captured, was an eighteen-year-old farm boy from Louisiana.

Where do they come from? How do they sneak up on us in such great numbers without making the least bit of sound? They wear black uniforms and sandals, the same as the civilians. Hell, we were told the VC was a ragtag bunch of outlaws, but these guys act like well-trained regulars and are armed with modern weapons.

We dread nightfall. Victor Charlie owns the night. They are masters of guerilla warfare and sneak into our camp a few at a time, or one at a time. This morning, we found a platoon leader with his throat cut, but nobody heard the enemy come or go. I think they sometimes kill just to piss us off. They target officers.

The constant smell of gunpowder makes me sick. My nose burns all the time, and my eyes water constantly, and I don't even know if I've killed anybody. When the attacks come, I just poke my rifle through whatever cover I think I have and pull the trigger. I hope I have killed some of them.

The little yellow people are yelling again over a loudspeaker. "Down with America!" they shout. Shit, it sounds like they're right in front of me! This damn war is nothing like I was told it would be. My dad was in WWII, and his old war stories were a lot different from what I'm living. Dad said he was in active combat for sometimes ten days a month. In Vietnam, we are in combat 240 days out of a year.

The general population walks around the compound as though nothing is going on. Mortars come in and the Vietnamese just keep doing what they're doing, oblivious to shells bursting around them. It's like they're in a trance. I honestly don't think they give a shit who wins this war. War is all they have ever known.

The whole platoon is running low on ammunition. I have about twenty rounds left. We don't have the ammo to sustain us much longer. This could be my last letter, Sue Ann. I'm glad I carry this pad and pen with me even in battle. I just hope my letter makes it to you. I look at your picture every chance I get, and even though you haven't answered my other letters, the hope that you will keeps me going.

I hear noise. Sounds like choppers. Damn! They are near the LZ. Choppers cover the sky over the jungle like bands of angels! I hear footsteps running, close above me, and hope it is my buddies. I have to leave the tunnel and try to get James to the choppers. I hope I will live to write to you again, my darling. I love you.

Tate

Chapter Six

Custer left Sue Ann and Betsy curled up on the couch in front of the fireplace, reading the author's proofs of *The Gully Path*. They each had a mug of coffee, with a shared box of tissues in front of them, ready to build mountains of tear-soaked fibers. Hawk had decided to take a day off work and spend it with his son. He, like Custer, knew this was a mother/daughter day, with interruptions not allowed. Custer was okay with this and had a mission of his own to accomplish.

When he pulled in at Tobi's, he found him sitting on the porch looking up at his side of the Beartooths. Custer and Sue Ann had surprised him the day before with four Adirondack chairs, accompanied by soft, kapok-filled cushions, for his porch. Tobi was relaxing in one with his feet crossed on the footstool. His tool belt lay on the floor beside him.

"Just in time. Pull up one of my fabulous chairs, Custer, but I'm not leaving my chair to greet you."

"Not necessary. Glad you're enjoying the chairs." Custer looked up at the mountains. "And the view. It never gets old, does it?"

"Nope, and it never will." Tobi watched as Custer took a seat and noticed he had a small grocery bag in his hand.

"What do you have there? Did Mom send me something to eat?"

"No, but she's got a moose stew simmering on the stove while she and Betsy read the author's proofs of *The Gully Path.* She wants you to come over tonight to eat with the family—kind of a simple celebration for getting the proofs."

"I'd be happy to oblige." Tobi pointed at the sack. "So what's in the bag?"

Custer handed the bag to Tobi. It's something Elizabeth, your mom's friend, sent from Mississippi. She wanted me to read them and make the decision of whether to tell your mother or not. Elizabeth thinks they might add too much stress to your mother's recovery."

Tobi pulled out the stack of letters and removed the yarn tie.

"Who are they from?" Tobi counted the letters. "Five letters. They look old."

"They are letters from Tate Douglas, letters your mother never received. Elizabeth thinks Sue Ann's mother hid them from Sue Ann and never let her know she had gotten them. According to Sue Ann, her parents, or at least her mother, never knew about Tate, but I think this disproves that belief."

"When did you get these?" Tobi had a scowl across his eyebrows.

"About a week ago. I've read them, several times, but I still don't know what to do with them. After talking to you yesterday, I figured you needed them to help you in your quest." Custer watched to see what Tobi's reaction would be.

"My quest? Like a vision quest?"

"In my world, it would be a vision quest. In your world, Tobi, it is a quest for truth, for answers as they exist in the here and now."

"So Mom and Betsy don't know about these?"

"No. I think for now, we should keep it that way. Hawk knows about them but hasn't read them. He agreed with me that you should have them."

"Why me?" Tobi held the letters but seemed more interested in Custer's reasoning. "What do you think I should do with these?"

"Read them. You will know what you need to do." Custer did not look at Tobi as he talked. Instead, he looked toward the mountain, where a mist had formed, hiding the top.

"I think you will have to leave the mountains to find your truth, son, but that is your decision."

Custer left a few minutes later, knowing Tobi was anxious to read the letters.

Tobi read through the first three hurriedly, but when he got to the fourth one, he slowed down, trying to feel what his father was feeling.

February 1967 (I do not know the day)

Dear Sue Ann,

I just got back from two days of R & R on a beach somewhere of insignificance—two days' reward for thirty days of fucking hell. Pardon my language, but this war can only be described using the most despicable terms. I remember nothing except the false illusion of happiness expressed by all those with me on the beach "paradise." The men drank and whooped as girls clad in skimpy bikinis danced and shook their butts in the ravenous soldiers' faces. I removed myself to a corner of the makeshift bar and drank myself into a coma. It was the most wonderful two days of my Vietnam nonexistence. I remember none of it. Joy and consciousness are reserved for assholes who carry no guilt. My life has plunged to the lowest point possible, and I'm wondering if I will be able to climb out of my misery.

Last week, I saw a pretty little girl running through the camp. She was new to the area and had the biggest brown eyes I've ever seen. She looked straight at me without smiling. Her hair was not short like most of the children have but hung to her waist like thick, black velvet. As I walked away, I could hear her little feet scampering lightly across the dirt like a tiny fawn. She looked so sweet and innocent, about nine or ten years old, and I thought I'd look for her later and give her a chocolate bar. She reminded me of my best friend's little sister, who was adopted from Korea.

Later, I saw her again at the edge of the jungle across the barbed wire that encircles the camp. This time, she was carrying a small bundle. I headed toward her, and when I was within an arm's length, I reached into my shirt pocket for a chocolate bar, ready to make friends. With my rifle held loosely under my left arm, I smiled and held the candy out to her across the wire. She stared at me, her brown eyes expressionless. The little girl had it! That same stare soldiers get when they've been in the shit too long—the thousand-yard stare. Her eyes never left my face as I inched a step closer. Then she looked back as if someone was waiting for her in the jungle. I expected her to run, but she didn't. She just kept staring at me across the barricade.

Too late, I realized what was happening. As I motioned for her to take the candy, she reached into the bundle and pulled out a grenade. She struggled a little, pulling the pin out, giving me time to raise my rifle and do the job I'd been trained to do.

I fired point blank with no hesitation. Her little face exploded like a tomato; a volcano of black velvet and red human shrapnel emanated in every direction. Then, as if that were not enough, the grenade detonated under her where she had dropped it as she fell. I dove to the ground as shrapnel split the air like Fourth of July fireworks.

When the smoke cleared, members of my platoon ran to me and helped me to my feet. I was unscathed physically and stood staring down at the spot where the girl had stood. The only thing left was a piece of the bundle that she carried.

What kind of army sends children to fight their wars? Nobody came to collect what little remained of the girl. The villagers did no more than glance at where the child stood only minutes before. No one seemed to care or to acknowledge the child's ever "being" in the first place.

Vietnam is slowly killing me. The girl's blood and flesh cover my uniform, but I refused to change my clothes. I feel no remorse, only numbness. I will go into the jungle tonight on patrol wearing the splattered remains of this tiny Viet Cong girl.

Emotionally, I am dead, Sue Ann. Maybe I will be dead physically soon. Shit, I hope so.

Tate

Chapter Seven

Tobi sat on the airplane waiting for takeoff, still trying to decide if he was doing the right thing. Custer had told him again to "follow his heart" and he would be okay. Custer was the only one who knew where Tobi was really going. The rest of the family thought he was going back to Denver for a while to visit Carrie.

Tobi had read the war letters over and over, but he still did not know Tate Douglas.

He sounded so desolate. Maybe Tate Douglas had his reasons for not coming back to Mom. I need to find out before we tell Mom—if we tell her.

Tobi thought about his detective friend whose dad had been in the Vietnam War at the Battle of Hamburger Hill in 1969. He was so traumatized by the horrors of that battle that he had to be institutionalized when he returned home. When he was released, he could never hold a job, and when Tobi's friend was a grown man with his own family, his father committed suicide. Tobi hoped his dad was not a victim of the war, but there was only one way to know.

In a small satchel, Tobi carried a copy of *The Gully Path,* one of the author's proofs his mom had given him, as well as a copy of the article from *The Billings Gazette.* She had no idea he would be taking these to New York.

Hell! I didn't even know I'd be taking these to New

York.

Tobi had the address of his grandfather's office from Tate's first letter, the letter of apology, and that would be where he would begin his search. The yellowed letters from the war were also in the briefcase. He had made copies of them, put them in a safety deposit box, and left a key with Custer.

"Twelve hundred Brookvine Avenue," Tobi told the cab driver. He had checked into a hotel but immediately left to begin his quest, as Custer called it. All he took with him was his satchel.

The building was in an older section of the city, and though it was several stories tall, it was not a skyscraper, and Tobi was glad, thinking back to 9/11.

Suite 35, Evers and Wainwright, Attorneys at Law.

Tobi opened the door and was greeted—not the right term for what awaited him—by a stern-looking older woman who barely glanced up through the glasses perched on the end of her nose.

After he'd cleared his throat twice, the woman said, "Yes?" in a long-drawn-out question like she was irritated with his intrusion. It was obvious she did not want to be bothered. She was the quintessential rude New Yorker.

"I hate to bother you, but I'm trying to locate Robert Tatum Douglas, who once had his law office in this suite, back in the 1960s. Do you have any idea of his whereabouts now?"

"I'm old, but I'm not that old. Go down the hall to Suite 42. The receptionist there is older than dirt." With this, the woman put her eyes back down, giving Tobi his order to leave.

"J. B. Turner, Attorney at Law," read Tobi in a

whisper before opening the door. This time, he was greeted by a very pleasant, "older than dirt" woman who seemed glad to see him. Actually, she looked as if she would be glad to see anyone as she sat almost hidden behind two giant plants.

"Hello there," she said. "May I help you?" The small sign on her desk read "Jeannette Turner."

"Ms. Turner...as in J. B. Turner?" Tobi pointed to the sign on the door.

"In a way." The woman smiled at Tobi, a genuine smile that formed huge crevices in her thick pancake makeup. Her eyes twinkled and her dark pink cheeks cracked with aged friendliness.

"Actually, J.B. is my son. How else would someone eighty-nine years old still be able to get a job?" She chuckled into her hand that looked like a road map to the afterlife with thick, dark blue lines—highways, or freeways—marking the mileposts of a long, long journey. Her fingers, crooked with arthritis, curled around her lips as she covered her laugh.

"J.B. only lets me answer the phone, and the pay is pretty bad, but I know you didn't come in here to hear about the trials and tribulations of growing old." She placed her trembling hands back on the desk in front of her.

"What can I do for you? Do you have an appointment with J.B.? If so, I can direct you to the secretary." Her fingers cupped her lips as she whispered. "She's young and pretty and very single."

"Oh, no, ma'am. I came to talk to you. The lady down in Suite 35 told me you might could help me." Tobi motioned back out the door with his thumb.

"Lady? Oh, you poor young man. The first person

32

you confronted had to be the wicked witch of New York. I am so sorry for how rude I'm sure she was to you." Jeannette shook her head in sincere sympathy.

Tobi smiled to let her know she was exactly right before he continued.

"I'm looking for Robert Tatum Douglas. He once had a law office in Suite 35. Did you know him?" Tobi felt at ease and motioned to the chair in front of Jeanette's desk. "May I?"

"Of course, dear." The woman began to smile. "Robert Douglas—oh, yes, indeed, I knew him. Handsome devil, with the prettiest blond curly hair I've ever seen." She looked at Tobi. "A lot like yours, young man. I bet you don't have any trouble with the ladies." She pulled her glasses down her nose and gave Tobi the onceover before resetting her glasses and continuing. "Actually, I went to dinner with him a few times after his wife died. My, my, wouldn't I love to have dinner with him now?" She did a "tsk, tsk" and then realized she was off track. "Well, that's too much information. What did you want to know about Robert?"

"For starters, is he still alive?" Tobi felt comfortable with the soft-spoken lady and leaned closer so he could hear her better.

"The last I heard, Robert was alive. He is rather feeble, though—was the last time I saw him, too. Walked with a cane for years. He has arthritis and doesn't get out much anymore, from what I hear. In fact, I believe he is in assisted living somewhere. His law practice has been shut down a long time." She put her finger to her cheek, as if thinking. Then she pulled out a phone book and began searching the yellow pages, stopping to lick her fingertips to aid in her arthritic page turning. "Here it is—Fairfield Manor. That's where he is." Picking up a pad, she wrote down the name, address, and telephone number of the facility and handed it to Tobi.

"Thank you so much, Ms. Turner. You are a very nice lady, nothing like"—Tobi used his head to motion down the hall—"you know who."

Jeannette giggled aloud. "You are so welcome. I'm sorry I didn't get your name."

"Tobi…Tobi Parish."

"Well, Tobi, if you find Robert, you tell him Jeannette said 'hello.' You might mention to him that I'd love to visit with him some time."

Pay dirt from "older than dirt." But what a nice lady!

Tobi hailed a cab and gave the address for Fairfield Manor.

"Long way…two hundred…advance." The cabbie had a thick accent and was abrasive, but Tobi didn't worry. He had come across all kinds in his line of work. He pulled two hundreds and a twenty out of his wallet and threw it over the seat.

"I pay…you drive." Tobi answered in the same tone as the driver and immediately wished he could recant when the cabbie floored it, almost giving his passenger whiplash.

****

Tobi was a little disconcerted when he walked through metal detector doors at Fairfield Manor, but then he remembered he was in New York City, and it all made sense. At the reception desk, he was pleasantly surprised to find another friendly woman, this one probably in her fifties.

34

"I'm here to visit Robert Douglas, please."

"And your name is?"

"Timothy Harden." Timothy had decided he had better give the name still on his driver's license. "I'm a relative of his, but he has never met me."

"We don't turn visitors away, Mr. Harden. We just wish our residents had more of them. Since you have never been here before, I will need to see your ID."

Tobi showed his driver's license, and the woman seemed satisfied.

"I guess Robert Douglas doesn't get many visitors either." Tobi was hoping to get information about his father.

"Once a week, every week, but that's it, other than church people and social workers. Robert is a sweet man if you catch him on a good day. His mind can be as sharp as a tack or as dull as a razor left in a homeless mission bathroom." She reached for a pen and handed it to Tobi. "Now, if you'll just go right over there to that registry and sign your name and time in, I'll give you directions to Robert's room."

Tobi signed his name in the book and looked to see if the receptionist was watching. She seemed to be engaged in something on the other end of the station and was paying no attention to him, so he looked back at each page of the book until he found the name Douglas. No visitor named Tate Douglas had signed in, but there was an Andrew Douglas who visited every Thursday morning at ten o'clock. He had just been there the day before. Tobi leafed back through several pages of the book and found Andrew Douglas had not missed a Thursday morning visit in at least six weeks, the length of time contained in the registry. This was good information even if the name was wrong.

A few minutes later, Tobi stood outside the room of his grandfather, Robert Douglas. He hesitated for only a second before knocking, even though he had no idea what he was going to say when he confronted the man.

"Come in." It was a female's voice, but Tobi, thinking perhaps it was an attendant or a nurse, opened the door and walked in.

"Hi, I'm looking for Mr. Douglas? I was told this was his room." Tobi was surprised to see a very attractive young woman sitting beside the bed. She had a notebook, of the electronic variety, in her lap and seemed to be taking some kind of notes.

"Hello, I'm Dr. Hoskins. I'm a social worker. Robert is one of my clients." She smiled at Tobi. "Robert should be back from therapy any minute now."

"Oh, all right. I'll just wait, if that's all right with you." Tobi could not help but stare at this petite young woman with long, velvety dark hair and piercing eyes so dark they added a mysterious gypsy quality to the woman's already striking appearance. Next to Betsy, Dr. Hoskins was the most beautiful woman he had ever seen.

"And you are...?"

Tobi suddenly realized he had been so consumed with the beautiful doctor's eyes he had forgotten to introduce himself.

"I'm sorry. My name is Tobi Parish." Tobi caught himself blushing, something he had not done since high school. "Your eyes are so dark and beautiful—if I may say so."

"Thank you, and yes, you may." She smiled and

looked into Tobi's eyes. "And I could say the same for you. I've never seen eyes the color of yours. Must be a family trait."

"Yes…from my mother. My twin sister and I both have these green eyes and the curly hair." Tobi combed his hand through his curls that had grown out to where they reached his collar.

"Well, Tobi with the beautiful eyes and hair, is there anything I can help you with? And if I may ask, what brings you to visit Robert? I suspect you are some relation since you have his—or what used to be his—blond, curly hair." She closed her notebook, giving Tobi her full attention.

"Yes, I am related, but at the risk of sounding mysterious, I'd rather hold off on the rest of the information until I've met Robert Douglas."

"Fair enough." She turned her head toward the door. "I'm thinking you are about to get your chance."

The door opened, and a stooped elderly man entered. He walked with a cane as a male orderly held to his arm. The resident was dressed in gray sweats, but he shuffled along in moccasin-type slippers rather than running shoes. With his eyes on the floor, he did not look up until he sat on the edge of his bed.

"Well, what a pleasant surprise, Star. I hope you have time for a long visit today." He was smiling at Dr. Hoskins, and Tobi sensed a fondness for the beautiful young woman.

"As a matter of fact, I intentionally came to see you for my last appointment today, just so I would not be rushed to leave." She looked over at Tobi and winked. "But you have another visitor, Robert." She directed her gaze to Tobi, who stood and extended his hand to

Robert.

Robert turned his head slowly as he moved his gaze from Star to the young man walking toward him. Catching a glimpse, he turned sideways to get a better look. The smile left his face, and his expression became strained, a look bordering on alarm.

"Tate? Tate?"

Tobi stopped when he saw Robert's shock.

"How can this be?" Robert looked to Star for an answer.

Not understanding her friend's reaction, Dr. Hoskins rose and stood beside the man, putting her hand on his shoulder as she turned her eyes to Tobi.

"I'm Tobi, Mr. Douglas. Tobi Parish." Tobi stood still and let his hand fall to his side.

"Oh, my. You look…just like my son…before he went to war…except for the eyes. Tate's eyes are dark." He looked to the young woman who still stood beside him. "Can you help me to my chair, Star? I want to visit with this young man sitting, not lying down like an invalid." His eyes went back to Tobi and did not move from his face as Tobi moved beside the man and took his other arm to help him into the chair.

One phrase stuck in Tobi's mind after Robert stopped talking. "Tate's eyes are dark." His father was alive.

Tobi turned to go back to his chair but was stopped by Robert's hand on his arm. The hand was gnarled with arthritis and shook intensely. He clutched Tobi's sleeve with two fingers.

"Please. Pull your chair closer so I can see you more clearly. My eyesight is not that good anymore." Robert still did not take his eyes off Tobi. He motioned to the window, and Star walked over and opened the blinds fully, so that the day's remaining sunlight streaked into the room.

Tobi did as he was asked, pulling up his chair directly in front of Robert. He should have felt uneasy with the stranger's stare, but he didn't. Instead, he leaned closer, resting his forearms on his knees and clasping his hands together. Tobi smiled at Robert, trying to put him at ease.

"Tobi Parish." He repeated the young man's name and continued to stare for a few seconds longer. "Tobi Parish." He paused, staring deep into Tobi's eyes. "Tobi Parish, are you the son of my Tate?" Robert's voice cracked with emotion like he already knew the answer.

Tobi glanced at Star, who had pulled her chair closer to Robert and had her hand on his. She sensed her client, her friend, was on the verge of an emotional breakdown. She, too, kept her eyes on Tobi, anxious to hear his answer.

"Yes." Tobi paused and looked into his grandfather's eyes. "My mother is Sue Ann." He paused giving his grandfather time for it all to sink it. "And I have a twin sister. Betsy. You have a grandson and a granddaughter."

Robert Douglas began to sob and reached out his hands. Tobi left his seat and knelt in front of his grandfather, who pulled him into his embrace. Star put her arms around both and cried with Tobi and Robert.

When the group regained their composure, Tobi opened his satchel and pulled out the yellowed letters and placed them in his grandfather's lap. Robert picked up the letters and held them close to his eyes.

"I was the go-between and sent all of Tate's letters on to Sue Ann. I never got to read any of them, though, and I never got any back from Sue Ann to send to Tate. I know it broke my son's heart, but he never mentioned it in his letters to his mother and me."

"Mom's mother never gave the letters to her. My mother still doesn't know about the letters or that Tate, my father, survived the war." Tobi waited a few seconds as his grandfather ran his fingers over the envelopes.

"Mom is recovering from breast cancer, and we just found out about these letters when her friend in Mississippi found them. We didn't want my mother to have to deal with all of this until we felt she was strong enough."

Next Tobi brought out pictures of the family. Robert grasped the picture of Sue Ann and her twin children, holding it close to his eyes; his smile never ceased as he tenderly moved his finger over each one's face. The last items Tobi pulled out were the book and the article from the newspaper.

"My mother and my sister are authors. Mom wrote this book as the first one in a series about her life. This one is her autobiography, more or less, and includes her time with my father. I will leave all of this with you. Maybe Star can read them to you."

"I want you to read the letters to me, Tobi, before you leave. There is so much I want to know—things your father would never talk about." He looked up to see Tobi's questioning face. "I know you want to know about your father, but I'll have to get in touch with him before I can introduce you. I need to know everything first. My son has some problems he has been dealing with ever since that son-of-a-bitching war almost took him away from me forever." Robert's hands began to shake more, and his speech became slurred with anger. His whole body shook as he talked about the Vietnam War.

"Don't get upset now, Robert. Tate is doing great. Remember?" Star looked from Robert to Tobi. "Maybe you need to rest for a while, Robert. You know your blood pressure goes up when you get upset. I bet Tobi will come back tomorrow."

Tobi stood as if this was his cue to leave, but his grandfather grabbed his hand.

"Please don't go yet, Grandson. Help me into bed, and I promise I'll relax. Star, please stay with us." Tobi and Star helped Robert into bed, propping him up so he could see Tobi.

"The letters…please…read them to me." He held his hand up and pointed to his chair, where he had left the letters. "And, Tobi, please call me Papa. It is what I called my favorite grandfather and is what I always wanted my grandchildren to call me. I thought it was a dream never to be fulfilled." His eyes filled with moisture again, and his chin quivered. "And now you are here."

"I can think of nothing I'd like better, Papa." Tobi patted his grandfather's hand and took the seat he had vacated, pulling it closer so his grandfather could hear.

Tobi began reading the letters in the order they were written. Star and his grandfather wept, and sometimes Tobi had to stop to give his audience a temporary reprieve from their emotions. He was glad he had read the letters many times and was now in control of his own feelings.

"Hearing you read is like hearing my son. Your voices are so similar. For the first time, I'm hearing Tate talk about the war, something he still refuses to do." Robert closed his eyes, imagining it was his son telling him about the war rather than a grandson he'd just met reading old yellowed letters written by a father he still did not know.

Tobi could tell his grandfather was getting tired, but he would not allow his grandson to stop until all the letters had been read.

"This is the last one, Papa." Tobi paused. "I need to warn you. It was hard for me to get through this one, and I don't know my father." Tobi looked at his Papa, who closed his eyes and signaled with his hand for Tobi to read. Star moved to sit on the foot of Robert's bed.

1968 (The date does not matter; all days run together into hell)

Sue Ann,

The Tate you knew is dead. I can never look into your eyes again. These shaking, murdering hands will never hold you. I look in the mirror but do not recognize the monster looking back at me.

Guilt should consume me, but I am numb. The dead are all around me and refuse to leave. I see their faces in my sleep; their whispers fill my ears every second. I smell them in the dirt, in the jungle, in the tent barracks where I pretend to live. I am the devil and can never return from hell.

I killed a man with a knife yesterday. A damn knife, Sue Ann! Kill or be killed? Who knows? He was a villager, a skinny little man I had helped carry water just the day before. He ran into his shack when he saw me coming. When he ran out carrying something long, I thought it was a homemade spear with a poison tip. My knife was the only weapon I had on me, and I gutted him without blinking an eye. The man crumpled, still clutching the object. His open dead eyes stared up at me, asking "Why?" After I pried the pole out of his lifeless hand, I saw it was nothing but a bamboo stick with what remained of a shredded American flag wound around it. The little man's blood ran on to the flag, mixing with the GI's dried blood. I stared down at the man and the flag, dropped the knife, and walked away. Fuck! The villager's blood covers my hand and is even under my fingernails.

We went out on patrol at dawn today and got hit hard. I don't even remember how we got back to camp. I am wounded, Sue Ann. Shot in both legs. I catch a chopper out of here in the morning to the hospital in Saigon. The medic says he thinks they can save my legs. If only they could save my soul. My regret is leaving these men, my friends. A bigger regret is not dying in the jungle.

The wounds I carry inside are more serious than my mangled legs. I cannot be saved, and no amount of morphine can ease this pain. The little girl, the one I murdered on the fence line—the one with the haunting stare, cannot be saved. The villager who died trying to give me a souvenir, the American flag of a fellow soldier fallen in battle, cannot be saved. The unnumbered gooks I've killed, maybe even some women I don't know about, cannot be saved. My soul has vanished.

Shit, it's hot! I'm tired of sweating. I'm tired of the stench. How can we do this to each other? Men killing men! Wallowing in blood and mud day after day, night after night! Why the hell are we here? I wish I had run off to Canada and never joined this fucking war.

Early this morning, I listened intently as Andrew whispered in my ear and pointed. "Look ahead...just there." And there they were—the ambush that was waiting for us. Andrew, the farm boy from Louisiana, was right again. He always sees them before they see us and warns me. Andrew's been dead for months. The platoon found his tortured skeletal remains, with his dog tags still around the bones that had been his neck, three weeks ago after we came back to retake the hill we had taken months ago and then abandoned, along with Andrew. I wish the angels, or the grim reaper, would come and take Andrew home to heaven or hell. I wish the fuck he'd leave me alone.

You will never see me again, Sue Ann. You will never see the dead man, the murderer I have become. I feel them watching over my shoulder even now as I write. They watch me with sad eyes, hating eyes, eyes filled with terror. They sit beside me in the jungle while I wait to kill their brothers.

This is the last letter I will write to you. I am not coming back. Tate Douglas is dead—vanished, or perhaps banished, with his soul. I am returning your picture. I no longer wish to remember.

"He did not sign his name to this letter." Tobi looked deeply into his grandfather's eyes. "I'm not sure he knew who he was by this time."

As Tobi had done every time he read the last letter, he carefully unfolded the frayed, cracked picture of a young Sue Ann with her long, blonde curls blowing in the wind as she posed leaning against the post of an old log cabin, probably her writing studio at the back of

Parrish Oaks. Her beautiful smile was hidden in one of the many torn folds of the picture. A brown stain, possibly Tate's blood, was smeared across and had distorted most of the picture so that only her face, still beautiful, shone through the battle-scarred paper. Tobi carefully handed the picture to his grandfather, who shared it with Star.

"I remember this picture. Tate showed it to me when he first told me about Sue Ann, the only girl he ever really loved, as far as I know. He said he would carry it into battle, and it appears he did just that." Tears ran down Robert's cheeks.

Tobi put the letters back in his satchel but left the book and the article for Star to read to his grandfather later. Upon his grandfather's insistence, Tobi also left his mother's picture. He tried to shake his grandfather's hand, but the old man wanted to be hugged by his grandson instead. Tobi withdrew after several seconds of one of the best hugs he'd ever received, second only to the ones given by his mom and Betsy. Tobi's grandfather looked weary, but it was a happy tiredness.

"You will come again, won't you, Tobi?"

"Yes, Papa. I promise. I'll come as much as possible before I leave to go back to Montana."

"If you'll wait just a minute or two, I'll give you a ride to your hotel. Getting a cab around here can be tricky, and it's getting dark," Star remarked as she, too, rose to leave.

Tobi stepped into the hall to wait while Star said goodbye to her client. He knew from the conversation that Star had information about his father and wondered if she would be willing to share it with him. It was worth the wait. Besides, he was attracted to Star. *She has looks and intellect, and she loves my grandfather.*

During the long ride to the hotel, Tobi was thankful not to be riding in another New York cab. They each rode in quiet solitude for a few minutes, until Tobi broke the silence.

"So, are you going to tell me where I can find my father?"

Star remained silent for a few seconds longer and then glanced at Tobi.

"If I did, I would be breaking my code of ethics. I can't break Robert's trust." Her hands were nervous on the steering wheel. "However, I actually know more about Tate Douglas than his own father knows."

"You mean Andrew Douglas, don't you?" Tobi watched for Star's reaction.

"How do you know that?" Star cut her eyes at Tobi. "Robert still calls him Tate."

"I snooped when I signed in at Fairfield. The only Douglas I saw was Andrew Douglas." Tobi paused. "Besides, I used to be a detective with the Denver Police Department." He looked straight ahead and waited a few seconds before continuing. "It's just a guess, but did my father take the name Andrew because of the Louisiana farm boy he felt so guilty about?"

"Now that I've heard his letters, I think that could have been part of the reason, but Tate's middle name is Andrew. He is not a junior. Mostly, he just does not want to remember the old Tate and the war. He also likes to pretend Tate Douglas is dead."

"PTSD...Post Traumatic Stress Disorder...right?" Tobi asked, keeping his eyes fixed on Star.

"To know nothing, you certainly do know a lot, former Detective Tobi Parish." Star went back to drumming on the steering wheel. "I met Andrew, or Tate, by accident. His father had talked about him incessantly and had asked me for information about PTSD. One day he was leaving Fairfield just as I came in to visit Robert, and Robert introduced us. About a week after that, there was a big article in the newspaper about St. Michael's Mission in upstate New York. Andrew's picture was in the article—in the background, mind you, but I knew it was him. I did some snooping and found out he is one of the directors who run the mission."

"A mission? I thought churches ran those," Tobi remarked.

"They do. I think your father is an ordained minister, Lutheran maybe, from what the article said. St. Michael's was established by a Catholic priest, but he included ministers from other churches in order to attract and help Vietnam vets of all faiths. There's even a Jewish rabbi on the board. I know all of this from being a social worker."

"Does Robert, or rather, Papa, know all of this?"

"Yes, but he doesn't talk about it. He wanted Tate to come home and live with him, but Tate refused. I actually live in Robert's house. He wanted me to live there and take care of it. In his will, Tate gets the place whether he wants it or not."

"So where is his house? I'd like to see it some time. My roots are extremely screwed up, so anything of family interests me. In fact, my legal name is Timothy Harden, but as soon as I can, I'm having it changed to Tobias Ezekiel Parish, the name my birth mother gave me. You'll understand when you read the article. You did bring it with you, didn't you?"

"Yes. Robert insisted. He wants me to give him a detailed synopsis of it and the book rather than read them to him."

"And then what will you do with the book and the article?" Tobi thought he knew the answer but looked at Star, waiting for confirmation.

"Robert asked me to take them to Tate." Star stared straight ahead.

Chapter Eight

Star pulled up in front of the hotel but stopped in a parking area rather than up front where she could just let Tobi out at the curb.

"Just pull up front and I'll hop out. You don't have to park, unless you want to come up?" Tobi raised his eyebrows and gave Star a suggestive smile.

"No. I'll stay here and wait for you to go up and get your bags and check out."

"What?" Tobi gave Star a look of confusion.

"More orders from your grandfather. I'm taking you home with me. Your grandfather was adamant no grandson of his would be staying in a hotel in the city when he had a perfectly good home outside the city." Star smiled at Tobi, who sat still, not knowing what to do.

"Go on, Tobi." She gave him a brushing away motion with her hand. "You've come this far, now keep coming. It's a big house, more of a mansion if you're from the same socioeconomic status I'm from. I promise you will have your own space, and I won't bother you." Star made the statement emphatically. "Besides, this hotel costs a fortune. You even have a car you can use. It's a little on the vintage side, but Robert has a mechanic friend who keeps it running. It's a 1985 Cadillac, black and shining like the day it was bought." Star smiled, knowing what Tobi's reaction would be.

"You're kidding, right? I'll be pulled over for pimpin'." Tobi left Star laughing as he stepped out of the car.

A few minutes later, Tobi was on his way to his father's childhood home. His mind was still reeling from all the newfound knowledge of his real family history.

"So, you're probably trying to soak all of this in and make sense of it. It has to be hard, even though you're no kid."

"I'm fast approaching forty, if that's a hint to find out how old I am." Tobi smiled at Star, who kept her eyes straight ahead.

"You're just three years older than I am, then." She still did not look at Tobi. "Divorced? Married? Gay?" A smile formed at the corners of her mouth as she kept her eyes on the road.

"And why do you want to know, Dr. Hoskins? Or is it Mrs. Hoskins?" It was Tobi's turn to direct his gaze at the road.

"Even if I were married, I would still be Dr. Hoskins. Dr. takes preeminence over Mrs., which is a bit obsolete anyway." She paused for a few seconds. "But I'm single—divorced for many years, with no children."

"If I told you I, too, am single and divorced, would you reconsider the promise not to bother me?"

Star let out the best laugh Tobi had heard in a long time, and he did not know how to take it.

"Do you want to be bothered, Tobi?"

"We'll get to know each other a little better and see how things go." Tobi smiled. "But we will be living together." Tobi turned his smile toward Star, and she gave him a pretend shocked expression with mouth open. But even in the dark, the twinkle in her black eyes gave her away.

Star had been driving for almost an hour, and her passenger was getting restless. Tobi fidgeted in his seat, kept seeking radio channels, and finally turned the radio off.

"So just how far out of the city is this house?"

"We're almost there. It's in the country. I better warn you. It's an estate, Tobi. You are part of the rich and famous, whether you like it or not."

"Rich and famous, huh? What's not to like?" Tobi shrugged his shoulders and held his hands up.

Star turned off the road and stopped in front of a large gate. Reaching up to her visor, she punched a button and the gate swung open. As they wound around the long, paved driveway, Tobi found himself more than a little excited at seeing the "estate," as Star had called it.

Star pulled up in front of a towering three-story Victorian mansion that was well lit, giving a dramatic first impression. It was snow-white, with green roof and shutters. The windows of the downstairs were lit up as if a large family were home.

"Damn! Papa must have been a hell of a lawyer!" Tobi sat still, looking up the full height of the house through the car window.

"Actually, Robert married well. His wife, your grandmother, was a wealthy socialite, a very charming but controlling woman, from all accounts." Star reached for the door handle and turned to Tobi. "Well, grab your suitcase. You ain't seen nothing yet, my dear."

Star removed her briefcase from the back seat

51

while Tobi grabbed his suitcase.

Tobi stopped after reaching the top of the steps and gazed both ways down to the ends of the massive porch that ran the full length of the house. "So do you have an entourage of servants, or do I have to keep my own bathroom clean?"

Star unlocked the front door and went in ahead of Tobi. "Hate to mess with the image, but the Scrubbing Bubbles are under the sink in your bathroom." Star stopped in the entry to watch Tobi take in the boyhood home of his father.

"Wow! This kind of puts my little log cabin in the mountains to shame! Well, not really. I'll take the Beartooth Mountains over an estate any day, but this is beautiful." Tobi set his suitcase down at the bottom of the stairs and walked into the sitting room on his right. Star came in behind him, picked up a remote, and instantly the gas log fireplace roared to life.

"No big-screen TV?" Tobi grinned, knowing this would get a reaction out of Star, and was surprised when she left the room.

She stepped backward in the doorway and gestured to Tobi. "Well, do you want to see the media room or not?" Star left again, but this time Tobi was right behind her. She led him through a set of double wooden doors, mahogany like the walls and trim as well as the winding staircase in the entry.

"This is the study-slash-media room, or as Robert calls it, his office."

The walls were covered in shelves of books, with a big gas fireplace in the middle of the outside wall. Star turned on the fireplace as soon as they entered the room. Leather sofas stressed from age and wear sat in front of the fireplace, inviting guests to sit and read a while. Once again, Star picked up a remote, and instantly doors opened above the fireplace to expose a huge flat-screened TV.

"Satisfied?" Star handed the remote to Tobi, who smiled at her.

"Actually, I'd rather check out the books on those shelves. Good books are in my blood, and I just found out why not long ago." Tobi walked to the shelves and did a quick look. "But right now, my sweats are calling my name, and these boots are demanding removal."

Tobi left the room and picked up his suitcase.

"I assume my room is upstairs?"

"Your assumption is correct." Star headed up the stairs and looked back over her shoulder to smile at Tobi. "And so is mine." She proceeded at a faster pace, not waiting for his reaction.

Star turned right at the top of the stairs, stopping at the second room.

"I think you will be very comfortable here. It's one of ten bedrooms, but I only use a small portion of the house, the side with four bedrooms." She opened the door and let Tobi enter first.

"Wow!" Tobi put his suitcase down and did a 360-degree turn.

The room was massive, with a huge king-sized mahogany bed centered on one wall and a sitting area in front of a fireplace. Tobi found the remote and clicked the logs to life.

"You know, I have to carry logs inside to have a fire in my cabin."

"Sounds wonderful. Gas logs have their place, are efficient and clean, but I'll take a real wood fire any day. I grew up in apartments in the suburbs of New York City and only dreamed of fireplaces, cabins, and mountains. I guess that's why I jumped at the chance to live on Robert's estate." Star stood with her arms crossed, looking at Tobi. "You will have to tell me all about your mountain cabin, Tobi Parish, and everything about yourself and your family out west. But first, I'm soaking in a tubful of bubbles, putting on my flannel pajamas, and preparing for the reading of *The Gully Path*."

Thirty minutes later, Tobi, clad in sweats, T-shirt, and socks, sat in the sitting room reading John Grisham's *The Firm* for the second time. But this time he read it from a different perspective, knowing he had lawyer genes. His Papa was obviously a Grisham fan. First editions of all his novels lined the shelves and included *A Time to Kill*, the self-published version Grisham had sold from the trunk of his car and now worth a fortune. Grisham's last two books were not among the collection, and Tobi surmised that by the time they were published Robert Douglas was no longer able to read, due to his failing eyesight.

A few minutes later, Star entered the room, dressed in baggy red-and-navy plaid pajama pants and an oversized sweatshirt, no makeup, wet hair pulled up in a loose ball on top of her head, and looking even more tantalizing than when he had met her earlier that day. Tobi wondered how he would be able to concentrate on Grisham with Star sprawled on the couch across from him, her little feet with bright red toenails, begging to be rubbed.

"Start at Book II, Star. *Where the Gully Path Ends* is where you find the love story of Tate Douglas and

Sue Ann Taylor." Tobi watched as Star pulled out the book, stretched her feet out, and opened to the middle, searching for Book II.

An hour later, Star sniffed and left the room, returning with a box of Kleenex, her reading glasses that consumed half her face, and two bottles of water, plus two cups of gourmet coffee. Also on the tray was a plate heaped with cheese, crackers, and grapes.

"It's what's for dinner, in case you don't recognize it."

"Looks just right. Thank you." Tobi helped himself and smiled as he realized Star was already into the book again.

"Oh, my gosh! This is so good." A few minutes later, Star was crying again, and Tobi enjoyed seeing her so wrapped up emotionally in what had become his story. He closed his book and put it aside and moved over beside Star. Then he picked up her feet and rested them in his lap.

"May I?" He took the book and began reading aloud. Star leaned back, putting her head on the armrest, and moaned as Toby began rubbing her feet with his free hand, except when page turning was necessary. Tobi's voice had his audience mesmerized, and she sat as attentive as a child being read a bedtime story by her mother or father.

Star openly sobbed as Tobi came to the end of the last chapter:

As I held her in my arms in the back seat of my parents' car on our way home from the hospital, I made a vow to myself, one that I would never break.

"I am Sue Ann Taylor Parish, daughter of a new Mississippi. Nothing can prevent me from being what I

want to be. I will not tolerate condemnation and will not stop until I have made a name for myself, a name Betsy can be proud of. With God's help, all is possible.

"Tomorrow will be a brilliant forever, Baby Girl. No regrets."

Tobi closed the book and looked at Star, who was now sitting beside him with her arms tight around her knees.

"I'm sorry, Tobi. I'm afraid I'm one of those who reads, and listens, vicariously." Star's voice cracked and she sniffed, not able to get control this time. She started to get up, but Tobi caught her hand.

With no warning, Tobi pulled her into his arms. He held her for as long as it took for her to regain her composure and continued to hold her close when she did not move. Finally, she raised her face to look into his and smiled.

Tobi removed her oversized glasses and put them on the side table. He caressed her cheek with his fingertips and then moved them to her lips, parting them with his fingertip. His romantic move was rewarded when she opened her lips wider before tightening her lips around his finger like a kiss, a very seductive move, in Tobi's thinking. His lips soon followed his fingers, and he kissed her lightly but with his tongue requesting more.

Neither of them said a word, but words were not needed. Tobi reached beside him and turned out the lamp, leaving them with only the glow of the logs. When Tobi turned back, he found Star loosening the pin in her hair. Dark hair tumbled across her face and onto her breast, giving her a sensual look as she moved even closer.

Star put a hand on either side of Tobi's face. Her lips devoured his as they lay back on the sofa. The kiss seemed to go on forever with neither wanting it to end. Then Tobi sat up, smiling down at Star, who sat up also, leaning on her elbow and returning a bigger smile. He pulled his T-shirt off and gazed down at Star.

"Would you mind too much…if I…bothered you, Star?"

Star answered Tobi's question by sitting up and removing her sweatshirt and then her pajama pants.

Tobi's hands found Star's small, firm breasts, but soon lips replaced hands.

Quickly, as if afraid Star might change her mind, Tobi finished undressing and pulled the black-eyed woman into his arms. Their passions met and were complete in the childhood home of Tobi's father.

Some time in the night, Tobi awoke and found Star gone from the sofa where they had made love. After pulling on his sweats, he left to search for this woman who had captivated his heart and soul in one day of knowing her. Seeing no lights in the media room or the kitchen, he made his way to the dimly lit staircase. He did not stop at his room but made his way down the hall to the room at the end, where a light shone around the door that was left ajar—hopefully, as an invitation.

He gently knocked, but when he got no answer, he took the liberty of opening the door and peeking in, and there she was. She was half sitting up, her big reading glasses still on, the article from the *Billings Gazette* laid across the covers. She was asleep, with her head lying sideways against the plump pillows that held her upright. Her hair had escaped the rubber band on top of her head again and cascaded across her shoulders.

Gingerly, Tobi walked to her side of the bed and sat down by her.

"Star?" he whispered not wanting to startle her. He caressed her cheek with his fingertips as he had done earlier that night, and a smile began to form at the corners of her mouth. Dark eyes peeked at him as she scooted to the other side of the bed and held the covers up for him to enter.

Tobi removed his sweats and crawled in, cuddling her in his arms. It was then that he noticed she was wearing his T-shirt, only his T-shirt, and he became aroused.

"What's this? A new fashion in lingerie?" He fingered the shirtsleeve that hung almost to her elbow.

"It's my favorite," Star answered with a grin before removing it and sinking back under the covers to cuddle in her newfound lover's arms.

****

When Tobi awoke, Star was gone. He pulled on his sweats and headed downstairs, but she was nowhere to be found. On the kitchen table, he found blueberry muffins, cereal, a box of Pop Tarts, and a note propped against a bowl.

The coffeepot is set up. Help yourself.
I am on a mission. Will be home around 5:00.
Looking forward to being "bothered" again.
Star

Tobi went back upstairs and removed his laptop from his suitcase. Returning to the kitchen, he turned on the coffeepot and then his computer. In the search box, he typed in St. Michael's Mission, New York, and rubbed his hands together while waiting for his options.

Two muffins and a big mug of coffee later, Tobi

knew that Andrew Douglas, a Lutheran minister, was now one of the directors of St. Michael's Mission, a halfway house for soldiers returning from war with "demons of battle." Tobi stared at the picture on the page. It was like seeing himself as an older man, and he knew then how his grandfather had mistaken him for his son at a younger age even with the different-colored eyes.

Chapter Nine

Andrew returned to the mission late that day after meeting with a group of potential contributors. On his desk, he found a large envelope with a note attached. It was from Star, saying she had delivered the package at his father's request. The part that was most interesting was her last sentence.

You have a visitor who is staying with me. He is anxiously waiting to meet you when you are ready.

Tate opened the envelope and pulled out a book. Inside it was a newspaper article. When he pulled the article out of the book, something else fell out with it, something contained in a small plastic bag. He opened the bag and pulled out a frail yellowed photograph that had been folded twice, its creases worn with age.

Carrying the package with him, he moved to the easy chair by the window, where the last rays of sunshine were washing through his office. He removed the white clerical collar that he wore on occasions such as today and put on his reading glasses. Carefully, he unfolded the picture, fold by fold, with each crease threatening to tear apart.

As he unfolded the last section, emerald eyes smiled at him, eyes surrounded by a mass of golden curls. The past roared to life in his hands as he leapt to his feet, allowing the book and the picture to tumble to the floor. With both hands grasping his head, he stumbled backward, falling to the floor.

Green and black oozed out of nowhere and surrounded him, the suffocating smell of rotting flesh tormenting his senses. He could taste death. The skeletons laughed, taunts of tortured souls, both gook and GI. In the next second, the green and black of the jungle became swallowed up by blood red as the river of no life consumed him and pulled him under.

"Don't fight it, Tate! Join me, brother."

The whispers of Andrew, the first Andrew, the dead Andrew, wafted through the breeze. Andrew, the farm boy from Louisiana, stood by the girl with the grenade who reached out her hand to save the drowning soldier as if accepting the chocolate bar he offered. Tate reached, trying to grasp her tiny fingers, but she jerked them back, her devilish laugh echoing through the sludge as she disappeared.

The skinny little man showed up next, shoving a bamboo pole in his direction. Tate started to grab hold as the bamboo dangled inches from his face, but he stopped when he realized a frayed American flag was wrapped around it.

"No!" Tate yelled and tried to kick himself away, sure it was a trick, the villager's retribution.

Flailing, sinking, unable to continue kicking with his blood-coated, mangled legs, he called out, "Sue Ann!" But only silence answered as Tate was sucked to the unfathomable depths of hell resurrected. Deeper, deeper he sank, his eyes open, looking up, watching for the end, begging for death, but the end refused to come. A hand, a large smooth hand, not a soldier hand, penetrated the murky water and pulled him to safety.

"Andrew? Andrew?"

Andrew opened his eyes. A man, his friend, wearing the collar of the Catholic Church, was holding his head in his lap.

"Benjamin! It's back! Hades has its clutches on my throat!" Andrew sat up and covered his face with his hands and sobbed aloud.

Father Benjamin helped Andrew back into his chair, then stepped to Andrew's desk, opened a drawer, and took out a bottle of pills. Picking up the opened bottle of water from the desk, Benjamin went back to Andrew.

"Here, Andrew. Take your pill. You'll be fine. The demons are not back. You destroyed them a long time ago. They are just trying to scare you into submission again."

Seeing the picture on the floor, Father Benjamin picked it up and looked at it.

"Is this what triggered your attack?" He held the picture out to his friend, but Andrew turned his head, burying his eyes in his arm.

"You know the routine, Andrew. I expect the same thing from you that we expect from those we try to help. You have to take the picture and look at it. Talk it through." Father Benjamin's voice was loud, demanding.

Andrew knew Benjamin was right. He took the picture and looked at it again through moist eyes. He stared at Sue Ann for several minutes, searching for his voice, Tate's voice.

"It's the last battle, the one where I was shot. I was desperate. I wrote a letter to Sue Ann, the girl I was in love with, telling her I was dead. I told her I was going to vanish and wanted no more memories and put her picture, this picture, in with the letter telling her goodbye." Andrew left his chair and walked closer to the light from the window.

"This picture was with me every step, with me for every shot I took at another human being, but I knew I could never let her see me like this, like I was then, like I was a few minutes ago. Besides, I had written her numerous letters and she never answered any of them. Her love for me was dead, and so was I. At that moment, I wanted to die, and I almost did."

Father Benjamin picked up the book. "What is the significance of the book, Andrew?"

Andrew took the book and looked at it. Then he turned it over and read the author's bio on the back. The picture above the bio was Sue Ann, an older Sue Ann, but she was still every bit as beautiful as the day he had left her.

"Evidently this is a book written by Sue Ann and coauthored by someone named Elizabeth Larson. It says it is the first book in a series, Sue Ann's autobiography." Andrew continued to stare at Sue Ann's picture.

"Who sent it to you?" Benjamin asked.

"Star brought it. She left a note saying my father sent the book, this newspaper article, and the picture, so I assume Dad knows what's behind this. Star said I have a visitor, a male, at her house, and he wants to meet me."

"Go home, Andrew. Read this information." Father Benjamin picked up the newspaper article that still lay on the floor. "Your past has found you. It's time. You can no longer hide behind the misery that is St. Michael's, nor can you hide behind your collar. Your heart is no longer purple, Andrew. You must let it heal."

Chapter Ten

Tobi passed the days getting to know his grandfather better. Each day he took a different picture album from the office for his Papa to go through and talk about Tate's growing-up years. Even Tobi could see how much he looked like his father, as a child and as an adult, but a hole many years deep was left from the Vietnam War years until his father started working at St. Michael's Mission.

On his third day's visit, Tobi got up the nerve to ask about those lost years.

"Papa, will you tell me about my father after Vietnam? Why are there no photos, no family history, for all those years after he came home from the war?"

Papa's face took on a sad, worried expression.

"I feel like that is your father's to tell, Tobi." The old man's hands began to shake.

"I know he suffered from Post Traumatic Stress Disorder, and I assume that is how he ended up at St. Michael's Mission. A little of his story is told on the mission's website. I can only surmise how very awful it was for him when he came home." Tobi added what little he knew to his questioning, and Papa lowered his eyes to his hands, folded in his lap, and began to talk.

"Tate was in the hospital in upstate New York for months undergoing therapy, both physical and mental. He became addicted to morphine and other painkillers.

Once he could walk, he left the hospital and disappeared. That is when he began calling himself Andrew. Of course, he was still, and always will be, Tate to me. His mother and I tried to find him, but to no avail. I really believe the stress of losing our son is what caused his mother's death in 1975."

"It must have been horrible." Tobi shook his head as he talked. "As a father myself, I can't imagine the pain of not knowing where your child is, if he's alive or dead or suffering."

Tobi watched his grandfather closely for signs of his becoming upset emotionally with this painful remembering. After a pause of a few minutes, the old man began reliving a parent's horrendous nightmare.

"I hired a private detective, who found Tate on the streets of Albany, New York. He was an alcoholic and a drug addict, although I never found out how he got the money for those addictions. Actually, I never wanted to know. Andrew, as he called himself, suffered from hallucinations and was always trying to protect himself from the imagined VC who fed his paranoia. This landed him in jail on numerous charges of assault." Robert paused. "I paid his bail every time, without him knowing it."

"Did you ever try to get him committed to an institution?" Tobi tried to think what options might be available under such circumstances.

"Once, I did get him into an institution, but the first chance he got, he ran away. This time he found his way farther upstate, into the Adirondack Mountains. It was there he attempted suicide." Tobi noticed how upset his grandfather was becoming and decided it was time to end the conversation. He moved to sit beside his grandfather and put his arm around his shoulders.

"It's okay, Papa. You've told me enough. Just remember that your son, my father, is fine now. No demons. I just hope he will want to meet me as much as I want to meet him."

Papa smiled at his grandson and patted his hand. "He'll come around, Tobi. I just know he will."

"I hope you're right, but I have to leave in two days. I have to go back to Montana and finish my cabin so I can bring my daughter out during her summer break from school."

****

Tobi drove the old Cadillac back to his grandfather's home. He loved being with his Papa but knew his time with him was limited, not only due to his return to Montana but to his grandfather's age and medical condition. He had learned from Star that his grandfather had a heart condition as well as suffering from arthritis.

As Tobi came within a few miles of the house, the excitement of knowing Star should already be home took over his thinking. Tobi had not had a serious relationship in the three years since his divorce. It would be so easy to let himself fall in love with this girl, but it would not be an easy romance.

If only she lived in Montana instead of New York. If only...

Tobi parked in front of the house and smiled when he saw Star's car. He looked forward to each night— cuddling with Star as they read together, watched movies on the big screen TV, looked at more family picture albums, and, of course, made love. Tobi had not slept in his own room a single night since he moved from the hotel.

As he opened the door, he was greeted by Star, who kissed him with the newfound passion they shared. Before he could begin what had occupied his mind the whole way from the city, Star drew back, holding to his hands, and gave him a big smile.

"What's up, Star? You act a little strange, maybe even giddy."

Star held to Tobi's hand and led him to the sitting room, her smile never leaving her face as she gave Tobi quick glances.

As they entered the room, Tobi saw a man sitting in the chair by the fireplace. He was leaned over with his elbows on his knees and his hands clasped.

Tobi stopped in front of the fireplace, and the man stood to face him. It was like looking in a magical mirror, one that aged a person considerably. Tobi had imagined what his reaction would be if his father ever decided to meet him, and now he was finding out in person.

Tate Douglas extended his hand.

"I presume you are Tobi." He paused for a few seconds and stared at the likeness of himself. "Hello, Son."

The two stood staring at each other, their hands locked in a tight handshake. One had curly blond hair and green eyes, the other curly gray hair and dark eyes. Both men were on the short side but had muscular builds; both were fit and looked as if they were disciplined to a regimen of exercise and outdoor living.

Tobi broke the silence, smiled at his father, and moved closer, still holding onto Tate Douglas's hand.

"I've been waiting and hoping you'd come." Tobi

watched, not knowing if his father was feeling the emotions he was feeling. Then, both moving at the same time, father and son embraced.

****

After hours of Tobi sharing pictures, answering Tate's questions, and summarizing his life with his other parents and grandmother, the two became quiet, contemplative.

"What's next, Tobi? Your finding me is the most important event of my life, and now I want to meet my daughter and my grandchildren." Tate looked at Tobi. "And I want to see your mother." Tate dropped his eyes to his hands that were once again clasped in his lap. "But I don't want to hurt Sue Ann. I'm sure she has her own life, maybe even her own love. I don't want to cause her pain ever again."

"I don't know..." Tobi almost said "Dad," and Tate caught this from the inflection in Tobi's voice.

"Tobi, if you can find it in your heart, could you please call me 'Dad'? It would be the sweetest sound I've ever heard."

"I would like nothing better, Dad." Tate's smile was all Tobi needed to bind them together as son and father.

Tate stayed at his childhood home that night, not wanting to leave the son he had just found. He was glad Star had come to the mission to see if he had made a decision about meeting Tobi. Tate's answer had been to pack a small bag and return home with Star. There would be no sleep in the Douglas house tonight. Too much time had been wasted already, and neither father nor son was willing to waste even a minute of their time together.

The next day, Tobi made the call he had been dreading. Custer answered on the first ring.

"Custer, it's Tobi." There was silence on the other end. "I found him. I found my father."

Chapter Eleven

Star took Tobi to the airport the next afternoon. The time had come for him to get back to the new life he loved in Montana, but leaving his grandfather and Star was hard.

"You promise you'll come out later in the summer, Star?" Tobi had his arms around her and caressed her cheek with his fingertips like he had done their first night together.

"I'll be there. I can't wait to see your cabin and the Beartooth Mountains, and yes, I've become quite fond of waking up to those green eyes."

Tobi and Star kissed a passionate goodbye, and Tobi headed for his gate.

He put his bag in the overhead compartment and was about to take his seat next to the window, ready to catch up on sleep on his way to Billings, when a voice behind him interrupted his thoughts.

"I hope you don't mind, but I asked for the seat next to you."

Tobi turned and looked into the eyes of his father.

"Dad?" Tobi smiled and gave his dad a quick hug. "You're coming to Montana with me?"

"Yes. I prayed about it and talked to Father Benjamin for a long time, seeking his advice. As usual, he told me I alone could make the decision. Somehow, I think it's what I'm supposed to do. Either it will result in closure or a new beginning, not just for me but for Sue Ann, too. But it has to be in person this time. You and I both know letters are not the answer."

****

Montana

Custer took solace once again in his old cabin in the woods. He had told Betsy of his conversation with Tobi, and she had cried, knowing that soon she would meet her father. Custer's vision was coming to its conclusion, and in his heart he knew he must leave the final answer to Sue Ann to discover. He had tried writing her a letter telling her he was leaving and removing himself from the picture so she could decide her own destiny, but in the end he wadded it up and threw it on the floor.

If Tate Douglas loves Sue Ann as much as I do, Sue Ann will be all right with him. What happened was not his fault, and he deserves a chance. And Sue Ann deserves another chance with Tate, her "knight in shining armor" as Elizabeth so facetiously described him in the epilogue in the book. Sue Ann's happiness is all that matters, all that has ever mattered, and I'll not stand in her way.

Custer laced his moccasins, packed his backpack, got his rifle, ammunition, and fishing gear, and headed to the high country, to the forestry cabin where he had spent many winters trapping. He never went to the cabin in the summer, and that made it the perfect location for his disappearance. Only Hawk knew where his uncle was going, and Hawk had been directed to tell Sue Ann she was on her own quest, one that only she could experience, to determine what it was that would make her happy. Custer felt he had to leave her life in order for her to make this decision without his presence to influence her.

****

Betsy sat with her mother while she read the copies of the letters from Tate. Custer had left the letters with Betsy and told her to be there with Sue Ann when she read them. Betsy and her mom cried and talked about the prospect of Tate finding out about his son and daughter and coming to Montana now that *The Gully Path* was on bookshelves in every state. Sue Ann had used real names, since it was her autobiography, so Tate could easily find out. She had convinced Betsy she would be fine seeing Tate again and not to worry.

"We share children, and Tate has the right to get to know his wonderful son and daughter and his grandchildren." Sue Ann kept the letters, at Betsy's insistence, and reread them many times after she left. At the end of the day, she tied the yarn around them and put them in the drawer of her writing desk. She had to pack for a trip she was making.

Back to life. What will be will be.

****

Betsy had not told her mother about Tobi finding their father. Nor had she told her that Tate was coming to Montana. Her mother was in her element right now, and Betsy would not put a damper on it. Sue Ann was on the Big Horn River, volunteering with Casting for Recovery, the charity organization that she supported through her book sales. As an avid fly fisher and member of Sisters on the Fly, Sue Ann always gave fly fishing instruction at the retreats paid for and sponsored by Casting for Recovery. Betsy had told her mom to call when she was on her way home from the retreat, but she was not due until the next day. This would give Betsy time to decide how to give her mom the news.

****

Tobi and his dad talked all the way from the airport in Billings to Red Lodge. The big Dodge truck seemed to surge, unsure why it was not traveling its usual five miles over the speed limit, but its driver was enjoying the leisurely ride with his dad, still trying to catch up on a lifetime of experiences and events as well as to point out the beautiful scenery on the way to Red Lodge. During a lull in the conversation, Tate asked the question that had been on his mind ever since he left New York.

"Did Betsy tell Sue Ann I'm coming? I do not want it to be a shock to her." Tate looked at his son, anxious to hear his reply.

"Mom is away at a Casting for Recovery retreat right now. She is quite a fly fisher and teaches casting to women who are survivors, or who are trying to be survivors, of breast cancer. She's always been a sponsor for CFR with her book sales, but after fighting her own battle with breast cancer, she feels even stronger about the organization. Betsy does not want to tell her until she is on her way home. She's due home tomorrow."

"Fly fishing, huh? You know, I taught Sue Ann how to fly fish when we lived together in the little cabin on the lake in Paxton, the semester she did her student teaching. She loved catching those little bream on a popping bug. I remember she called it 'the dance across the water' when she'd reel in a fish." Tate smiled at the knowledge that he had been a part of Sue Ann's future even though he had not been there to share it with her.

When Tate pulled up his truck in front of Betsy and

Hawk's cabin, the door opened and Trapper ran out, fully clad in boots, jeans, and cowboy hat. He ran to Tobi and jumped in his arms. Following him were Betsy and Hawk.

Betsy, smiling through teary eyes, practically ran to the man who was exiting on the passenger side of the truck. Tate smiled and opened his arms, and his daughter fell into them, resting her head on her dad's chest and holding tight like she was afraid he might escape. Tate caressed her long golden curls and was amazed at how like her mother she was in every detail.

Next came a handshake that quickly dissolved into a man hug with Hawk, and then the introduction to his grandson Trapper, who immediately left his uncle's arms for the grandfather he was meeting for the first time. Trapper, all smiles and feeling comfortable after seeing his mom's reaction to this stranger, gave his grandfather a big hug and kiss.

"I'm your Papa, Trapper, and I am so glad I have you for a grandson." Tate kissed and hugged Trapper until the boy had had enough and wiggled to get down. The little cowboy took his grandfather by the hand and began pulling him.

"Poppy, come see Dakota. He's real friendly, but you're too big to ride him."

"Wait until later, Son, and we'll put Poppy on a big horse and take him for a long trail ride. Sorry, Tate, but I think Trapper has picked another name for you." Hawk took Trapper's other hand and redirected him to the porch, with Trapper giggling and pulling his dad to go faster.

Trapper grabbed his stick horse off the porch and began galloping around his grandfather, whooping like a Crow warrior, doing his best to impress his Poppy.

Tate laughed at the antics of the boy and had already fallen in love with him.

Later, the family lingered at the table, drinking coffee and enjoying their new togetherness. Betsy had cooked a hearty elk stew, cheese biscuits, and rhubarb pie. The group was laughing and talking so loudly they didn't hear a car come up.

"Sounds like a party in here!" Sue Ann yelled from the front door.

The group became silent. Tate looked to Tobi for help, knowing Sue Ann would not be expecting to see the ghost from a romance past. But before Tobi could get to the door to warn his mother, Sue Ann was at the table.

"Something smells good. Hope there's some left for me." Sue Ann reached and hugged Trapper who began to kick in excitement.

"Sudi!" Trapper began to point. "Poppy's here!"

Sue Ann glanced in the direction Trapper was pointing and froze as Tate stood and faced her. He could only stare at this beautiful woman, this woman he had loved and yet hurt so deeply.

"Tate?" Sue Ann stared for only a second, and a smile covered her face as she moved toward him. Tate left the table and met Sue Ann with open arms. Sue Ann fell into his embrace just as her daughter had done, but with her arms around his neck and her face held tightly to his. Betsy and Tobi left the table and joined in the family embrace and were soon joined by Hawk holding Trapper.

Sue Ann, holding Tate's hand, led him back to the table, where a bowl of stew awaited her. She could hardly eat for staring at Tate, who took the seat beside her.

"You look wonderful, Tate. Except for the gray, you really have not changed much at all."

"And I can say the same for you. You are still just as beautiful as the last day I saw you in Mississippi. But let's not talk about that." Tate kept his eyes locked on Sue Ann's.

"Mom, you came home early." Betsy poured coffee for her mother. "I was going to call and tell you, but I wanted you to get finished with your retreat first."

"This being my first retreat since my own battle with breast cancer, I was getting a little too tired and decided I'd better come home early." She reached across and put her hand on top of Tate's. "I'm really glad I did." Tobi and Betsy could do nothing but smile, watching their parents react to each other. After taking a bite of stew, Sue Ann looked around and then at Hawk.

"Where's Custer? Betsy, I can't believe he let you cook this stew without him hovering over you telling you to add a little more salt or pepper, or sneaking in a secret ingredient or two." She took another bite, waiting for someone to answer.

Hawk hesitated and looked to Betsy for help. When she did not offer, Hawk decided it was his responsibility to tell her.

"Sue Ann, Custer is gone." He paused. "Indefinitely." Hawk watched, anxiously gauging Sue Ann's reaction. She dropped her spoon in her stew and stared at Hawk.

"What do you mean 'gone indefinitely?' " Sue Ann's face took on a look of panic.

"Custer knew Tate was coming and said for me to tell you not to worry about him. His exact words were, 'Tell Sue Ann this is her quest. Only she can make decisions about her future happiness, and I will not stand in her way.' I can't tell you where he is, Sue Ann, but I promise I'll keep in contact with him."

"Then you get on that cell phone, or whatever, and tell him to get his old Crow butt home. I'm sure he's on that mountain somewhere, and he does not need to be alone. His heart is not to be trusted. He needs to be here so I can take care of him." Sue Ann looked at Tate. "And besides, I want him to meet Tate."

Tate strained a smile as he listened to Sue Ann. Perhaps it was too late for him, but he, too, wanted happiness for Sue Ann, even if it meant continuing her life with Custer.

"And I want to meet Custer. Tobi has told me how special he is to all of you. I appreciate his care for you, Sue Ann." Tate's eyes scanned the table. "And my children." Tate turned to face Hawk. "Please give him that message for me, Hawk."

"Custer doesn't listen to me or anyone, Tate. It's best for me to simply relay the messages and not to try to convince him. Somehow, he always knows what he needs to do. He'll come back when the time is right."

The afternoon raced by with all of the catching up, but Tate did not talk about his lost years. He knew he would talk about these to Sue Ann in private, but that would come after they became reacquainted.

"Well, I hate to put an end to this, but I am really tired and need to get home." Sue Ann hugged everyone with extra hugs for Trapper, and headed to the door. "Betsy, the meal was heavenly. What a great afternoon!" Sue Ann looked to Hawk. "Call your uncle, Hawk, and tell him what I said." Hawk nodded, letting her know he would.

"Tate, get your bags. You're coming home with me. You have plenty of time to get to know your kids, but I need to be caught up on those years we lost."

Tate stood but looked to Betsy and Tobi for what he should do.

"It's okay, Dad. You go on with Mom. We'll see you tomorrow."

"Tobi is right." Betsy moved beside Tate and gave him another big hug. "But Mom won't be hogging you the whole time you're here. I want to know my dad, and I want Trapper to know his Poppy."

****

Sue Ann drove in silence for a while, even though there was much she wanted to talk about with Tate. Her mind was racing, filled with "what if's."

How different things would be if my mother had only given me the letters. But now there's Custer. He's left me to my own "quest" as he called it, and I can only hope he comes back. I can't imagine life without Custer, but it is just like him to not want to interfere at this time. Custer, the selfless, caring man whom I have loved for so many years.

Chapter Twelve

Sue Ann made coffee while Tate built a fire in the fireplace. Even though it was June, nights in the mountains tended to be chilly, and Tate was glad, thinking back to another time he had sat with Sue Ann before the fire.

As Sue Ann came back into the room bringing the coffee, she noticed Tate staring at the large portrait that hung over the fireplace. Sue Ann turned her gaze to the portrait and smiled, remembering the greatest of her loves, Shade Dubois.

The scene was Betsy and her mom, surrounded by an Alaskan night brightened by fresh, deep snow. Sue Ann and Betsy stood close, their heads almost touching, wearing matching heavy dark green Alaskan coats with ruffs of white wolf fur. Long blonde curls cascaded from under loose green suede hoods. Streaks of northern lights undulated overhead, the heavenly green dancers reflecting on the scene below, playing off the green of mother/daughter emerald eyes. Sue Ann remembered posing that night as Shade, an artist, took pictures of her and Betsy, in preparation for this painting, his masterpiece as he had called it. Moose Springs, Alaska, was the little village where Sue Ann met and fell in love with Shade Dubois. She had taken a job as principal/teacher in the summer of 1982, when she made her move from Parrish Oaks to what would become her favorite place in the world.

"Thank you." Tate took a sip and smiled at Sue Ann, who sat beside him on the sofa. "You remembered after forty years?"

"A spoon and a half of sugar, and no cream." Sue Ann took a sip, smiling over her mug, and waited for Tate to begin talking.

"Tell me about the picture of you and Betsy. It's beautiful! Whoever painted it captured the essence of your beauty and the beauty of my daughter."

"Shade Dubois was his name, and I loved him more than anyone in the world other than my Betsy. He was an artist with a past, one that included Vietnam but not as a soldier."

"What do you mean by 'not as a soldier'?" Tate turned his gaze to Sue Ann.

"It was a long time ago, Tate. Seventeen years after you left me, to be exact. Shade taught me how to love again, something I refused to do after you. But mostly, he was a warrior and hero to Betsy and me. He died saving Betsy in the spring of 1983, leaving me with the worst pain of my life, even more than when you left. But I don't want to talk about Shade. He is gone, and you have been miraculously reincarnated, and I am overjoyed."

Sue Ann put her hand on Tate's leg, and immediately Tate covered her hand with his own, locking his fingers in hers.

"I guess it's a little late to say I'm sorry." Tate put his cup down and took on a serious look, staring into Sue Ann's eyes. "Sue Ann, you have no idea how much I missed you, missed staring into those mesmerizing eyes. I tried to blame the whole engagement thing on my mother in my first letter to you, but it was my fault for not standing up for what I wanted. I wanted you. I loved you, Sue Ann." Tate squeezed Sue Ann's hand, and gained the courage to continue when she did not pull away.

"I know I have no right to be here with you, but I have to be truthful now that God has so graciously given me this chance to make things right." Tate turned to face her more directly, moving his arm to Sue Ann's shoulder, where he began twisting her curls just as he had done in 1965.

"I still love you, Sue Ann. God help me, but I do. I never stopped, not even when I was so possessed from the war that I wanted to die."

Sue Ann looked down, unsure of what to say or do. Her words were guarded as she answered him.

"Tate, I am glad you're here, but right now, my feelings are muddled. You are the father of my children, and that certainly counts for a lot. But the hurt of your leaving and of going through the birth of the twins, burying the baby boy I thought was Tobi, and raising Betsy by myself left me numb where love was concerned." Sue Ann put up her hand. "Don't get me wrong. Eventually, I was able to love again, twice, in fact. First Shade in Alaska and now Custer." She looked into Tate's face and saw the same look of passion he had given her the first time he had kissed her in the old cabin at Parrish Oaks. A shiver covered her just as it had that day, and she wondered if it was a warning.

"I know I don't have the right to love you. Custer was here when you almost died, and I was not. I could have found you after the war if I had tried, but I was too messed up. I kept my distance from everyone, including my parents. All I thought about was staying paralyzing drunk, or high, or both." Tate released Sue Ann's hand and stared at the fire, unable to look at Sue Ann as he made this confession.

"Where did you go after the war, if you weren't with your parents?"

"I honestly don't remember. I was so violent, Sue Ann. Even if I had wanted to stay in my parents' house, I wouldn't have. I was afraid to go to sleep and refused to go home. Even in the hospital, my biggest fear was that I would hallucinate and murder some innocent person. Every person who stared at me in the gutter or on the streets was VC in my eyes. I attacked people randomly and scared everyone away, even the others who were down and out, many of whom were vets like me who lived on the streets."

"You lived on the streets?" Sue Ann gave Tate her most concerned look. "Oh, Tate, I am so sorry. I was so swallowed up in my own pity, I never thought about what you were going through during the war or after." She reached over and picked up his hand before continuing.

"I called your house when I found out I was pregnant, and your mother told me you were going into the military and were at a going-away party at the home of your fiancée. My heart almost stopped at that moment. But then I put my unborn child before myself, and I got through it. I got my doctorate just so I would never have to be called Miss again, changed my last name to Parish so my child would not have to explain Taylor as a last name, and I let my world revolve around Betsy."

"My mother never told me you called. If only she had, things would be different now." Tate clasped his hands and remained silent, thinking. "I have been off the streets, alcohol and drug free and, for the most part, free of the demons of war, for over thirty years, but even now, things can trigger a relapse. I take medicine to keep the hallucinations under control, so please don't be afraid of me." Tate put his hand on Sue Ann's shoulder again and leaned closer to her.

"When I saw your picture the other day, the one I had carried through the war and sent back to you in my last letter, I had a reaction, a recurring event from the war. I blacked out, and the devils of Vietnam took control of me again. If I had not been in St. Michael's Mission among friends who are always willing to help me, I would have gone off the deep end. Father Benjamin brought me back. He told me my past has found me and I have to stop hiding behind St. Michael's. His words were, 'Your heart is no longer purple, and you must let it heal.' "

"What did he mean by 'your heart is no longer purple?' " Sue Ann asked.

"I received a Purple Heart when I was wounded in Vietnam. In one of my hallucinatory stages after I ran away from the hospital, I threw the medal off a bridge, one I was planning to jump from to put myself out of my misery. Before I could jump, two teenage boys walked by and began taunting me. In my eyes, they were VC. I lit into them and knocked one over the rail. Fortunately, the kid was a good swimmer and saved himself, but I was locked up for a few days and charged with assault. A by-passer came to the police station a few days later and said he had seen everything. He told the police I was defending myself, so they let me go."

"You tried to kill yourself?" Sue Ann's face took on a look of horror and shock.

"Several times, but God had something planned for me. The last time I attempted to take my life, I was in upstate New York trying to keep warm in an alley. I had found part of a bottle of whiskey in the trash behind a bar and had drained the bottle. Not wanting to live like this any longer, I broke the bottle, took a piece of the shattered glass and slashed my wrist. Blood poured down my hand and dripped off my fingertips. I staggered down the street, subconsciously hoping someone would save me before I crossed into hell. Then I saw a purple light shaped like a heart that flashed on and off, pulsating like a real heart or like a beacon. It was hypnotizing, and I dragged myself to it and collapsed on the front steps."

"St. Michael's Mission," Sue Ann said.

"Yes. Father Benjamin, a Catholic priest, saved me from myself that night. My heart and soul were revived, and I have been at the mission ever since. Now I help other vets with PTSD. I'm actually one of the directors at the mission." Tate searched Sue Ann's eyes for understanding and was rewarded, not with a look of pity but one he interpreted as concern and caring.

"The purple heart signifies the wounded souls of Vietnam vets like me. The mission is also open to young soldiers today who suffer from Post Traumatic Stress Disorder from the wars in the Middle East."

"Oh, Tate. I should have known there was a reason I never heard from you. If only I had received your letters, I would have forgiven you and would have waited for you." Sue Ann's voice cracked and tears flooded her eyes. She opened her arms to Tate, who eagerly fell into her embrace. They both cried, and when they did finally part, Tate ran his fingers over Sue Ann's wet cheek, wiping away her tears.

"I love you, Sue Ann." Tate spoke softly. "I don't deserve you, but I still love you. You have given me the greatest gifts any man could ever receive—a son, a daughter, and grandchildren—but I want more." Tate put his hands on both sides of Sue Ann's face and pulled her mouth to his. Without hesitation, Sue Ann's lips joined Tate's, and they kissed with the same passion they had in the little cabin on the lake over forty years earlier. Tate pulled his lips away but kept his face close to hers.

"I want you, Sue Ann."

Before she could stop herself, or think of Custer, Sue Ann found herself wrapped in the arms of Tate Douglas. The old longings resurfaced, and they made love as if no years, no wars, no pain had ever separated them.

Sue Ann woke up lying next to Tate Douglas in the bed she had shared with Custer. Guilt overtook her, and she questioned her actions and her feelings. She started to move from the bed, but Tate opened his eyes and caught her by the arm. He looked at her and smiled.

"Tate, this is wrong. I shouldn't have... We shouldn't have..."

Tate propped on his elbow and put his fingers to Sue Ann's lips.

"You're not sure if you still love me or not. You're thinking of Custer."

"Yes, on both counts."

Tate put his arms around Sue Ann and pulled her

head to his chest. He ran his fingers gently over her scarred chest and remembered the first time they'd made love as two young crusaders with their heads and hearts in the clouds. Tate admired Sue Ann's bravery in fighting this terrible disease and respected her even more for offering no apology for her disfigured body, her own "battle scars" as she referred to them. She had explained how she had made the decision not to have reconstructive surgery and to just accept the curve life had thrown her in her own way.

"You think you are the only one feeling guilty? I'm an ordained Lutheran minister. I haven't made love in so many years, I'm surprised I remembered how." He smiled. "Am I going to repent? Probably not. It would be too dishonest. Given the chance, I'd make love to you again and again. Besides, I know I love you, Sue Ann. There is no one else in my life and never has been, but I promise I won't put you in this position again, if you don't want to be."

Sue Ann raised her face and looked into Tate's eyes.

"It felt so right, Tate. It's like someone, the only person who could make it right, finally said I was not a cheap, condemned-to-hell unwed mother and that my children were born out of love, not sin. Yes, I loved you more than any man alive at the time, but I also love Custer that way now, or I did before you came back into my life."

Sue Ann left Tate's arms, pulling the cover around her. She stopped and looked down at him. "Give me some time to think all of this through and to do the right thing." She paused and looked away for a moment before returning her gaze to Tate's. "But please, Tate, don't leave me until I know the answer." Sue Ann reached down and kissed Tate again, with the passion of the young rebellious girl from Mississippi. She stayed close for a second, smiled, and turned away from him again.

"So I might still have a chance, Sue Ann?" Tate's voice pleaded, making her face him again. "I feel like we've never been apart, and I want to pick up where we left off. I want you to marry me, sweetheart, like we promised so long ago, and let's share our children as a real family. It's not fast; it's late, but I know where my heart is, where it never left. Is it an impossible dream?"

Sue Ann sat on the bed again beside Tate and took his hand in hers.

"You were my first real love; you are the father of my children; I will always love you, Tate Douglas. But I don't know if I can love you enough to make me forget Custer."

"Can you try, Sue Ann? Starting here, starting now?"

Sue Ann tucked her head down, as if in deep contemplation, and then removed the cover she was wrapped in, returning to Tate's arms.

****

Betsy and Tobi each wanted their father to stay with them while in Montana, but he would not leave Sue Ann. The twins were confused by their feelings. They loved having their father in their lives, but they also loved Custer, especially Betsy, who thought of Custer as the only father figure she'd ever had, other than Shade. Sue Ann must have sensed their questions and feelings and called them both to come out to the cabin while Tate had gone into town.

They sat on the sofa, quiet, waiting. Both were anxious to hear what their mother had to say.

"My thoughts are very confused right now, my children, but I felt you needed an explanation." She paused to gather her words. "Your father says he loves me and wants to marry me so we can be a real family."

Betsy and Tobi looked at each other, but no shocked looks appeared on their faces.

"How do you feel about that, Mom? And what about Custer?" Betsy asked the questions both she and Tobi were thinking, although they had not discussed it with each other.

"Custer is my greatest concern." Sue Ann paused, gathering her thoughts. "Do I love Tate? Yes. I would be lying if I said otherwise, but I'm not sure if it's real love, or if it's just the acknowledgement I've been seeking that what we had, what resulted in you two, was real and right. It's like justification for what transpired forty years ago between us."

"And Custer?" This time Tobi asked the question.

"I love Custer, too. And I can't explain it. Is it possible to love two men and choose between them? I don't know. All I know is that I don't want to lose either of them."

"So Dad staying here with you… Is that…" Betsy could not get the words out.

"Are we once again living like an old married couple, as I said in *The Gully Path*?" Sue Ann smiled as both Tobi and Betsy nodded their heads, letting her know that was exactly what they were asking.

Sue Ann walked to the window and gazed at the mountain.

"Let me give you a scenario, my precious children,

one that you might possibly understand as adults. Since you both are connoisseurs of wine, here it goes. You are offered two rare, priceless wines, but you may have one, and only one, for the rest of your life. How can you make a decision about which wine you will savor unless you taste each?" She paused to let this sink in, cocked her head to one side and cut her eyes at Betsy and Tobi. "Within the same timeframe, that is?"

Tobi and Betsy looked at each other and laughed.

"Oh, Tobi. You have missed so much by not being raised by an author mother all your life."

Chapter Thirteen

May the stars carry your sadness away.
May the flowers fill your heart with beauty.
May hope forever wipe away your tears,
And, above all, may silence make you strong.
                                    ~Chief Dan George

Custer sat motionless, gazing at the mountains, Sue Ann's mountains, and he missed her. He tried not to think of what was happening in the cabin in the valley, but his heart kept interrupting the silence, pushing away the blankness he coveted. A week had gone by, and he knew from his nephew's one call, the only one Custer had allowed, that Tate Douglas was there. He refused to let Hawk talk of Sue Ann and Tate, only listening when Hawk told him Sue Ann wanted him to come home. Custer knew this was premature, something Sue Ann wanted at that moment but not necessarily what would be her choice in the end. Custer had turned the cell phone off, condemning himself to silence.

The first stalk of Indian paintbrush had presented itself to him as he walked the trail to the high mountain lake he planned to fish that day. He had been so overcome with emotion at seeing Sue Ann's favorite wildflower he could not continue, choosing instead to sit on a boulder, hold the flower, and stare at the mountains. This was no vision quest. He did not cleanse himself in a sweat lodge; he did not pray to the Great One; he did not call out to the mountain peaks for answers. He only swore to silence, the giver of the strength he would need to live without her if that was what she chose.

The eagle, his animal spirit, kept vigil over him, but he found no comfort in it.

Is it protectiveness for the never-ending pain to come? Is it a sign of hope that things can be back as they were before Tate Douglas re-entered her life? Or perhaps it is nothing but Crow superstitious nonsense, as Isabelle called it, that keeps me thinking something is about to happen for the good, or not.

No chickadee had shown itself, and Custer was thankful. The animosity Custer had transferred onto the small intelligent bird, the animal spirit of Tate Douglas, was not something the Great Spirit could overlook. Custer held to the medicine bag containing the braided lock, his and Sue Ann's, and the single curl from Tate Douglas, and wished he could throw Tate's symbol away.

Was I right not to stay and fight for Sue Ann? Am I a coward, only pretending to sacrifice my happiness for hers? And what if he wins? Is Tate Douglas the right man for her? Will he protect Sue Ann and care for her like I have and always will if given the chance?

Custer wanted silence, not just from human voices but also from the thoughts and fears that threatened to destroy him. Sometimes he wished for death, like Tate Douglas had, not from battle weariness, although he had experienced plenty of that, unbeknownst to his loved ones, but for wanting his forever with the only woman he had ever loved. Perhaps he should have jumped at the chance when Sue Ann told him she wanted to marry, but he sensed there was something in her future, a great decision she must make, and it was a decision that might not include him. The possibility had marked the end of his vision quest, and Custer could not turn away from it, and neither could Sue Ann.

Custer left the boulder and made his way back down the trail to the forestry cabin. He would wait. He would be silent.

Chapter Fourteen

Star missed Tobi. She found it harder and harder to sleep with each passing night after he left, and her lack of sleep was showing itself as she drove to her office, yawning every few seconds. He called every day and told her he missed her and begged her to come to Montana. Visiting Robert was the only comfort she found, since all he wanted to talk about was Tobi, and Tobi was all she thought about.

The ringing of Star's cell phone interrupted her thoughts. She knew it would not be him. He had already called her that morning, and he knew she would be on her way to work. She looked at the caller ID and became alarmed when she saw it was Fairfield. She hoped and prayed nothing had happened to Robert.

"Hello?" she answered sharply.

"Star, it's Robert. I need to see you as soon as possible." Robert was talking loudly, and she had to hold the phone out from her ear.

"Robert? Are you okay?" Star pulled to the shoulder so she could talk.

"I've never been better. Get on over here. I've got a proposition for you."

The phone went dead before Star could question him further.

When Star walked into Robert's room, he was sitting in his chair, fully dressed, even wearing his walking shoes. A suitcase lay packed on his bed.

"What's going on, Robert? Are you changing rooms?"

"No. I'm changing states, and I need an escort."

"What?" Star sat down on the bed.

"I've been doing some checking—had the nurses Googling, whatever the hell that is, and I've found a privately owned assisted living facility in Red Lodge, Montana. It's called Pioneer Home, and it is beautiful. Has all this glass looking right into the mountains, and the old women residents they show in the ad are real natural beauties. Not like these grotesque floosies with too much makeup and no spunk who sit around in the recreation room here trying to remember how to play bridge. Says in the ad that they have a fly fishing stream that runs right through the property." Star started to speak, but Robert kept going. "It shows a bunch of old codgers like me out there wetting a line. I'm going, Star, and you're escorting me, on my dime. Already talked to your boss and got us two first-class tickets on an early flight tomorrow."

Star grabbed the edge of the bed with both hands and stared at Robert with her mouth open.

"You're serious about this, Robert?"

"Damned right. I'm going to meet my granddaughter Betsy and my great-grandchildren. I want to be with Tobi and get to know Sue Ann. Hell, Tate's out there now, and he may not come back."

"But what if Tate does come back to New York? You won't see him every week. Can you live with that?"

"Once a week? What a trade for getting to be with Betsy and Tobi and that little cowboy Trapper and

Carrie that Tobi talks about all the time."

Robert's happiness was contagious, and Star couldn't stop smiling.

"My boss said I could go? For real?"

"For real. Now get your pretty little butt home and pack. Stop by the desk and get my paperwork. They're expecting me at the Pioneer Home day after tomorrow. Got my room all ready. Tobi will put me up tomorrow night. And from the look on his face when he would mention your name when he was here, I think he'll have a spot for you, too." Robert winked at Star. "I'm getting me some boots and a hat, and I'm gonna become a real cowboy." Robert rubbed his hands together and laughed. "Hot damn! Montana, here I come!"

****

Star called her boss on her way home and, sure enough, she was approved for a two-week leave to escort Robert to Montana and get him settled in his new residence. When she got home, she took down her biggest suitcase, then changed to a medium-sized one when she realized she had nothing in her closet appropriate for Montana. She grabbed her three pairs of designer jeans, a few shirts, a pair of semi-hiking boots she had never worn, and her one pair of designer cowboy boots. At the last minute, she put in a couple of girly, going-out clothes that she might, or might not, be able to wear out west, especially in ranch country.

Tobi called while she was packing and could not contain his excitement. Fairfield had called him and given him the information he would need to get his grandfather registered at Pioneer Home. He was on his way to his mother's cabin, where he was meeting the rest of the family to tell them the good news.

"I'll pick you and Papa up at Billings airport tomorrow afternoon, sweetheart. I can't wait."

Star's body shivered like a teenage prom queen when he called her "sweetheart," and she jigged in place thinking of the handsome cowboy.

"Cowboy! Montana!"

With one quick move, Star grabbed the two New York outfits and threw them back in the closet.

"I'll buy Montana clothes when I get there."

Star put on her cowboy boots and began boot scootin', or what she thought might be boot scootin', as she watched herself in her full-length mirror. Laughing, she clicked her heels and snapped her fingers.

"Hot damn! Montana, here I come!"

****

"You really like Star, don't you, Tobi? I could see it in the way you looked at her at Dad's house." Tate put his hand on Tobi's shoulder.

"Yeah, I do, Dad." Tobi turned to face Betsy and the rest of the family. "I can't wait for all of you to meet her. She has these gorgeous dark eyes, like caves full of mystery and intrigue." Tobi smiled just thinking of her. "And I really can't wait for Papa to get here. Can you believe he's moving here, at ninety?"

"That's my dad. I'd believe almost anything from him now that he knows he has grandchildren and great-grandchildren." Tate reached down and tickled Trapper, who had crawled up in his lap.

"I love you, Poppy." Trapper gave his grandfather a hug and then jumped down and galloped into the other room.

"I love you, too, little man." Tate smiled and

looked at Betsy and Hawk. "Good thing he decided I needed to be called Poppy and not Papa, since the senior Papa will be in his life as of tomorrow."

"I'm going to get to know Papa." Betsy put her arm around Hawk, who hugged her to him, smiling with his wife. "It just keeps getting better."

"This is great news, Tobi. Trapper has so much family now. We just have to get Carrie here, and the family is complete." Hawk made the statement but noticed Sue Ann was quiet. "You okay, Sue Ann?"

Sue Ann realized she was not sharing in the happiness and began to smile.

"Of course. I'm happy. I've never met Mr. Douglas myself, and I'm looking forward to it."

Hawk sensed there was something else on Sue Ann's mind and figured it concerned Custer. He found Sue Ann alone on the porch later, looking toward the mountain peaks while the others played Twister with Trapper.

Hawk pulled his rocker over by his mother-in-law.

"Before you ask, no, I haven't heard from Custer, Sue Ann. He told me not to call anymore, that he was turning his cell phone off."

"Do you think he's all right, Hawk? What if he has a heart attack up there? Nobody will know until it's too late." Sue Ann's face was lined with worry.

"It's the way he wants it, and you and I can do nothing to change it," Hawk reminded Sue Ann.

Hawk and Sue Ann rocked in silence, both looking at the mountains.

Hawk wanted to ask her if she had made her decision, but he knew that would be intrusive. Besides, Custer had told him not to worry Sue Ann about it.

He'd said that when Sue Ann made her decision, he would know and would come down to face it, whatever it was. Hawk had no idea how his uncle would know, but he trusted Custer would, just as he had known when his nephew needed his help to overcome alcoholism. Hawk thought about the months he had spent away from Betsy when she was in Tennessee with Patrick, how alone he'd felt, and how overwhelming his despair had been. It broke his heart to know his uncle was going through the same thing, especially after waiting for Sue Ann through all those years when she was in Alaska.

After everyone left, Sue Ann remained on the porch. Tate joined her and reached for her hand, squeezing it. She smiled at Tate but kept her gaze fixed on the mountains.

"Where do you think he is?" Tate followed Sue Ann's gaze.

"I don't know. Custer was in the forestry service for years, so he has access to any number of cabins. He's a rugged outdoorsman and a survivor, but I still worry about him. He has had two heart attacks, and the last one was very serious."

"Was that when he saved Betsy and Hawk?" Tate asked, but he already knew the answer.

"Yes. Custer is a strong, brave man. He would gladly give his life for those he loves."

"You miss him, don't you, Sue Ann." Tate dropped Sue Ann's hand, keeping his eyes on the mountain.

"Yes, Tate. I miss him. This is the worst and the best position I've ever been in. For most of my life, I had no one, at least not a soul mate, or someone who could make me think about vows, and now…" Sue Ann paused and turned her attention to Tate. "And now, I have two men I love very deeply, and I can't stand the thought of losing either of them."

****

Later, as she lay in bed with Tate spooned tightly to her back, her tears soaked her pillow. When she finally closed her eyes, she dreamed of Custer. He sat on a boulder, his eyes searching the mountains like a lost soul. In his fingers, he twisted a single stem of Indian paintbrush, the flower she had said she would carry in her wedding just as Betsy had carried in hers; that is, if she ever had a wedding.

Her dream shifted, and she was walking slowly down the aisle of a small rustic chapel with Tobi on one side and Betsy on the other. As she approached the altar, both Custer and Tate were smiling at her, each reaching for her hand. As she held out her hand, waiting for the man she would marry to take it, her dream was interrupted by the howl of a lone wolf somewhere up the trail toward Custer's old cabin. It was a haunting howl, and she sat up, turning her head left and right, trying to hear the sound again. Pushing back the covers and trying not to wake Tate, she left the bed and walked to the window.

The moon was bright, and as she looked down, she thought she saw a figure standing at the trailhead at the edge of the yard. Sue Ann moved closer to the window and cupped her hands over her eyes to get a better look. She thought she saw the shadow move back into the trees.

****

Tate sensed Sue Ann's absence and left the bed to stand beside her. He put his arms around her and hugged her tightly to him and turned her face to his. He caressed her hair and kissed her with the passion of a man deeply in love. As always, Sue Ann melted with his kiss and allowed him to escort her back to bed.

****

Custer stood in the shadows, looking up at the bedroom window, his and Sue Ann's bedroom window. But it was not his arms holding her. And it was not his lips kissing her in the moonlight streaming in, lighting up her beautiful face. Feeling his heart skip a beat, Custer turned and headed back through the darkness that consumed him, back to the silence that would either strengthen him or kill him.

Chapter Fifteen

Tate and Tobi met the plane in Billings the next day. Star might have wanted to run to Tobi when she saw him, but she was pushing Robert in a wheelchair. When she did reach Tobi, she threw herself into his arms, and he picked her up and twirled her around before kissing her with passion unashamed. Several passengers smiled and stared at the handsome couple, but it didn't prevent Tobi from giving Star another kiss before turning to his grandfather, who was clearing his throat.

"I feel like I'm being ignored. What do you think, Tate?"

"I think your grandson is preoccupied." Tate patted his dad's shoulder. "How are you, Dad?"

"Never better, Son. Never better." Robert glanced at Tobi and Star who were finally looking toward him. "Give an old man a ride home?" he asked with a grin the size of Montana's big sky.

"You bet, Papa." Tobi hugged his grandfather and began pushing him toward the baggage claim with one hand. His other hand had a grip on Star's hand.

"Let me have that, Tobi." Tate took control of the wheelchair and smiled at how happy his son was with Star.

That night, another family celebration was held in Betsy and Hawk's cabin. Trapper's Papa gave him too much attention, and every time Robert had to get up, he had to hunt for his cane, which Trapper found worked entirely too well as a stick horse, especially with his daddy's sock tied around it for reins.

After much deliberation and Tate's noticing that his father was looking very tired, the decision was made for Papa to stay the night with Betsy and Hawk. Hawk warned Robert he might have company in the night, in the form of a little boy wearing cowboy boots and pajamas, and Robert grinned from ear to ear and said he hoped that would be the case.

The best part of their time together was when Hawk left the room and came back with a gray cowboy hat and a red western scarf for Robert. Robert wore both the rest of the evening, even though he was told cowboys always remove their hats when inside. He pointed to Trapper as proof it was okay to wear such things inside.

No one was surprised when Tobi left early, taking Star to his cabin. In fact, everyone was surprised he stayed as long as he did, given the way they looked at each other. Before he left, he helped get his Papa settled in his bedroom for the night and promised to come the next morning bright and early to take him to Pioneer Home.

****

Sue Ann was quiet all the way home, and Tate kept eyeing her with concern.

"Are you all right, Sue Ann? You're terribly quiet." Tate did not get out of the truck after parking in front of the cabin, waiting for Sue Ann's answer.

"I'm just a little tired and a little overwhelmed. My family grew from Betsy, Hawk and Trapper, and then, of course, Tobi, to…" She paused, trying to figure up the number. "I can't even figure out how many in a short period of time." Sue Ann gave a low laugh.

"Are you sorry I showed up, Sue Ann? I mean, if Tobi had not found me, you and Custer would still be together, and your family would be manageable, to say the least."

"You know I'm glad Tobi found you." She squeezed his hand in reassurance. "And there is no such thing as too much family. Look how Trapper thrives on all this attention, and your father is a wonderful, fun-loving man regardless of his age."

"But your thoughts are still on Custer."

"I won't lie to you, Tate. I am worried about Custer." She paused and looked down. "And yes, I miss him."

Tate held Sue Ann that night without making love. Her sadness and worry were of great concern to him. His mission in life was to help people, not cause them pain, especially people he loved, and he loved Sue Ann with all his heart.

Chapter Sixteen

The next day, Tate and Tobi settled Papa into Pioneer Home. Tate had told Sue Ann that he would be gone most of the day.

Sue Ann tried to read one of the new books she had bought, but she just could not wrap her mind around it. Pulling out her cell phone, she called Betsy.

"How about meeting me in town for a little shopping and lunch?"

Betsy jumped at the chance to have some one-on-one with her mom. Betsy, always tuned in to her mother, had noticed the worry on her face. Her mom pretended to be happy, but Betsy knew this was not the case.

As they sat eating lunch in the Pollard Hotel, Betsy reached across the table and put her hand on her mother's.

"Mom, I know you love Dad, or at least you think you do, but you can't get Custer off your mind, can you?"

"Very perceptive, as always, Betsy. I suspect Hawk told you about our talk the other night on the porch."

"Yes, but he didn't ask you what I'm about to ask you. He said Custer would be angry if he did. In fact, Custer told him not to badger you about it."

"You want to know which one I choose, your father or Custer?"

"Yes. I know I can't help you with this decision. I love my dad, and I am so happy to have him in my life, but I love Custer, too, probably as much as I do Dad, but I've known Custer longer. Please don't tell either of them I said that."

"Custer was always there for you, as a teenager and as an adult." Sue Ann smiled, remembering those first years when the three of them fished and camped together every summer. She also remembered the nights she sneaked out of the tent she and Betsy shared and spent time with Custer in his tent, with Betsy never knowing.

"The main thing I want you to know is I will be happy with whatever decision you make, and I'll support you. Tobi and I talked, and he feels the same way."

"What does Hawk think about all of this?" Sue Ann noticed Betsy looked down as if not wanting to answer.

"Custer is like Hawk's father. He is worried about him the same way Custer worried about Hawk during his crises."

"Crises? Is this a crisis, Betsy?" Sue Ann looked concerned with her daughter's choice of terms.

"For Custer, yes, if you choose Dad. And if you choose Custer, then I guess it is a crisis for Dad. I just know I'm glad I'm not in your shoes."

The waiter brought their lunch, and they dropped the conversation while they ate, choosing to talk of happier times such as Betsy's adopting Trapper and of Betsy and Hawk's wedding at the waterfall.

"That was the most beautiful ceremony I've ever witnessed." Sue Ann had her elbows on the table and her chin resting in her hands, smiling at the remembrance of Betsy in her white Indian wedding dress.

"I bet your wedding will be that beautiful, too, Mom. That is if you ever decide on a groom." Betsy and Sue Ann laughed and decided it was time to shop.

****

Tobi and Tate left Papa flirting with the western women in the recreation room. He was most impressed when he saw they were playing poker, and he could not wait to join the ladies. He told Tobi he felt just like a real cowboy in a saloon, surrounded by gorgeous women, but these were playing cards rather than hustling the gamblers. His first stop when he had walked into the home was in front of the floor-to-ceiling glass windows that looked into the heart of the Beartooth Mountains. As he leaned on his cane, gazing at the panorama of mountains still tipped in snow, he turned to Tate.

"It's like a page from *National Geographic.* Those mountains are so damn big even I can see them." Robert and Tate stood in silent awe, keeping their gaze on the mountains. "Beats the hell out of New York skyscrapers, Tate. Don't you agree?"

"Yep, Dad. I have to agree with you." Tate put his hand on his dad's shoulder. "I think this was the right move for you. You will never lack for visitors."

****

As Tate and Tobi pulled out of the parking lot, Tate was overwhelmed with sadness, not knowing if he, too, would be close enough to visit his father like he had done all these years since he had finally gotten his life together. The two weeks he had been with Sue Ann had been the most wonderful of his life, but she had become sad the last few days. He knew she was worried about Custer.

What is Custer to Sue Ann, and more important, what is Sue Ann to Custer? Custer removed himself to allow Sue Ann room and time to love the father of her children. What kind of strength and selflessness does it take for a man to do that for the woman he loves? Would I do the same for Sue Ann if the circumstances were reversed?

Tate knew there was something he had to do for Sue Ann, and when he left Tobi's cabin, he did not head back to her.

****

Hawk was surprised to see his father-in-law enter his counselor's office at school. Hawk was wrapping up for the summer, getting student records ready to be sent off to universities and planning for the new school year in the fall.

"Come in, Tate. This is a pleasant surprise." Hawk took a chair in front of his desk and directed Tate to the chair opposite. "Call it a wild guess, but I bet this has something to do with Custer. Am I right?"

"You are a true counselor, Hawk. You know me well, although you know me hardly at all." Tate looked away before beginning.

"Hawk, Sue Ann is struggling, and I'm afraid my being here is causing her too much stress. I'm concerned about her health, but the thought of leaving her is unbearable."

"Tate, I don't know that I can help you in this. This decision is between you and Sue Ann, and possibly Custer, although he refuses to have anything to do with it."

"But he should be part of it." Tate leaned toward Hawk. "I know Sue Ann loves me, and I love her as if we were never separated."

"I hear a 'but' in your voice." Hawk leaned back, rubbing his chin.

"Yes, but—I also know that Sue Ann loves Custer. She is afraid something will happen to him on the mountain and she won't be there to help him like she did when he had his heart attack."

"And I fit in this where, Tate?"

"I need to talk to Custer. No, let me rephrase that. I need to know Custer." Tate emphasized the word *know*. "You know where he is, and I need to go to him, to talk to him, since he won't come to me. Custer and I both love Sue Ann, and we need to help her choose."

Hawk shook his head vehemently.

"I can't take you to him, Tate. You don't know my uncle. I can't even call him." Hawk kept his eyes on Tate. "My uncle is a strong man or, perhaps, I should say a strong-willed man, and he won't talk to you."

"So you won't take me to him?" Tate's eyes pleaded with Hawk.

"I don't see how it will help. What you're wanting to do is honorable, and my uncle respects honor, but he's made it clear that I am to leave him alone and to tell no one, not even Sue Ann, where he is. I have to respect his wishes." Hawk left his chair and walked to the window. Keeping his back to Tate, he spoke.

"You know, Tate, Custer worked for the Forestry Service here for years. A lot of his friends still work for the service." Hawk turned and looked at Tate to see if he understood his meaning.

Tate nodded and left Hawk's office.

****

Sue Ann and Betsy each bought a western jacket in Whispering Pines, their favorite shop for clothing, and then made their way down Main Street to their favorite antique store in Red Lodge. Twice Touched had an amazing collection of primitive antiques, and both had purchased many pieces for their cabins. They were just about to leave the store, after adding to their collection of candles as they always did, when Betsy noticed a dress hanging behind a cupboard door almost out of sight. Betsy moved to the cupboard to get a closer look.

"Mom, come here!"

Sue Ann could tell by her daughter's voice that she had found a treasure.

Betsy took the hanger down from the cupboard door and held it up to her mother.

"Perfect!" Betsy grinned an impish grin and shoved it into her mother's hands.

"Oh, my goodness! It is beautiful!" Sue Ann touched the fragile, cream-colored dress made of muslin. The cuffs of the puffy long sleeves were trimmed, like the long skirt, in rows and rows of lace. The bodice was separated from the skirt by a peplum that gathered at the fitted waist before dropping six or eight inches in symmetrical pleats over the skirt. The front of the bodice was covered in rows of delicate French lace, alternated with rows of tiny mother-of-pearl buttons fastened with tatted loops, the rows running from the mandarin collar all the way to the waist.

Enjoying the mother/daughter response to the vintage dress, Mitsy, the storeowner's mother, came over to Sue Ann and Betsy.

"I told Lynette this dress would not last long. Isn't it beautiful?" Mitsy caressed the dress as Betsy held it.

"Yes, it is. How old is it?" Sue Ann asked. "It looks like it's from around the late 1800s, or maybe the turn of the century."

"Let's see…" Mitsy pulled the tag around to where she could see it. "It says 'circa 1900.' That sounds about right to me. I know it came from an estate sale in Absarokee. Mrs. Kendall, the previous owner, just recently put herself in Pioneer Home. Since she had no heirs or children to take care of her, she sold everything at auction last week."

"That is so sad. I can't imagine having to give up a family heirloom like this. Do you know anything about the bride who wore it?" Betsy asked, knowing how her mother loved local history.

"No, but if you want to know about it, pay Mrs. Kendall a visit. She is quite a character. Loves talking about her ancestors and her family history."

Sue Ann left the store with the dress, just as Betsy knew she would.

"Wouldn't the dress make a beautiful wedding dress?" Betsy smiled but did not look at her mother. She could feel her mother's grin even though she could not see her face.

****

When Sue Ann got back to the cabin, the Jeep that Tate used was already sitting out front. She found herself looking forward to seeing him and wondered if she had just needed an outing with Betsy to get her joy back. But when she entered, she found a large new backpack, fully packed, sitting by the front door.

"Tate?" she called up the stairs.

Tate descended the stairs and smiled when he saw Sue Ann. Before she could ask any questions, he grabbed her and kissed her hard letting his tongue relay the passion he felt for her. When he released her, he walked to the door without saying a word. As he picked up the pack, she noticed he was wearing new hiking boots, zip-off fishing pants, and a cap from a local fly shop. A sheath holding a knife hung from the side of his belt, and a Winston fly rod case stuck out of a side pocket of his pack.

"You're going fishing without me?" She stared, not knowing what was going on.

"That's right. I am still an avid fly fisher, and I, like Custer, am a pretty serious outdoorsman." Tate raised his eyebrows and smiled. "I have a forestry map and everything I need, and I'm going to fish some Montana high mountain lakes, something I've wanted to do all my life."

Sue Ann stood with her mouth open. Tate, seeing the unanswered questions on her face, retraced his steps and took her in his arms again.

"You won my heart a long time ago, and I feel the same about you today as I did then, but you can't make a decision with me here any more than you can with Custer here. I love you, Sue Ann. Custer loves you, and we both know you love each of us. But Custer and I need to know which one of us you want to spend the rest of your life with, and I need to leave and let you decide." And Tate put on the backpack and walked out the door. Sue Ann walked onto the porch and watched as Tate Douglas rounded the old fencepost and disappeared on the trail.

Chapter Seventeen

Tate checked the map again and located the forestry cabin where he thought Custer would be. Tate had gone by the Forestry Service office and told the forest rangers, Custer's friends, he was an old buddy and was going up to fish with Custer. But being new to the area, he did not know exactly where his old friend was. The head ranger took out a map and marked the trail to Second Rock, famous for indigenous cutthroat trout.

"Custer told us the other day he was going to this cabin." He marked the cabin with an X. "Anybody can use the forestry cabins, but they are supposed to be reserved through us. Custer has it for a month, not that anybody else even knows about this cabin. Can't remember the last time anybody stayed there other than Custer." As the ranger folded the map and handed it to Tate, he asked, "You been in the wilderness much? It can be dangerous, and getting to Second Rock is no hike around Central Park. The boulder fields can kill a serious mountain man." The ranger hesitated for a second. "Do I detect a New York accent?"

"Thanks for the concern, but I know what I'm doing. I hike and fish the Adirondacks often, not to mention I'm a Vietnam vet who did not sit behind a desk, if you catch my meaning."

Several hours later, Tate stopped to apply moleskin

to the areas of his ankles where blisters were forming. Time was important, and none could be wasted breaking in the new hiking boots. He had comfortable, broken-in boots in New York but had not had time to think of what he might need for the trip west.

Several miles later, Tate reached Keyser Brown Lake. This would be where he would camp for the night. After putting his tent up, he put his rod together and began fishing for his dinner, poached trout to add to the instant brown rice he had thrown in at the last minute.

****

Custer was at September Morning. He had needed a change of scenery and had made his way back down the trail. It was getting late, but he really wanted to make it to Keyser Brown. The waterfall where he liked to shower was not far from there, and he needed a good scrubbing after too many days in the wilderness. He chuckled to himself, remembering the waterfall scene from *The Hawk and the Deer*, in which Betsy named Hawk "the Neopolitan Man," something Hawk was still having to deal with from the locals who had read Betsy's novel.

As Custer approached the lake, he noticed a tent was set up and someone was fly fishing at the water's edge, not a surprise to Custer, since it was the first good fishing lake on the trail. Custer called out to let the angler know he was there, so whoever it was would not be startled.

"How's the fishing?"

Tate turned to see a tall, muscular Native American man with shoulder-length gray hair. His face was covered in thin stubble, and Tate knew it wouldn't be long before his own face would look like a diehard outdoorsman's also.

Custer stopped when he came closer. The angler had taken his cap off and was combing his collar-length curly hair back away from his face. The man had on fishing pants and had zipped off the legs to make shorts. His legs were covered in deep, purple scars, and Custer knew immediately who he was. Besides, he looked just like an older version of Tobi.

"So you still fly fish?" Custer asked.

"Yes, Custer, I do." Tate cast his line again and continued to talk with his back to Custer. "No, Sue Ann did not send me. You're not the only one who can give her time to think." Tate stripped his line in when a small brook trout hit his fly. Tate released this one back into the lake and turned to Custer.

"Your friends at the Forestry Service said you'd be at Second Rock."

"I was. Just needed to pass some time, so I came down here. There's a waterfall just down the trail that's the best shower in the wilderness. I think I'm ripe enough for it." Custer sat on a boulder after taking off his pack. "You cast pretty good for a city slicker."

"Thanks. But I'm not a city slicker all the time. I fly fish and camp in the Adirondacks every chance I get." Tate reeled in his line and moved closer to Custer, propping his foot on a rock. Neither spoke for several seconds.

"So why did you come looking for me? I made it pretty clear I wanted to be left alone." Custer looked at the lake and not at Tate. "And I know you didn't leave Sue Ann to catch a trout."

"I told you. Sue Ann needs time away from both of

us. She has a decision to make, and it's not fair for me to be there and you here." Tate cast his eyes on the lake before turning back to face Custer. "Besides, my being there was putting too much stress on her. That's not good for someone recovering from cancer."

"Is she well, other than being stressed?" Custer still did not make eye contact.

"She is, but she misses you, and she's worried about you being alone up here." Tate waited for Custer's answer, but it was not to come for several seconds.

"I tell you what, Tate." Custer looked at Tate. "I'll take a day or so for us to get to know each other, if that's what you want, and I'll even take you up to Second Rock to catch some native cutthroat, but the deal is we do not mention Sue Ann. If you can't agree to that, then I'll forget the shower and head back up."

Tate moved to stand in front of Custer, facing him man to man.

"Deal, but with one exception. I just found my children. Whatever happens with Sue Ann, you and I will still have these ones we love in common, and I will talk about them." Tate emphasized the word *will*. "Can you live with that?"

Custer stood and held out his hand.

"Deal." The two shook hands, and Custer set up his tent.

The next day found Tate and Custer making their way toward Second Rock to the forestry cabin. The boulder field was exactly as the forest ranger had warned Tate, and he had a hard time keeping up with Custer. *Sue Ann was right. Custer is a strong outdoorsman. I'm no match for him in the mountain man department.*

After depositing their packs in the cabin, the two men headed to the lake above Second Rock to catch cutthroats. They had talked little the day before, and neither mentioned Sue Ann, just as they promised. They did talk about Betsy, and Tate enjoyed hearing Custer tell about Betsy as a teenager and a fly fisher.

That night, they grilled trout over the campfire and baked potatoes in the coals. While they drank coffee, Custer began talking.

"I read your letters from Vietnam." Custer waited in silence for Tate's reply.

Tate took a sip of coffee, gazed into the campfire, and answered Custer's probe.

"Then you know how crazy I was when I left there. The scars on my legs do not represent my deepest wounds." He took another sip and began his explanation.

"I was messed up for years after coming back, lived on the streets as an alcoholic and drug addict, and in addition to suffering from my addictions, I was also at the mercy of the elements of New York winters and harassment by the good citizens who still hated the Vietnam War. The jail provided me with a warm bed many times for assaulting some poor soul that moved wrong, spoke wrong, or just happened into my hallucinations of the Viet Cong surrounding me." Tate stopped and added another log to the fire. "When I saw the picture…" Tate caught himself before mentioning Sue Ann's name. "You know from my last letter how it would have triggered a flashback from the war, the first episode I've had in years. It was unnerving, to say the least, since I thought I was cured. I take pills, and that prevented it from becoming a full-blown episode, but it was still terrifying."

"I was never in a war as such, but I have been in the middle of some of what you experienced, something I'm not proud of. Fortunately, I realized the error of my ways and got out of it before it consumed me. As a result, I did battle alcoholism for a long time, trying to forget. My medicine was the mountains." Custer paused and then added, "And the spiritualism of my ancestors. Same medicine I use today."

The next day, Custer took Tate higher up the mountain to the small lake with no name, a very difficult hike. The cutthroat hit at practically every cast, and Custer had a hard time convincing Tate to leave.

"It will be dark soon, and it's a hard trek back to the cabin. Easy to get lost." Custer warned.

Custer was right, and darkness fell before they got back to the cabin. Custer stopped every once in a while and waited for Tate to catch up. Tate's stride was nothing like Custer's, so he was always a good ways back, catching up to Custer when Custer stopped to wait on him.

"You don't have to go so slow, Custer. I know my short stride is wearing you out. I promise I'll catch up. Go ahead at your own pace."

"I'm a patient man. Rarely get in a hurry." Custer looked around at the star-and-moon-lit scenery. "Especially when I'm in the wilderness. I'll go ahead, but I'll stop and wait on you every few minutes. Just follow the boulder fields down."

****

After crossing the boulder field, Custer rested, waiting for Tate to catch up. Custer knew Tate would struggle to get through the dense brush he was about to enter and wanted to make sure he was close behind him. After too many minutes of waiting, Custer became concerned and backtracked searching for Tate.

****

Tate had enjoyed his day of fishing but was not enjoying going over the boulder fields with a flashlight in one hand and, in the other hand, a stick he had picked up to help him with the long stretches needed to boulder hop. This was one of those many times in his life he wished he had inherited his dad's height rather than his mother's. As he stretched, trying to get over a wide gap, he lost his footing and fell, adding cuts and bruises to his scarred legs. In the process of trying to stop his fall, he dropped his flashlight. He sat on a boulder trying to get his bearings and thought about waiting there for Custer, who would surely come back for him, but his ego got the best of him, and he headed out again.

Soon he was over the boulder field, but Custer was nowhere to be seen. He started to call out when he saw the dense brush in the moonlight and remembered coming through this on his way from Second Rock. From his experience in the jungle and his own knowledge of hiking, he knew he should stop and wait, but again his pride got in his way. He did not want to look like a wimp in the eyes of his competitor. As he stepped into the marshy underbrush, the mud oozed around his boots, and his mind took control, taking him back to the jungles of Vietnam.

****

When Custer reached the last place he had seen Tate, he tried not to panic, but Tate was nowhere to be found.

Surely Tate will stop when he realizes he's lost. Everyone who goes into the wilderness knows this. Besides, he's a Vietnam vet.

Custer knew the dangers of being lost in the Beartooths and followed his instincts. The quarter moon added some light to the small maglight he used, enough for any outdoors person who knew the Beartooths, but it would be difficult traveling for someone, like Tate, who did not know his way. Custer decided to take another trail, in case Tate had lost his sense of direction or maybe fallen. When he was halfway down the trail, Custer cupped his hands over his mouth and called Tate's name.

"Tate!" Custer wailed hoping the breeze would carry it. He waited a few seconds between calls, moving his head in all directions, but no answer came.

****

"They're coming, Tate! You've got to hide!" Andrew shoved Tate, who was already struggling in the black jungle muck, and Tate fell to his knees. "You've got to go faster!"

Tate pulled himself up, lifting his heavy feet out of the mud, and finally found footing in a stream with a rocky bottom. Something pricked at his legs, and he wondered why his uniform pants were not protecting his skin.

"Fuck! I must have torn the bottom off my pants legs in those bushes."

It was then Tate realized he had dropped his rifle somewhere in the jungle. He bent and reached into the bank, dipping his fingers in the mud. With three fingers spread apart, he streaked his face and arms for camouflage and covered his khaki pants with mud so he

120

wouldn't stand out in the darkness of the jungle. Reaching to his side, he pulled the knife out of its sheath. The Marine crouched behind a big fallen tree and waited, his knife drawn, ready for the kill and to take the VC's weapon.

****

Custer moved fast, boulder hopping. He felt sure Tate had lost the trail and gone down the wrong side of the boulder field. As he stretched to reach the biggest boulder, he noticed something shining in the gap between the two giant rocks. Directing the flashlight beam down, his light reflected off the gold top of Tate's rod case. He lifted himself down between the rocks and retrieved the rod. Beside it he found Tate's flashlight. At least he knew Tate had come this way but was traveling in the dark now.

Custer attached the Winston rod to the outside of his pack and held a flashlight in each hand. He used both flashlights, trying to pick up Tate's trail, and was rewarded with boot prints in the marshy ground where the thick brush began. Custer moved slowly, keeping his eyes on the ground and stopping every few yards to call Tate's name, but he received no answer.

At one point, he lost Tate's trail in a small stream but picked it up again on the other side after walking down a few yards. The brush was thick, and the marshy ground made tracking hard, but Custer was a master at tracking, with the keen eye of an eagle. His ability to follow signs unobservable by most men had landed him a job with the CIA in his younger days, but no one knew of his secret missions, not even Hawk.

****

"I hear him coming, Tate!" Andrew whispered in

121

Tate's ear. "Get ready! You can kill him, but be quick. There might be others behind him."

"I'm ready, Andrew! Now be quiet!"

****

Custer stopped and listened. He thought he heard whispering and turned his head to the right, sensing something, or someone, ahead. He hoped it was not a bear. Not that he feared any animal, but he didn't want Tate lost with a bear close by. As he inched his way forward, he shined the flashlight on a big tree trunk lying across the path. He worked his way to the right of the tree and had started to call Tate's name again when something lunged at him from behind the tree.

Custer realized a knife was coming at him fast, and behind the knife was Tate, his wild eyes glaring from behind streaks of mud. Custer, remembering his moves from the old days, put his arm up to ward off the attack and pushed Tate to the ground, knocking the knife out of his hand. Straddling him, Custer had to summon strength from deep within to keep the madman pinned to the ground, even though he was smaller than Custer. Tate gave a grunted yell, his face tightened, and his eyes glared in panic and anger, pumping his adrenaline to fight his imagined enemy even harder. Custer knew this required desperate action on his part. Lifting his right arm, he doubled his fist and knocked Tate unconscious with one blow.

Custer sat back, breathing hard, and shined the flashlight in Tate's face, hoping he had not seriously hurt him. Custer knew the cabin was close, so after binding Tate's hands behind him with his bandana, just in case, he picked Tate up and slung him over his shoulder.

Chapter Eighteen

Two days had passed with no word from Tate. Sue Ann now had both of the men she loved in the mountains, but somehow she felt more relieved than she had felt in the two and a half weeks she had spent with Tate. She slept soundly at night with no sense of guilt but with the same recurring dream, the wedding dream. In each episode, she was wearing the Victorian dress.

Sue Ann was sitting on her porch drinking her mug of coffee when her cell phone rang.

"Mom, Trapper and I are going to visit Papa today. I've got a surprise for him. Why don't you go with us?"

An hour later, Sue Ann met Betsy and Trapper at Pioneer Home. Betsy was carrying a long package wrapped in very masculine-looking paper covered in dry flies, and Trapper was carrying a smaller gift wrapped the same way.

"I bet I know what that is. What a great idea, Betsy!"

Papa was sitting looking at the mountains, chatting away with a beautiful elderly lady who was wheelchair bound. She had a long white braid lying across her shoulder and reaching almost to her waist, and her face was almost flawless, with only a few wrinkles. She wore no makeup and was dressed in faded jeans, a Red Lodge sweatshirt, and moccasins. Betsy and Sue Ann caught the tail end of the conversation and knew the lady was telling Papa all about her life as a rancher.

Papa rose when his family entered and chuckled at the sight of Trapper grinning from under his big black cowboy hat. Papa was wearing the red scarf around his neck, blue jeans, and a new pair of gray cowboy boots, a present from Tobi, that matched the hat Hawk had given him. His hat lay beside him on a chair.

After being showered with hugs and kisses, Papa turned to the lady sitting beside him.

"Kathryn, I want you to meet my granddaughter Betsy and her mother Sue Ann. And this handsome big man is my great-grandson Trapper." Trapper stopped in front of the lady and gave her a big smile and tipped his hat just like his daddy had taught him.

"You are a handsome young man, Trapper, much like your Papa, here, and what good manners you have."

Trapper giggled and plopped the package he was carrying in Papa's lap.

"Here, Papa, from me." Trapper propped his elbow on Papa's knee, anxious for him to open the present.

"A present for me? Why, thank you, Little Man. Whatever can this be?" Papa began tearing the paper off and motioned for Trapper to help him. Trapper tore away until the box peeked out.

"Open it, Papa! You'll like it!"

Papa opened the box, and a big smile covered his face.

"A fly fishing reel! Oh, my, Trapper, what a beauty!" He dug deeper in the box and pulled out fly line, fishing tools, and a Wheatley box full of flies. "Thank you, precious boy." Papa reached for Trapper, and the little cowboy climbed into his Papa's lap, allowing him to hug him tight.

"Guess you might need something to put that on, Papa. Here's another gift, from Hawk and me." Betsy handed her package to her grandfather.

Trapper didn't wait around to help this time and began exploring the huge room with the big window.

"A Sage rod! My, my, my! This is better than my old rod at home I used for all these years. Thank you, sweetheart. You've made your Papa a very happy man. As soon as I get this rigged up, I'll be down there on that stream showing those old ranch hands how to catch a big rainbow."

"I'll help you rig your rod, Papa. Let's move over to the table, and we'll get you ready to fish."

"Sue Ann, are you coming?" Papa called over his shoulder as he followed Betsy to the table.

"I'll just sit and talk to Kathryn while you two get your rod rigged." Sue Ann did not have to worry about making conversation. Kathryn was a talker.

"Robert is a fine man. I like him. He's not the rancher type like my Bill, but then old Bill went and died on me. Robert is fun to talk to, a good listener." She leaned toward Sue Ann. "He laughs at my ranching and rodeo stories."

"Oh, yes, he's quite a character." Sue Ann moved to the other side of Kathryn where she could hear her better. "Where are you from, Kathryn?"

"Absarokee. Lived there all my life. My grandmother homesteaded our ranch in 1910. She was divorced, something unheard of in her day, but she didn't give a prairie dog's ass what people thought. She had two children to raise, one being my mother, and she figured she could do anything a man could do and do it better."

"How long have you been at Pioneer Home, Kathryn?"

"Oh, only about a week. I just couldn't stay by myself anymore, and couldn't find decent help to stay with me that wouldn't steal me blind." Kathryn whispered the last part.

Sue Ann immediately knew who Kathryn was.

"Is your last name Kendall, by any chance?" Sue Ann smiled, anticipating the answer.

"Why, yes, it is. How on earth did you know?" Kathryn cocked her head to one side, keeping her eyes on Sue Ann's.

"I think I bought a wedding dress the other day that belonged to someone in your family. I found it in an antique shop in Red Lodge."

"Oh, my goodness! You bought Grandmother Lily's wedding dress. She made it herself. Is it two-pieced, with a lot of lace?"

"That's the one. It's beautiful. I was planning to find you later to ask you about the history of the dress, and you found me first. Imagine that!" Sue Ann liked Kathryn, just as Mitsy had said she would.

"I would love to tell you about the dress and Grandmother Lily." The twinkle in Kathryn's eyes told her audience of one she was in for a treat.

"My grandma was the strongest, most independent woman Absarokee had ever seen and didn't weigh much over a hundred pounds. She was small, like you, Sue Ann, but she could 'bout carry her weight in horse feed. Chopped her own firewood, too. She homesteaded a hundred fifty acres, with help only from books she read about ranching, and she made a go of it. She sewed to help make ends meet until she could get the ranch producing enough for a good living. Before she died, she owned five hundred acres and was one of the top horse breeders in the area."

"She didn't have a husband?"

"She did before she came to Montana, but he beat her and controlled every move she made. She hated being under his thumb, and one night when he was drunk and 'bout to beat her black-and-blue again, she took a stick of wood to him, and—pardon my language—beat the hell out of him. He never touched her again and ran off with a prostitute. Grandmother filed for divorce and headed west."

"Where was Lily from originally?" Sue Ann was fascinated by the story, and in her head she could see a novel in the making, even though she had promised to end her writing career as soon as she could write *Under Northern Lights*.

"She was from Chicago. Can you believe that? She was a city girl who just wanted her freedom. She always told me not to marry any man who wouldn't let me be myself and be free, and I took her at her word. Bill and me were happy as a pair of loons on a lake, but if I decided I wanted to buy something, go on an adventure, or run barrels in a rodeo, he never tried to stop me. Last time I ran barrels, I was seventy-two years old. Can ya believe that? Bill did try to talk me out of that one, but it didn't do any good. 'Course I ran the barrels so slow that the clock 'bout stopped, and that was when I hung up my spurs." Kathryn chuckled. "But Bill never said 'I told you so.' He liked me being adventurous. He'd kiss me before I'd leave and say,

'Don't forget your way home now, Kat.' "

Sue Ann laughed with Kathryn as she told her stories.

"Yep, I'd say I got a big dose of Grandma Lily in me. Least Bill always told me I did."

"So Lily never remarried?" Sue Ann was intrigued with the story and thought about her own exploits in Alaska as a single mom.

"Oh, yes. Four years after she came to Montana, she decided she needed help on the ranch, but she wasn't willing to pay anybody, so she put an ad in all the big papers in Montana and Wyoming. She was specific about what she expected and conducted fifty or more interviews before she found a man who was willing to work hard, love harder, and leave her the hell alone when she wanted her independence." Kathryn's infectious laugh added to the story of Lily, and Sue Ann laughed with her. "When she finally decided on my grandfather Pete, the local newspaper wrote an article about the wedding with the heading 'Miss Lily Gets a Mail Order Groom.' She was the talk of Montana."

****

The next day, Sue Ann spread Lily's wedding dress out on her bed and scrutinized the intricate handwork. Miss Lily had made the dress with her own hands, calloused hands that ran a ranch, chopped wood, cooked on a wood stove, and tenderly cuddled two children who had no father. This pioneer woman's life had been so similar to her own. Miss Lily's dress had found Sue Ann in Red Lodge, and she wondered if it was a sign.

Sue Ann took the dress and her sewing and moved to the porch, where she planned to reinforce some of the seams. For what purpose, she did not know.

Oh, Lord! What am I to do? Sue Ann let the dress fall with her hands to her lap as she looked up at the mountains.

Her thoughts were interrupted by a call from overhead. An eagle soared above the cabin, closer than she had ever seen one, and she was reminded of Custer. The eagle was his animal spirit, and seeing this awesome bird made her heart beat faster. The eagle flew closer and landed in the top of a huge ponderosa pine that stood beside the trailhead.

Sue Ann watched the eagle for several minutes until she noticed another bird on the other side of her front yard, high up in the tallest spruce tree. The raven looked strong and regal, not flinching as the eagle cast his eyes toward him. The two seemed to be having a staring contest.

"Raven wings." Sue Ann whispered remembering Shade's dark hair and piercing blue eyes. This raven had light-colored eyes, not dark like most ravens she had seen, and she wondered if Shade, or his animal spirit, was channeling her, trying to help her with her decision.

"Oh, Shade. If you were here with me, there would be no decision to make, and I would not be in this stressful dilemma. But you left me, and now I must choose between the other two men in my life. I do not want to be alone for whatever time I have left in these mountains. Help me, my darling, to choose between these two men who mean so much to me."

Her eagle and raven sightings were interrupted by the chirp of a smaller bird, a chickadee, that flew right through the porch over her head, stopping at the old rotting fencepost that Custer had said he was tearing down but never did. The bird had a red berry in its mouth and soon disappeared into the fencepost. After only a few seconds, it left the nest and flew off into the woods.

I wonder if that's the same chickadee I saw in late summer carrying twigs to build the nest.

Sue Ann left her chair and walked toward the fencepost, being careful not to scare the female bird incubating her eggs. Custer had told her male chickadees feed the females while they are sitting on eggs awaiting the hatching of the fledglings. He also said chickadees mate for life, just like ravens.

Humans could certainly take a few lessons from these intelligent creatures.

Sue Ann tiptoed the last few feet to the post, not wanting to disturb the mother, but when she was ready to peek in, the mother left her nest and flew over the intruder's head, giving a panic-filled call, probably to her mate for help. Sue Ann's motherly instincts kicked in, and even though she was sorry for frightening the tiny bird, she had to see the eggs.

Holding her breath, she peeked into the fence post and was rewarded. Two eggs lay touching each other, reminding her of how close Betsy and Tobi must have been in her womb. The brown speckles of the gray shells were camouflaged against dry mud and brown twigs, but she could see them.

How unusual that there are only two! Usually there are five or six eggs in a nest.

Sue Ann backed away from the nest and noticed the pair of chickadees nearby, chattering in panic as the intruder left their home and their soon-to-hatch babies.

As soon as she was a safe distance away, the pair fluttered by her, making their way to the nest.

At least she has support in caring for and raising her babies. I have no concept of this, but Betsy and I did all right, and so did Miss Lily. Even with a mate, every female should feel independent if they are to feel secure and totally fulfilled. The possibility of being alone looms over every woman, married or not.

Sue Ann reentered the cabin and laid the dress aside. She took her Casting for Recovery Cap off the coat tree standing by the door and headed for the trail. It was time to visit Custer's old cabin. She had the feel and smell of Tate, her first real love, all around her, and she loved it, but she needed the same from Custer right now. The time had come to end this, once and for all. She needed to choose a mate for the rest of her life, however long that might be.

Chapter Nineteen

The sun burst through the forestry cabin window and awoke Custer, who was sitting with his back to the wall, facing the sleeping bag where a muddy Tate Douglas lay sleeping. After stoking the fire, Custer set up the coffeepot and placed it on the stove.

Custer was exhausted from carrying the unconscious man but had managed to get him inside and into his sleeping bag and had zipped the bag tightly under his chin, not only for warmth but to prevent Tate from trying to attack him again. Custer had not slept soundly. Not only did he fear another hallucination by Tate, Custer was afraid he might have hurt Tate with the hard blow he had given him.

As the sun spread across the sleeping bag a few minutes later, Tate began to squirm. His fingertips unzipped the bag and he sat up, looking around, trying to figure out where he was.

The fire crackled in the stove as the coffee perked, but Custer was nowhere inside. Within a minute, the cabin door opened and Custer entered carrying wood for the fire.

"Good morning." Custer spoke in a low voice as he placed the wood beside the stove. Custer sat on a stool beside Tate. "It's another beautiful day in the Beartooths." Custer smiled at Tate and was rewarded with a return smile.

"Good morning," Tate replied. Looking down at his hands and arms, Tate saw the mud and began pulling himself out of the sleeping bag. His boots and socks had been removed, but his legs were scratched and covered with a mixture of dried mud and blood. He fell back on the bag, covered his eyes with both hands and moaned.

"What happened, Custer?" Tate did not move and kept his eyes closed as if afraid of what Custer would tell him.

"It's okay, Tate." Custer moved to the stove. "You didn't hurt anybody." Custer paused. "But you scared the hell out of me." Custer chuckled, trying to relieve the fear and embarrassment Tate was feeling, judging by Tate's refusal to look at him.

"Coffee's ready." Custer moved to his pack. "But you might want to go down to the lake and wash up." Custer threw Tate a towel.

Tate rolled out of his sleeping bag and picked up the towel. He left his muddy boots and walked out the door barefooted. Tate sauntered toward the lake and squatted down at the edge. His reflection in the clear water confirmed Tate's worst nightmare and it all came back to him.

I heard Andrew again.

Tate stared at his image and took longer than needed as his tears helped to wash away the muddy nightmare. He wanted to stay at the lake indefinitely but knew, inside, he had to find out from Custer what had happened.

****

When Tate reentered the cabin, Custer sat silent, sipping his coffee.

"Did I attack you, Custer?" Tate stood at the door staring at Custer, who was sitting at the table. "I have to know. Did I attack you?"

"Yes." Custer looked up and patted the knife in the sheath on his belt, the knife he had taken away from Tate. "But you were not successful." Custer paused and took a sip of coffee. "I knocked you out with my fist, if you wonder why your jaw is sore."

Tate put his hand to his face and stretched his jaw from side to side.

"Oh, so that's why…" He did not finish his sentence. "Thank goodness."

Custer poured a cup of coffee for Tate and directed him to sit down. It was several seconds before either spoke.

"I am so sorry, Custer." Tate kept his gaze down on the table. "I was so focused on trying to locate you, I neglected to take my pill." Tate's gaze took refuge on the floor as he ran his hands through his curls. "And that is why I can't have Sue Ann, even if she chooses me." He held his hand up to stop Custer from saying anything. "I know we said we wouldn't talk about her, but what I did last night cinches it. What if I have a flashback and hurt her?" Tate ran his fingers through his hair again and pulled out mats of mud. "I can't risk it. When I get down from the mountain, I'm going back to New York, and I won't say goodbye. You've got to help me disappear again, for Sue Ann's sake."

Custer watched a distraught Tate Douglas holding to the cup with both hands but not drinking, still looking at the table and not at Custer, who sat opposite him. Several seconds of silence followed before Custer spoke.

"You've been with Sue Ann for over two weeks. You've slept with her every night." Tate looked up and started to speak, but Custer held his hand up to stop him. "I know. I saw you the other night. During a weak moment, I went to the trailhead in Sue Ann's yard. I had no intention of seeing her, but I had to be near. You were holding her as the two of you stood in the bedroom window." Custer waited for Tate's reaction, but none came. "You've shown Sue Ann love, and you've been there to protect her if she needed it." Custer kept his eyes on Tate and took another sip to give his words time to sink in.

"What's your point, Custer?" Tate kept his eyes focused on Custer.

"Did you ever once have a flashback and think she was VC?" Custer asked.

Tate shook his head. He had not. "But there's no guarantee I won't. I don't know why the terror is back, but I can't trust myself with Sue Ann or my children." Tate left the table and walked out to the porch.

Custer remained at the table to give Tate time alone, but after a few minutes, he joined him.

"Tate, would you let me help you?"

"What do you mean?" Tate turned to face Custer.

"The same way I saved myself. The same way I helped Hawk save himself from his demons. You know, there are other medicines besides pills, but you have to trust and have faith in yourself as well as in the process."

"You sound like the minister I'm supposed to be." Tate held to the porch post and did not speak for a few seconds. "Why would you do that for me, Custer?" Tate kept his eyes on the mountains. "I need to leave, and when I leave, you can go back to Sue Ann."

"This is not about Sue Ann. This is about one man helping another. Are you willing to try?"

"And what about Sue Ann?" Tate kept his back turned and did not look at Custer as he asked the question.

"Do you love her?" Custer asked.

"Yes. More than life itself, but so do you." He faced Custer, waiting for his reply, but none came. Instead, Custer took the knife out of the sheath, walked to the woods and began cutting limbs.

Before long, a sweat lodge had been built, and Tate sat beside it, naked, shaking from the swim he had just taken in the lake. He silently prayed to his own Great Spirit and waited for more instruction from Custer.

Chapter Twenty

Custer's cabin was unlocked, and Sue Ann entered. She walked around the one room and ran her hand along the table where Custer often had coffee when he needed alone time, and she inhaled memories of Custer. Custer's bed, with its soft down mattress, beckoned to her, and she sat on it, rubbing her hand across the Pendleton blanket and remembering. She was in her late thirties and had slipped away from Betsy at the log cabin where they spent each summer after a long school year in the Alaskan Interior.

Custer was always waiting for me, instinctively knowing when I was coming, and he grabbed me as I entered, kissing me with the passion of a man on fire and in love. How we struggled, getting out of our clothes as we made our way to his bed, with kissing never ceasing. Sunken in the feather mattress, exhausted from making love, we lay wrapped in each other's arms, not wanting the moment to end. But end it always did. I knew I had to retrace my steps to Betsy.

Sue Ann moved from the bed to the table and sat with her face in her hands; tears of indecision rolled down her cheeks and dropped to the table. As she stood to leave, her foot hit a piece of wadded up paper and sent it tumbling across the floor. She picked up the paper and unfolded it and laid it flat on the table, pressing it out so she could read the words. Tears came to her eyes as she sat down to finish reading it.

My love,

I am not a man of fancy words or long phrases, but what I say is from my heart, and you know I must follow it. Your happiness is all that I live for, and I only want what is best for you. You do not have to make this choice; I will make it for you.

You are free, Sue Ann, as free as you have always been, whether in Alaska or Montana, as free as you have always been when in my arms. Free is the only way I can think of you, and I love you more for it.

For you to have the love that you deserve, I will no longer be a part of your life. Go with my love, my blessing, and always, my heart.

Custer

Sue Ann folded the letter and placed it in her pocket. She took one more look around and closed the cabin door behind her.

Chapter Twenty-One

Sue Ann gazed at the panorama of the Beartooth Mountains through the big windows of the rustic log chapel on the outskirts of Red Lodge. No stained glass was needed, with the natural beauty streaming through, signifying God's approval of the scene below.

Wearing the Victorian wedding dress she had found in Red Lodge, Sue Ann was strengthened with the knowledge that Miss Lily, another strong, independent woman, had worn this dress a hundred years ago. Sue Ann could almost feel the presence of the pioneer woman.

But she would never forget Shade. As she looked down at her empty ring finger, she remembered Shade asking her why she did not wear rings. Her reply had been, "Empty finger...empty heart." There would always be an empty spot in her heart for Shade, but her ring finger was about to be filled with the ring given her by another man she loved, one who was about to become her husband. Shade's blue diamond now held its place of honor on her right hand.

Betsy stood by her mother's side, waiting to hand her the bouquet of Indian paintbrush she would carry down the aisle. As "Annie's Song" began to play, Tobi moved to the other side of his mother.

"Are you ready, Mom?" He held out his arm to usher his mother down the aisle to the altar. Sue Ann smiled at her son and nodded. It was time to take her vows, vows she should have taken a lifetime ago, and she was proud to have her children there to walk her down the aisle.

Sue Ann had made her decision, and in a few minutes, she would have the man she could not live without beside her for the rest of her life. It had been a difficult decision choosing between the two men she loved, but she knew it was the right decision.

Hawk stood in the front of the chapel and smiled as his eyes met Betsy's. He knew she, too, was thinking of their own special day at the waterfall a few years ago and of their love that grew deeper with each passing day. Hawk also had his eyes on the little cowboy ring bearer at the back, just in case he decided to wander away. Carrie, who had just met this part of her dad's family, also kept her eye on her little cousin, hoping Trapper would follow through with what they had practiced, with him staying behind her as she spread wildflowers behind her grandmother.

In the front of the church, Tate Douglas stood smiling and watched as Sue Ann approached the altar. In his mind, he was seeing the young southern rebel, this woman he had loved forever, with gold ringlets contained in a braid that hung to her waist. In reality, the braid had been replaced by gray curls that almost reached her shoulders now. But for Tate, time had stopped in the spring of 1965.

The bride took her place as she approached Tate and smiled at him. Her children kissed her cheeks and held tight to her hands for a few seconds longer before moving to the side.

Tate reached for Sue Ann's hand. As she placed

her hand in his, he moved in and kissed her, not a quick short kiss, but a kiss of passion, a man in love with the woman who would always be his soul. After pulling his lips away from hers, Tate looked deep into her eyes and mouthed the question he would ask for the last time.

"Are you sure?"

With the reassurance of her simple nod and eyes transparent with moisture, Tate smiled and whispered, "I always knew I'd marry you some day, Sue Ann." Tate took Sue Ann's hand and placed it in Custer's. "I just didn't know it would be to another man."

Custer nodded to Tate, letting him know he would take care of Sue Ann.

Tate took his own place in front of the couple and began the marriage ceremony.

"We are gathered together to join Custer Larson and Sue Ann Parish in holy matrimony..."

The final chapter, Sue Ann's chapter, was written.

Epilogue

"Is it done?" He answered the cell phone with a question, knowing the caller's purpose.

"Yes, Raven. She has chosen."

"And the nugget ring?" Raven asked the question but feared the answer.

"She wears it on her right hand and looks at it often." Long seconds followed before the caller spoke again. "She loves you still."

Eagle imagined Raven, a willing victim of unfulfilled dreams, pacing, rubbing his hand through hair now more gray than black. Raven showed no reaction to the caller's disclosure.

"Promise me…" Raven moved to the huge glass window separating him from his paradisiacal jungle hell. Eagle interrupted before Raven could finish.

"I will take care of Sue Ann as I promised, but not only for you. I love her, Raven, just as much as you do." Loss of words prevailed on the other end.

"I'm tired of thinking, Eagle." Raven broke the silence. "It's time to end this. Destroy the phone and forget me."

"I hear your pain, but my forgetting is not possible when married to one who refuses to put thoughts of you aside." Eagle held on to the phone, wishing he could help his old friend but knowing he could not.

Raven's eyes glistened as he held the cell phone,

knowing what he must say.

"Thank you for trailing me that day, Eagle, and for risking your life to pull me from the river. I never thanked you, and I'm sorry."

"It was my job. I was proud to do this for one who risked his life to save so many. It was not your time to die, even though you wished for death." Eagle paused, choosing his next words carefully, knowing what was in Raven's mind. "As men, we do not decide for ourselves when the Great Spirit is ready for us."

"No more calls, Eagle." Raven opened his other hand and stared at the L pill as he readied to end his call, but before he could disconnect, Eagle's final words resounded.

"Eyes to the sky, Raven—to the Sky Dwellers who still speak to you even though no longer visible in your night skies. Be still and wait. The mist may yet clear, and when it does, act with the courage of a man."

A word about the author…

Dr. Sue Clifton is a retired principal, fly fisher, ghost hunter, and published author. Dr. Sue, as she is known, can't remember a time when she did not write, beginning with two plays published at sixteen. Her writing career was placed on hold while she traveled the world with her husband Woody in his career, as well as with her own career as a teacher and principal in Mississippi, Alaska, New Zealand, and on the Northern Cheyenne Reservation in Montana. The places Dr. Sue has lived provide rich background and settings for the novels she creates.

Dr. Sue now divides her time between Montana, Mississippi, and Arkansas and enjoys traveling with Woody as well as with her fly fishing group of 6000-plus members, Sisters On the Fly. She loves all things vintage, including her 1950 canned ham camper "Spam I Am." Dr. Sue supports Casting for Recovery, a national organization providing fly fishing retreats for survivors of breast cancer. Ten percent of the profits from her Daughters of Parrish Oaks series goes to Casting for Recovery.

Dr. Sue is the author of nine novels: five in her Daughters of Parrish Oaks series with The Wild Rose Press, Inc., three paranormal mysteries elsewhere, and one nonfiction book.

Visit Dr. Sue at: http://www.drsueclifton.com and see Novels by Dr. Sue Clifton on Facebook.

Thank you for purchasing
this publication of The Wild Rose Press, Inc.

If you enjoyed the story, we would appreciate your
letting others know by leaving a review.

For other wonderful stories,
please visit our on-line bookstore at
www.thewildrosepress.com.

For questions or more information
contact us at
info@thewildrosepress.com.

The Wild Rose Press, Inc.
www.thewildrosepress.com

Stay current with The Wild Rose Press, Inc.

Like us on Facebook

https://www.facebook.com/TheWildRosePress

And Follow us on Twitter
https://twitter.com/WildRosePress

53211814R00160

Made in the USA
Charleston, SC
03 March 2016